Also by Jane

EARL
ON THE RUN

JANE ASHFORD

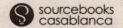
sourcebooks
casablanca

Published by Sourcebooks Casablanca, an imprint of Sourcebooks
P.O. Box 4410, Naperville, Illinois 60567–4410
(630) 961-3900
sourcebooks.com

Printed and bound in Canada.
MBP 10 9 8 7 6 5 4 3 2 1

One

JONATHAN FREDERICK MERRILL, APPARENTLY THE thrice-damned ninth Earl of Ferrington, known to himself and his old life as Jack, encountered the Travelers on the third day after he left London. They were ambling along the road he was walking, and he caught up with their straggle of horse-drawn caravans and swarm of children when the sun was halfway down the western sky. The sight of them was the first thing to lift the black mood that had afflicted him since he'd fled the city. "*Grālt'a*," he said to the man apparently serving as the rear guard.

This produced a ferocious scowl and a spate of words he didn't understand. "I only know a few words of the Shelta," he replied, naming the language these traveling people spoke among themselves. The adult men had begun to gather around him, looking menacing. "My mother was born to *an lucht siúil*, the walking people, over the sea in America," Jack added. "She left them to marry my father, but many a tale she told me of life on the road."

The first man surveyed the landscape around them, an empty stretch of forest. "You have no horse?" he asked contemptuously.

Jack had thought of buying a horse. He had a sizable sum in

a money belt, his passage home and more. But he'd put it off, thinking he would soon be leaving England. "Only my own feet and a bit of coin in my pocket. I'm happy to work for my keep, however." Nobody needed to know the extent of his funds.

The group scowled at him. Jack had already noticed that his accent puzzled the people here. They were accustomed to judging people by the way they spoke, but his mixture of North American with the intonations of his parents didn't fit their preconceived notions.

"Perhaps we just beat you and take your coins," the man said.

Jack closed his fists. "You could try, I suppose."

A wizened old woman pushed through the circle of men. Leaning on a tall staff, she examined Jack from head to toe.

Jack stiffened. He wouldn't be enduring abuse from another crone. He'd had his fill of that and more from his new-found great-grandmother. She'd discovered nothing to like about him. His brown hair, dark eyes, and "undistinguished" face were nothing like her noble English get, apparently. A poor excuse for an earl with the manners of a barbarian, she'd said. Though how she could tell about the manners when she'd hardly let him speak a word, he did not know.

"We are not brigands," said the old Traveler woman to her fellows. "No matter what they may say of us."

"Nay, fine metalworkers and horse breeders, or so my mother told me," Jack replied.

"Did she now?" Jack caught a twinkle of good humor in the old woman's pale eyes. Perhaps she wasn't like the ill-tempered Lady Wilton after all.

"She did," he replied. "And inspired me to be footloose. I've been a frontier explorer, a bodyguard, and a sailor." He'd been told he had charm. He reached for it as he smiled at the small woman before him.

"And now you are here."

Jack nodded. He wasn't going to mention inherited earldoms. That would be unwise. "Seeing the world," he answered. "I don't care for sitting still."

This yielded nods of understanding among his audience.

"Might I walk along with you?" Jack dared. "I'm headed north, as you seem to be." The truth was, Jack was lonely. He was a sociable man. He'd had many friends back home. Why had he left all that at the behest of a stuffy Englishman? He should have known that any legacy from his feckless father would be tainted.

"North to what?" the old Traveler woman asked.

It would be as unwise to mention estates as to reference an earldom, though Jack had decided to take a look at this Ferrington Hall he was supposed to inhabit. "North until I decide to turn in some other direction," he replied jauntily.

One man laughed.

"The road is free to all," said the woman.

"It is that. But companionship is a gift beyond price."

She laughed. "You have a quick tongue. If you wish to walk with us a while, we will not turn you away."

"*Maa'ths*," said Jack, thanking her with another of his small store of Shelta words. He was surprisingly glad of the permission.

The caravans started up again. Jack walked along beside

them. But with this matter settled, his thoughts began drifting back to the scene that had driven him from town. Much as he'd like to forget it, he could not.

Until the high-nosed Englishman had shown up in Boston with his astonishing summons, Jack had only half believed his father's stories of a noble lineage. His Irish mother claimed Papa bragged about being an earl's son before they wed, but once they were, he wouldn't take the least advantage of it. He refused to lift a finger to introduce Jack, his only child, to his rich relatives before he drank himself to death. And so she'd decided it was all a lie. Jack wished she'd lived to see the arrival of that "man of business" who'd lured him back here. He'd come partly because of her. How she would have reveled in the idea of her son as an earl.

His mother would *not* have stood for one single insult from his scold of a great-grandmother, however. She'd have scratched the harpy's eyes out.

Jack had been taken before this Lady Wilton as if he was a package to be dropped in her lap. And she'd received him like a delivery of bad meat. Facing her distaste, he'd actually felt as if he smelled. The small, gnarled woman with snow-white hair and a nose seemingly designed for looking down on people had proceeded to deplore his appearance, his lowborn mother, his upbringing, his accent, and the sins of his scapegrace father, whom she'd never expected to hear of again after she packed him off into exile. But there was no help for it, she'd declared at the end of this tirade. Jack was now the earl. She would have to force him onto Society. It might just be possible if he followed her lead in every respect and kept his mouth shut.

Of course, Jack had rebelled. No red-blooded man would stomach such words, particularly about his mother. The mixture of motives that had brought him across the sea evaporated in an instant. He had no interest in joining any society that included people like Lady Wilton.

Bruised and resentful, Jack had nearly boarded a ship and returned to Boston right after that meeting. But he hadn't quite. He'd set off north instead. Only when he'd been walking for a full day did his anger cool enough to acknowledge he was hurt as well as outraged. The truth was, he'd been drawn here by an idea of family, a homely thing he'd never had. He'd read stories about domestic tranquility and seen glimpses of it among his friends, but his childhood had been fragmented and contentious. His parents couldn't seem to agree on anything except their tempestuous reconciliations after a shouted dispute. Jack had been audience or afterthought, often left to fend for himself.

When the summons to England came, he'd actually imagined a welcome by a circle of kin, a place where he belonged. He'd found disdain instead, rejection without any chance to show his worth. It was painful to be the unwanted earl, the bane of his father's kin. The inner bruise had been expanding rather than fading as time and distance separated him from London.

"Are you a dreamer?" said a voice near his knee.

"What?" Jack looked down to find a girl of perhaps six or seven trudging along beside him. Tiny, dark-haired, and bright-eyed, she peered up at him.

"You didn't hear what I said three times. That's a dreamer."

"I beg your pardon. I was thinking."

"About what?"

"My great-grandmother."

"Do you miss her?" asked the little girl.

"No, she thinks I'm a disgrace."

"What did you do?"

That was the point. He'd done nothing but be born into Lady Wilton's precious bloodline. Half into it. His mother's lineage was not to be mentioned. Jack hadn't *asked* to come here or be an earl. "Not a thing."

The little girl took this in solemnly. She seemed to decide to believe him. "You're too old to be scolded."

"A man might think so."

"How old are you?"

"Twenty-four."

"I'm nearly eight. My name's Samia."

Jack stopped walking, doffed his hat, and gave her the sort of elegant bow he'd learned from his wayward father. He had absorbed a good deal from the man, whatever his great-grandmother might think. "Jack…" He hesitated. His last name might be better concealed. Lady Wilton was no doubt furious at his disobedience and perfectly capable of organizing pursuit. "At your service, Miss Samia," he added. "Very pleased to make your acquaintance."

She giggled, then looked around to see if any of her friends had noticed his bow. They had. Samia preened as they walked on, and she assumed a proprietary air as other children joined them and Jack told them tales of another continent.

When the group stopped for the night in a clearing

well off the road, Jack helped gather wood for the fires and carry water. Borrowing some lengths of cord, he set snares that might yield a rabbit or two by morning. He was given terse thanks and a tattered blanket to augment his meager belongings.

Later there was shared stew and music around the central fire. When he rolled up in the blanket and pillowed his head on his arm, Jack felt the first stirrings of contentment. He went to sleep in the pleasure of companionship, wondering only how he might best contribute to the group and earn his meals. His snares gave a partial answer to that question in the morning, yielding several rabbits for the pot. He vowed to discover more.

Jack fell easily into the Travelers' erratic schedule. Some days the caravans moved; others they stayed in a place to sell objects the Travelers crafted or offer repairs to the people of a village or farmstead. The old lady sometimes read fortunes for those who came to inquire. Jack didn't mind the slow pace. There was no particular hurry to see his ancestral acres, and he enjoyed the rhythm of the road. He did have wandering feet. He began to make—not friends, for this was a closed group, but cordial acquaintances. Some exhaustive conversations had established that his mother was not directly related to any of these Travelers, so he couldn't claim kin right. But similarity of spirit created bonds. He enjoyed them, along with the certainty that his continuing absence must be infuriating his noble great-grandmother. That was a solid satisfaction. He would see what others he could find as time passed.

❦

"Not that you would know anything about that," declared the fat, choleric-looking man taking up the entire front-facing seat in the traveling carriage.

"No, Papa," said Harriet Finch's mother meekly.

Harriet gritted her teeth to keep back a sharp retort. She'd had years of practice swallowing slights and insults, so she wouldn't let anything slip. But hours in a coach with her grandfather had tried her to the limit. From the less comfortable rear-facing seat, she looked at her mother's father, Horace Winstead. Winstead the nabob. Winstead the all-knowing, according to him. She'd never spent so much time with him before. They hadn't been thrown together like this during the months of the London season. Now that she'd endured a large dose of his company, she was afraid their new living arrangements were a mistake. How long would she be able to hold her tongue?

She hadn't met her grandfather until this year because he had so disapproved of her parents' marriage that he disowned his daughter. More than disowned. He'd vengefully pursued the young couple, ruining her new husband's prospects by saying despicable things about him. Horace Winstead had consigned Harriet's family to genteel poverty for her entire life. And then, suddenly, after the death of a cousin she'd never met, he'd turned about and declared he would leave his immense fortune to Harriet, now his only grandchild.

The reversal had been dizzying. New clothes, a lavish house in London for the season, a changed position in society.

Young ladies who'd spurned Harriet at school when she paid her way with tutoring pretended to be bosom friends. Young men suddenly found her fascinating. A thin smile curved Harriet's lips. They found her prospective income fascinating. Some hardly bothered to disguise their greed.

Harriet was expected to receive this largesse with humble gratitude. She couldn't count the number of people who'd told her how lucky she was. She was not to mind her grandfather's "abrupt" manners or ever lose her temper in his presence. He was to be catered to like a veritable monarch lest he change his mind and eject them. It was nearly insupportable. And one of the hardest parts of all was her mother had felt redeemed.

Harriet glanced at her sole remaining parent and received an anxious look in response. Mama knew she was annoyed, and her eyes begged Harriet not to let it show. Years of worry had carved creases around Mama's mouth and added an emotional tremor to her manners. She continually expected disaster, and she'd often been quite right to do so. Brought back into the fold of her youth, she'd been so happy. Had she really thought Grandfather had changed? He still treated her with something close to contempt, even though she agreed with everything he said.

Harriet gave Mama a nod and a smile, silently promising she wouldn't add to her burdens. Harriet might sometimes wish her mother had more fire, but Mama's youthful rebellion had brought her years of scrimping, an early grief, and very little joy. She deserved some ease and comfort now. Harriet could not take it from her.

She sat back and watched the landscape passing the carriage window. She took deep breaths to ease her temper, a method she'd learned at an early age. At least she could revel in the knowledge that she resembled her father, Harriet thought. Her grandfather must notice it every time he looked at her. She'd inherited her red-blond hair, green eyes, and pointed chin beneath a broad forehead from her papa. He'd been a handsome man, though bitterness had marred his looks as he aged. His fierce drive to support his family, continually thwarted, had broken his health. Harriet could not actually prove that her grandfather's meanness had killed her father, but she thought it. And this made her present life a painful conundrum.

"The countryside here is very fine," said the old man. He pointed out the window. "That is Ferrington Hall, the principal seat of an earl. A neighbor of mine."

Harriet perked up at this name and leaned forward to look. She'd heard of Ferrington Hall while in London. An acquaintance, Lady Wilton, had complained that its new owner, her great-grandson, was missing. Peering through a screen of trees, she could just see a sprawling stone manor. "Is the earl in residence?" she asked.

"Not at present," replied her grandfather.

She could tell from his tone that he knew nothing about it. Harriet remembered her friend Charlotte Deeping saying, "We will unravel the mystery of the missing earl." How she missed her friends! She'd been allowed to invite Sarah and Charlotte for a visit later in the summer. She couldn't wait.

Ferrington Hall disappeared as they drove on, and in

another few miles, they came to her grandfather's country house, the spoils of the fortune he'd made in trade. But Harriet was not supposed to think of that, let alone ever mention it. People in society despised business, and those who benefited from commercial success hid it like a disreputable secret. It seemed ridiculous to Harriet. Everyone knew. And how was it any better to have gained lands and estates with a medieval broadsword?

"Here it is—Winstead Hall," said her grandfather. "I changed the name when I bought it, of course."

Of course he had. Horace Winstead put his stamp on anything he touched. Or, if he could not, he demeaned it.

They passed through stone gateposts, traversed a tree-lined avenue, and pulled up before the central block, a red-brick building studded with tall chimneys. It was not large, but a sprawling wing constructed of pale-gray stone had been added at one end, and another was going up on the opposite side. The sound of hammering rang across the lush summer lawns.

Servants appeared at the front door, hurrying out to receive them. As more and more emerged, Harriet realized she was to meet the entire staff in her first moment here.

"They ought to be ready," grumbled her grandfather. "I suppose the coachman forgot to send word ahead."

She understood then that the servants were required to turn out every time he arrived. Her grandfather probably imagined that was how great noblemen were received at their country homes. She'd noticed he equated pomp with rank.

Horace Winstead longed to be accepted by the

aristocracy. He'd planned to purchase entry into those exalted circles by marrying his daughter to a title. That was one reason he'd been so vindictive when Mama met and married a junior member of his company. Papa's intelligence, diligence, and business acumen hadn't mattered a whit. He'd thwarted Horace Winstead, so he had to be punished. Now Grandfather expected Harriet to fulfill his social ambitions. She'd heard him say his fortune ought to net him a viscount at least. Harriet's fists clenched in her lap, and she had to wrestle with her temper once again. Her London season had been shadowed by Grandfather's demand for a lord. If she so much as smiled at a commoner or seemed to enjoy dancing with one, he scolded her mother into tears.

They stepped down from the carriage and walked toward the door. The servants bowed and curtsied as they passed along the line. Harriet saw no sign of emotion from any of them—certainly not welcome. Slade, the superior abigail her grandfather had hired to dress her, would not appreciate this ritual. In fact, Harriet couldn't imagine the thin, upright woman participating. She would view it with the sour expression she reserved for cheap jewelry and fussily ornamented gowns. It was fortunate this display would be over by the time the vehicle carrying Slade, her mother's attendant, and her grandfather's valet arrived.

They entered the house, moving through a cramped entryway into a parlor crammed with costly furnishings, Eastern silks, and indifferent paintings. It looked more like a shop offering luxury goods than a cozy sitting room. Harriet felt as if the clutter was closing in on her, strange and oppressive. Her mother wandered about, seemingly in a daze. She had not grown up here; her father had purchased the house after her marriage.

"You can see we will be quite comfortable here," said her grandfather with his usual complaisance.

Harriet's spirits sank as she thought of the days ahead. There would be long, heavy dinners, tedious evenings, and many difficult conversations. Indeed, all the conversations were likely to be hard. How would they manage, just the three of them? She knew her grandfather had not received invitations to fashionable house parties, and she doubted his neighbors here included him in their social round. As far as she had seen, he had no friends.

"We will settle in and plan our strategy for next season," the old man said. "You have not made a proper push to attract a noble husband, Harriet. You must try harder."

Harriet started to reply, saw her mother's worried frown, and bit her lip. She didn't know what she was going to do. She couldn't swallow her anger forever.

∽

Harriet slipped out a side door of Winstead Hall and moved quickly to a line of shrubbery that would hide her from the house. Strictly speaking, she was not supposed to wander about alone. It hadn't been specifically forbidden, however. Mainly because her mother didn't realize she was doing it. Harriet had evolved a variety of excuses to withdraw to her room during this visit, and so far, they had been working.

Slade might have noticed her absences, but the dresser was not the sort to tattle. She would speak to Harriet if she had concerns.

Fortunately, her grandfather spent his mornings on business matters, reviewing documents or conferring with employees up from London. If she avoided him in the afternoons, she only had to spend evenings with him. It was all she could bear. She thought she would burst if she had to watch every word for much longer than that.

Harriet opened the parasol she'd brought with her. Her pale skin tended to redden with the least exposure to the sun, and Mama would notice that. She walked through the gardens to a path she'd found that went across a grassy field and into a wood. It was well away from the hammering of workmen on Winstead Hall's new wing, and it led toward Ferrington Hall. Harriet remained curious about that neighboring estate. Lady Wilton had made such a to-do about its missing heir. Harriet had gone over to peek at the neglected house more than once.

She walked fast, eager to expend some of the energy that built up in her at Winstead Hall. It was better to be tired than mad with frustration.

A little more than halfway along her customary route, Harriet began to hear a chorus of unfamiliar sounds—children shouting, the ring of a smith's hammer, a barking dog. As she moved on, they grew louder. Finally, when they seemed nearly on top of her, Harriet looked through a screen of vegetation and discovered a band of Travelers camped in a meadow. They hadn't been there yesterday.

She drew back, not frightened but cautious. She didn't know very much about the nomadic Travelers. Some people complained of them, but the people she could see in the camp didn't look shiftless. They were busy with about a dozen tasks. She didn't think she'd be welcome in their midst, however. She also resented this intrusion on her woodland refuge. This was Ferrington land, where they had no real right to be. Perhaps they'd discovered the hall was empty.

Harriet watched the camp for a few more minutes. Children ran gaily between the roofed wagons, which were decorated with twining painted designs. Women sat together over some sort of handwork. Two men tended a picket line of horses. It looked more idyllic than threatening. She saw no reason to change her habit of observing Ferrington Hall. She didn't think any Travelers would enter its grounds.

She skirted the encampment and went on, slipping through a small, overgrown gate in the walls around the manor. She'd never seen anyone out on the estate, not even a gardener, though the plantings were in need of attention.

Harriet walked through the grounds, enjoying her solitude, feeling the tension in her shoulders ease. She *required* this respite from her grandfather's house and his hovering presence. She was grateful for it.

Her path gave her intermittent glimpses of the house. There were at least two people living in the substantial dwelling, and she'd never gone too close for fear of being seen. She didn't wish to be questioned.

She had completed most of her usual circuit when she rounded a clump of oaks and came face-to-face with a stranger. Broad-shouldered, powerful-looking, with brown hair and alert, dark eyes, the man looked as surprised as she. His clothes were worn and had a foreign feel. Though of good quality, they certainly were not the product of a fine London tailor. She'd seen enough of those garments to know. He didn't look as if he belonged here. But then, she was out of place herself. She backed up a few steps.

"Who are you?" they said at the same moment.

Neither answered the question. Instead, once again they echoed each other, asking, "Do you live here?"

Harriet shook her head. The man gave a kind of half shrug that she took as a negative. "What are you doing here?" she asked.

"Taking a look at the house," he replied.

He had an odd accent. Harriet couldn't pin down its origins. It was not that of the local countrymen. He must have come from the Travelers' camp, she realized, and thus should not be within these walls. Perhaps what people said about the Travelers was true. Ignoring the fact that she had no right to be here either, she said, "So you could rob it?"

"What? No, why would you… Ah, you saw the Travelers, did you? And you think them thieves."

"Aren't you?"

"I am not. Nor are they, mostly."

"Mostly?"

"Well, if a thing is left entirely unattended, perhaps forgotten, it might walk off now and then," he replied with a glint in his dark eyes.

He wasn't handsome as most would define it. His

features were too rough-hewn. Yet he was undeniably attractive. Perhaps it was that glint, which hinted at antic humor and something…more like a wild creature than tamed. "You condone robbery?" Harriet asked.

"I didn't say that now."

She caught an echo of Ireland in his voice. But only a trace; she didn't think he was Irish. "You're trespassing."

"And you are not?"

"I beg your pardon?"

"You said you don't live here," Jack pointed out to one of the prettiest girls he'd ever seen. She had hair as red as his mother's and a face like a fairy-tale sprite. Her dress and way of speaking did suggest she was part of his great-grandmother's capital-S society. Particularly the parasol. That was a drawback, but still, he couldn't resist. "You could come along and watch me if you're worried about my intentions."

"Watch you what?"

"Look at the house."

"No." She didn't walk away though. She seemed curious, as if she might be tempted.

Thinking he would very much like to tempt her, Jack said, "Shouldn't you make certain I don't break in and ravage the place?"

She blinked at him. Those green eyes were stunners. She hesitated, definitely wavering. "Someone will see us. There are people in the house."

Jack almost laughed. He'd nearly lured her in. He could feel the tug on his invisible line. "Not just now. The old couple who watches over the place have gone off in a gig."

"How do you know that?"

"I observed it."

The phrase seemed to startle and interest her. "You mean you've been snooping."

"If you care to put it that way. I might have said *reconnoitering*."

"Why? You said you weren't a thief."

He wasn't going to tell her the true reason. The less people knew about him, the better now that he'd reached his ancestral lands. "Curiosity. Wondering at the state of the place."

"There might be others inside."

He was winning her over, and a true pleasure it was. "I don't think so. The stables are empty with the gig gone. And the shutters are closed on the upper floors." In fact, Ferrington Hall looked as if it hadn't had any careful attention in years. "My name's Jack," he added.

She tossed her head.

"It would be polite for you to give me your name now."

"No, it would not. This is not a proper introduction."

Certainly a society girl, Jack concluded. And yet he couldn't resist. "Very well, I shall call you Miss Snoot." He turned toward the house. "Are you coming along with me, Miss Snoot?"

"Do not call me that!" But she followed him.

Jack enjoyed the sound of her footsteps behind him. He enjoyed the thought of her trailing in his wake.

For the first time, he went right up to Ferrington Hall, his father's birthplace, as he understood it. He peered through a tall window. He'd never seen such a large house. There were such mansions in America, but he hadn't moved in those circles.

"The furniture is all under covers," said his lovely companion. She'd put her nose to the glass right beside him.

"Those sheets spread over things, you mean?"

"Yes. No one can be living here."

"Didn't I say so?"

"I wonder what has become of the earl," she murmured.

Jack stiffened. "What's that?"

"The Earl of Ferrington. This is his house. He's missing."

"Is he now?"

"Yes. His great-grandmother Lady Wilton is concerned."

"You don't say so? Friend of hers, are you?" If she was, this would be the end, however pretty the girl was.

She frowned. "No. I have *met* her."

"A lovely old lady, is she?"

His companion shook her head. "I would not describe her in those terms." She wrinkled her nose. "I don't think anyone would."

Perhaps it was all right. Jack wanted it to be all right. "What term would you use then?"

"Irascible?" She put a gloved hand to her lovely lips. "Oh, I didn't mean to say…"

"Mean as a snake, is she?" Jack inquired, elated at the slip. A girl who didn't like Lady Wilton had definite possibilities.

She pressed her lips together on what might have been a smile. But she didn't answer.

"Shall we look in some other rooms?"

"We really shouldn't." But she moved along to another window.

They made their way around the house in this manner, Jack now and then saying, "After you, Miss Snoot." Her indignant objections to this label were a pure pleasure.

To Jack, Ferrington Hall was a confusing jumble of large chambers shrouded in white sheets, like the domicile of ghosts. He didn't see what a man would do with so many rooms. Once you had a place for sleeping and for sitting and perhaps a study with a desk, what else was needed? The large, unkempt emptiness of this place was daunting.

When they'd made the full circuit, his companion noticed the angle of the sun and said, "I should go."

"Leaving me alone to ransack the house?" asked Jack.

"Is that what you intend to do?"

Was there the suggestion of a twinkle in her green eyes? Or was he imagining it? Jack didn't think so. "It might be," he replied to keep her by him.

"I don't think you have nefarious purposes after all."

"Nefarious, is it? You expect me to know a word like that?"

"It means…"

"The sort of fellow who would plot a robbery. In short, a rogue."

She looked surprised. And perhaps interested? "Are you a rogue?"

"Would you prefer that I was or was not, Miss Snoot?"

"Don't call me that!"

"What shall I call you then?"

She turned away to hide her expression. The dashed parasol was useful for that. It dipped between them.

"I might be a bit of a rogue, now and then," Jack suggested. "But I never hurt a lady in my life and never will."

This won him a flashing glance. "I should go," she repeated.

"Home," said Jack.

"No, not home."

Her tone was bleak, and Jack understood its nuances far better than she could have imagined. "To the house where you're staying then?"

"Yes."

"Where's that?"

"Nearby."

It had to be, since she'd walked here. And on her own as well. She was a neighbor. "I'd be happy to escort you," he tried.

"No!" That had spooked her, clearly. She gave him the parasol again, turned, and hurried away.

Jack noted the direction she went, but he didn't follow. That might seem threatening, and he didn't wish to worry her. Heading back to the camp, he reviewed this unexpected meeting. He'd thought he would just take a look at Ferrington Hall and then move on, but now he decided he might as well stay a little while.

Two

WALKING BACK TOWARD WINSTEAD HALL, HARRIET scarcely noticed the turns of the path or the birds calling in the leaves. Her mind was full of this fellow Jack. Why had he made such a strong impression on her? She'd met handsomer men, certainly. True, some of them were perfect stocks, about as lively as a statue. Jack was the opposite of that. His zest and vitality drew one's gaze. She'd had to resist watching him, even when he wasn't indulging in a bout of impudent wit—of which he seemed to have a boundless supply. Miss Snoot, indeed. In the privacy of her solitude, Harriet smiled as she walked.

He was different from anyone she'd met before, she realized, and that made him memorable. This Jack had a jaunty sense of freedom. As if he might do anything at any moment, whatever he pleased, in fact. He made Harriet imagine boundless liberty, a thing she'd never had in her life. The very idea made her wistful. What would it be like to roam with the wind, to have no obligations?

Harriet had lived in a meager household as a child, become a sometimes-despised working pupil at her exclusive girls' school, and then had one whirlwind London season, during which she'd never quite found her feet. She'd not met a rogue outside the pages of a novel. Young ladies were carefully kept far away from such people, for good reason. But this Jack hadn't felt dangerous. As a poor girl with no social power, Harriet had learned to detect unsavory intentions. She'd had to fend off an oily dancing master at school, among others. And she'd felt no such threat from Jack. He seemed charming, fascinating, nearly mythical. Perhaps she would call him Jack in the Green when she saw him again.

And there, her train of thought stuttered to a stop. Of course, she wouldn't see him again. Now that he was lurking around Ferrington Hall, along with the Travelers, she couldn't walk there. He'd taken that option from her, narrowing her world, as so much seemed to do these days. Resentment bubbled up, tinged with a curiously mournful disappointment. But life was seldom fair. She'd learned that very young.

Harriet slipped back into the garden of her grandfather's house and entered the shrubbery. If she had been missed, she could claim to have been wandering in this evergreen maze designed for shelter on colder or windy days. She hurried through it, conscious of the hour, emerged on the side nearest the house, turned toward the door, and nearly bumped into the burly figure of her grandfather.

"Ha, Harriet," he said.

She hadn't seen him in the garden before, and he looked out of place. He was a creature of the city, of offices and counting houses and cobbled streets. She would be surprised if he could tell one sort of tree from another and was certain he didn't care. More worrying was the fact this would be their first private conversation. Her mother had always hovered over them before.

"Been taking a turn around the grounds? They're thought to be very fine, you know."

Anything he owned had to be superlative. Telling herself he had no reason to suspect she'd walked beyond his property, Harriet said, "Yes."

"You never take any luncheon, I believe."

"No."

"That's why you're slender as a reed. Shall we walk a little?"

Harriet wanted to refuse, but she could find no reason for such out-and-out rudeness. He started off, and she fell in beside him, using her parasol as a shield. She was nearly as tall as he, she realized. Though he was far broader.

Her grandfather took a gravel path bordered by a glory of flowers, turned left and then right, coming up to a circular bed of red blooms surrounding a statue Harriet hadn't noticed before. It depicted a plump man sitting cross-legged with a serene smile.

"Ah, there it is," said her grandfather. "I came out to be sure they'd settled it properly. You've never seen anything like that, I expect."

She shook her head. "What is it?"

"That is Buddha. An Eastern god, you know. I bought him because we're both fat." He slapped his ample stomach.

"You think him a god?" It slipped out. And Harriet could hear that it sounded incredulous. Her grandfather had never shown belief in anything besides himself.

"Of course not. I just like the shape of him." The old man nodded his approval of the installation and turned back the way they'd come. "You don't care for foreign lands?" he asked.

"What?"

"You look sour whenever I speak of places where I do business. Or perhaps your grand friends have given you a disdain for trade?"

She hadn't thought he noticed anyone but himself, and she couldn't interpret his tone. He didn't sound angry. Yet. "I don't know a great deal about it," Harriet replied.

"Next to nothing, I would think. Except that my money paid for your fancy gowns and such."

She couldn't resist. "I do know that we British have enriched ourselves in many places around the world. With little regard for the people who live there."

"Ah."

Harriet pressed her lips together. Her mother would have a nervous collapse if she alienated her grandfather.

"We've also spread a system of law. And industry."

She couldn't stop herself. "So we are benefactors."

"No, mostly we're just filling our pockets. I certainly did."

She couldn't interpret his expression. Was he simply self-satisfied?

"I suppose you would prefer I'd remained a shopkeeper, scraping by from year to year. But where would that leave you now, eh?"

For once in her life, Harriet was speechless.

"You don't like me." He gave her a sidelong glance. "Did you think I hadn't noticed? I'm not stupid."

Harriet let the parasol dip so she wouldn't have to face him. "It's because of your father, I imagine."

This was too much. "You ruined him!"

The old man nodded. "Yes, I took my revenge after he crossed me."

"You admit it. You have no remorse?"

Her grandfather shrugged. Clearly, he did not. Anger flooded Harriet. How could he be so shameless?

The old man clasped his hands behind his back as they walked on. "I liked Finch, you know. Admired his abilities. I had plans for him, before he stole my daughter away."

"Mama is not a…a piece of property to be bartered."

"They never should have met," he went on as if he hadn't heard her. "I didn't think… Well, I keep my business separate now. Have you encountered any of my employees?"

"No."

"And you won't. I shan't make that mistake again." His round face set in obstinate lines.

Harriet almost wished she could descend on his offices, seize one of his minions, and marry him out of hand.

"Your father must have known what would happen. He'd worked for me for years. He'd seen that I have a bad temper." He owned it as if a temper was as immutable as blue eyes or pale skin and not a trait he might control.

"He was in love," Harriet retorted. "As was Mama."

"Well, they got their love." He gave her a sardonic look. "That was the bargain they made. And perhaps came to regret."

Harriet would never admit that. Indeed, she didn't think

it was true. Which did not excuse her grandfather's attitude or his behavior. Nothing could do that.

"I married for capital and an heir," he went on.

Harriet had wondered about her grandmother, who had died before she was born. She knew nothing about her.

"I got the funds I needed all right and tight." His mouth turned down. "But a sickly son. He lived just long enough to produce a copy of himself, who didn't even manage that much."

This was the deceased cousin Harriet had never met. She wondered what had become of his mother.

"And Mama," she had to point out.

"Yes. A daughter who defied me." He spoke as if he still couldn't quite believe it, even after all these years. "So, you see, you must take care just what sort of bargain you make." He gave her a searching look.

Harriet blocked it with her parasol.

"I won't be cheated again," he added.

The threat was obvious. He saw marriage as a business transaction, and he expected her to use it, bringing him a link to the nobility. If she did not do as he wished, she would not be the heir to his fortune. On the contrary, she and Mama would be subjected to the same sort of revenge that had killed her father.

"I'm glad we had this talk," the old man said as they reached the house.

He seemed to think they'd resolved something. He had no idea how he'd fed Harriet's burning desire to thwart him.

✑

Over the next two days, Jack walked a spiraling path around
Ferrington Hall, widening his ambit with each loop, searching for the lair of the lovely Miss Snoot. Her real name would
have helped, but he had no doubt he would find her without it. Over the course of an errant life, he'd learned how to
observe and gather information without attracting too much
attention to himself. A bit of time and a few casual questions
would tell him who lived in any likely houses he found. And
it was no hardship to amble around the countryside on fine
summer afternoons. He liked knowing the territory.

He had high hopes at first for a manor to the east, but
he discovered it was inhabited by an old squire and his wife
with no sign of any visitors. A large and prosperous farmstead seemed unlikely, given the dress and manner of his
quarry, but he took the time to make certain. Finally, on the
third day of his wandering, he came upon Winstead Hall,
and something told him this was the place.

He circled the house at a distance, watching the builders at work on a new wing and the gardeners busy at their
tasks. Drifting out to the surrounding fields, he surveyed
the laborers until he found one with the look of a man who
didn't relish hard work. Leaning on the fence nearby, Jack
said, "Good bit of building going on yonder."

The man seemed glad to pause and lean on his hoe. "Aye.
Making it grand as a palace. Or so this Winstead fella thinks,
any road."

"Master of the hall, is he?"

"He is *now*. Bought the place ten years back and changed
the name. Brant Hall was good enough for everybody before

that." The man scratched at the front of his smock. "They say this Winstead made a packet of money in foreign parts."

"And now he's back with his family to enjoy it, I suppose," Jack prompted.

"Nobody reckoned he had any family, but he's brought a pair of ladies along this time. Daughter and granddaughter, I hear."

Jack felt certain Miss Snoot was the latter. And that he would soon find her. "Sounds like a lucky man," he said, ready to be on his way.

"I don't know about luck. They say he gets above himself. Tries to act like a lord when he ain't any such thing." The man hawked and spit. "We got a lord, over to Ferrington Hall. Don't need any other."

"Ferrington, is it?" asked Jack, diverted.

"The earl lives there. Always has."

Always seemed an exaggeration, but Jack couldn't help asking, "What's he like then?"

For the first time, the laborer looked uncertain. "Dunno. His lordship died near on a year ago. The Rileys are waiting for the new fella to show up."

"Rileys?"

"They've watched over the place. Well as they can with no help. It's all gone to pot, I'd say. The new earl ought to set things to rights."

"Why do you need some lord swanning about, giving orders?" Jack asked him.

The man frowned. "The earl looks after the people hereabouts, gives a helping hand where needed. Belike he'd put this Winstead in his place." This idea clearly gratified him. "The last lord weren't much for settling disputes. Folks are hoping for better with the new one."

"Sam, are you working or not?" called an older laborer from the other side of the field. "Cause if you're not, you may as well take yourself off."

Jack's informant made a sour face and turned away to ply his hoe.

Jack sauntered down the lane, maintaining his character as an idler while he thought over what Sam had said. He knew nothing about the duties of an earl. He hadn't realized that a neighborhood might rely on such a person.

Once he was out of sight, Jack began to look for a spot to observe Winstead Hall without being noticed. He found one quite easily. The place had no high walls and seemingly no thought for security. Builders, more than likely strangers to the household, swarmed over one end of it. He was unlikely to be marked.

In less than an hour, Jack had his answer. This was indeed the dwelling place, if not the home, of the lovely Miss Snoot. Who was perhaps really Miss Winstead. She walked out of the house and into the gardens at midafternoon, wearing another fashionable gown, again holding a parasol. Jack waited to see if she might venture out toward Ferrington Hall. But she began a circuit of the gardens instead, and he found he was disappointed. He'd thought she had more spirit than that, or more interest in him. He began to make his way toward her, using the cover the lush gardens provided.

Harriet walked fast, plagued by an excess of energy. This visit to the country was an unsettling combination of tedium and tension. She had books to read, a pianoforte to play, and her mother's company, but she was accustomed to the society of her friends from school. They'd still seen each other nearly every day during the London season, and she missed them very much. Instead of their pleasant company, she had what was now defined as her family. She was required to make amiable conversation with her grandfather each evening, under her mother's tremulous, anxious gaze. Any misstep brought her reproaches from both sides. It was oppressive.

The noise of hammering and the calls of the builders followed her along the paths. The Winstead Hall garden was noisy all day, even at the farthest end from the construction works. The tumult was another push outward, toward the small woodland and Ferrington Hall. But when she'd walked there again yesterday, Jack the Rogue had not been in evidence. Harriet had realized she'd expected him to be awaiting her return. She'd imagined he was as struck by her as she was by him, and his absence had stung. Though tempted to ask the Travelers about him, she hadn't quite dared intrude on their camp. She supposed she would never see him again, which was…too melancholy a thought for comfort.

And on that note of wistful regret, the man stepped out of the shrubbery and saluted her.

Harriet felt her jaw drop in astonishment. "You!"

"None other, Miss Snoot."

"Don't call me that." His smile was as dazzling as she remembered, a flash of white teeth in a tanned face, reaching and warming his brown eyes in a way that seemed to heat her as well. Though he didn't look a great deal older than her nineteen years, he had such a confident air. She imagined this man had lived a life crammed with adventure. "What are you doing here? How did you get in?"

"Not much to stop a visitor. I thought I'd see where you came from."

"You searched for me?" That was why he'd been missing yesterday.

"I asked about the neighborhood. Miss Winstead, is it?"

"That is not my name!" She hadn't meant to snap, but the idea of sharing her grandfather's name was repugnant.

"Ah? I understood that the owner of this estate was called Winstead. Named the place for himself, in fact."

"He is my grandfather." Who would summarily eject this intruder from his garden. Indeed, Harriet thought, her grandfather would deplore every single thing about Jack the Rogue. He would forbid her to speak to him, a connection far worse than any acquaintance with one of his employees. She could practically hear his sputters of indignation. How splendid. "I am Harriet Finch," she said.

The visitor made a surprisingly elegant bow. "Pleased to make your acquaintance, Miss Finch."

He had finer manners than one would have expected of a rogue. But then it occurred to her that a plausible facade was probably quite useful for...roguishness. "And now it would be polite for you to give me your full name," she said, echoing his earlier words to her.

"Ah."

"Or shall I call you Jack the Rogue, Jack in the Green?" She was glad to have gotten that in.

He smiled. "Jack Mer..." He seemed to bite off the last word.

Harriet waited, but he said no more. "Mere? Like Grasmere or Windermere?"

He looked uncomfortable, shrugged.

He didn't like questions. Unless he was asking them. Rogues would have secrets, Harriet acknowledged. They would be positively crammed with secrets. In fact, Jack Mere was a sort of human puzzle waiting to be deciphered. And she loved unraveling mysteries. "What do you do?" she asked.

"Do?"

"Have you a...a profession or a livelihood?" Some rogues played tricks to bilk people of their money. She hoped it wasn't that. "Gypsies breed horses, don't they?"

"What have gypsies to do with anything?" he asked.

"Well, you are living in the camp."

"Travelers and gypsies are two different things," he said. "Travelers are from Ireland and gypsies... Well, I don't know. Somewhere else."

"Egypt? I think I heard that." Harriet thought this probably came from her friend Sarah, who was always reading about arcane topics and delighted to share her gleanings.

He shrugged. "Could be. Travelers come from the Gaels. Or so my mother said."

"She was a Traveler?"

Again, he didn't seem to like being questioned. Finally, he said, "Yes."

"So then, you Travelers…"

"I am not really a Traveler. I've just been walking along with them for a space."

"Why? Are you hiding from the law?"

"No, I am not. Why would you think so?"

"Rogues often have to evade the magistrates, I believe. So I have heard, at any rate." She was teasing him a little. But she also wanted to know all about him.

"You're very fond of that word *rogue*. I think you've read too many lurid tales."

In fact, she hadn't read nearly enough. "You don't… deceive the gullible?"

He looked scandalized. "Never. I've done a deal of different things, but I always earn my keep fair and square."

"What sorts of things?"

He gazed at her as if evaluating something. "I went along on a frontier expedition two years ago," he said. "I managed the animals and supplies and helped the mapmakers."

"Frontier?"

"Out in the Missouri Territory." He cocked his head. "Never heard of it, have you? It has nothing to do with your own little country."

"We were rather occupied with a war two years ago," Harriet pointed out.

"Napoleon, aye, I know."

"You are American?" That explained the unusual accent.

Jack the Rogue hesitated. His reluctance to give out information made Harriet feel as if she was trying to pick his pocket. She rather liked the sensation. At last, he said, "My mother came to Boston as a child. My father was English."

"So you are here to visit his homeland?"

His expression was rueful. He gave a half shrug. "I suppose I am that."

"And then you will be going back to your…frontier?"

"To a fine, cultured city on the River Charles," he replied. "We have plenty of those."

"Rivers?"

"Cities."

"You are the one who spoke of frontiers. What do you do in your city? Boston, I suppose?" She had heard of it.

"You're quite an inquisitive young lady, are you not? Is this the way they talk in high society?"

"No. They don't wish to learn anything. Unless it is a piece of malicious gossip. Which they pass along with the *greatest* hesitation, of course."

"Assuring you that, more than likely, it isn't true," he replied. "Even though a great many people seem to be saying it." He grimaced. "Because the sneaking creature has been telling them all to be sure it's repeated."

"You've gone into society?" He didn't dress or speak like the people Harriet had met during the season.

"I know how damaging stories are spread."

Of course he did. He was a rogue. "Because you have done so?"

"No, Miss Snoot, I have not. And I shall call you that because it fits you better than your real name."

"It does not!"

"Indeed, it does. Finches are lovely little birds, as bright and innocent as the air. You, on the other hand, poke and pry and look down your nose."

"I do not!" The idea revolted her. "I'm far too familiar with contempt to ever indulge in it."

"What would a rich girl know about that?"

"I'm not rich."

He looked around, gesturing at the house, the lush gardens.

"My grandfather is," Harriet acknowledged.

"And this is his home, not yours." When Harriet blinked in surprise, he added, "You said it wasn't home."

"No, it is not."

"Where is your home then?"

"I haven't one." She bit off the final word. She hadn't meant to say that. Though it was certainly true. Mama had given up the rented house where they'd once lived. "My mother and I are his dependents. He will take it all away if we defy him."

"That's an uncomfortable state of being."

He said it with quiet understanding. No argument. None of the bantering that had laced their earlier conversation. Harriet looked into his dark eyes and found them full of sympathy. It felt as if he knew exactly what her situation was like and how rebellious and anxious it made her feel. She couldn't think what to say. The silence was stretching too long. Finally, she simply nodded.

"But you know, there's a kind of freedom in it, too," Jack Mere added.

The tremulous moment collapsed like a soap bubble. He didn't really understand. How could he? "For you, perhaps. You can wander and…blather and be a rogue. Do whatever you like. I cannot."

"I'm not really…"

Harriet heard her name called. She turned toward the sound. It was her mother's voice, which was unusual out of doors. "You must go. If my grandfather discovers you, he will have you thrown off his property."

"Will he now?"

"Oh yes." Harriet might have liked to annoy her grandfather. But she didn't want to distress her mother. Wasn't that the pinching point of her current life? She didn't want to see Jack insulted either.

"Might you walk toward Ferrington Hall another time?" he asked.

She wanted to see him again. That was clear, though not very wise. "Perhaps."

"I could take you to visit the Travelers' camp."

"Would they let me in?" Harriet was curious about these wandering people.

"If you come with me. Tomorrow, perhaps?"

"I will see. I cannot always get away."

"Trying is all we can do," he answered. And with a nod, he disappeared into the shrubbery. Harriet had no doubt he would not be seen if he didn't wish to be. He seemed a man of many unusual skills. She went to see what had brought her mother out to find her.

☙

Jack brooded over the deception about his name as he walked back toward the Travelers' camp. If he'd told her he was Jack Merrill, she'd have connected him with the missing earl. If not right away, then soon. And she knew Lady Wilton was after him. Could anyone resist passing along that information? He didn't want to find out. Such a revelation would bring his furious great-grandmother down on him and force his choices. He would have to take up the position the old lady wanted to thrust on him or leave, and he didn't want to do either of those things just yet. So he'd lied to a girl—as smart and lively as she was beautiful—who drew him more and more. Partly, he wished he hadn't, but his lips had literally not let him say the name.

So he'd deceived her. He'd meant no harm. He wasn't trying to put anything over on her. Except—she seemed to like the idea of a rogue, and he was playing that role as she appeared to see it. Jack shook his head as he walked through the flowering band of woodland between Winstead and Ferrington Halls. He'd met some real rogues, and she wouldn't have liked them. Nor would they have treated her well. The idea of young Harriet Finch chatting so artlessly with some of them made his blood run cold. Fortunately, he was not a man like that.

She didn't come the next day, and Jack's disappointment was sharp. But the day after that, he spied her walking along with her perpetual parasol, fresh as a daisy in a straw bonnet and a figured muslin gown. He intercepted her near the gates to Ferrington Hall and steered her away. The caretakers were in residence today. Indeed, the old man was in the kitchen garden pulling weeds.

"I couldn't get away yesterday. My mother needed me."

Her expression implied tribulations. "She's not ill, I hope?"

"No. Not…really. She's anxious, and sometimes it…gets the better of her."

The strain in her voice suggested this was an understatement. Jack didn't know what to say. He settled on, "I'm sorry to hear that."

"She'll improve with time."

This sounded more like a hope than a certainty.

"Are we going to visit the Travelers' camp?"

In other words, she was finished with the previous subject. As she had every right to be. "We're on the way," Jack replied. He led her along the wall around the gardens. "I wanted to tell you that Mere is not my real name."

"No? Is it a nom de rogue?"

"Eh?" She'd taken this admission more easily than he expected.

"Like a nom de plume, a pseudonym," she added, twirling her parasol as they walked along. "That's a name authors use when they don't wish…"

"I know what it is."

"It's because you don't trust me," said this forthright young lady. "And why should you? I don't trust you."

"Do you not?"

"We've just met. We don't know anything about each other. And you're a rogue."

"I am not." He'd become sick of the word by now. And her assurance that she didn't trust him rankled more than it should.

"What are you then?"

Well, that was the question. If he couldn't answer it for himself, he clearly couldn't tell her. "A fellow doing some traveling."

"On foot, with a troop of gypsies," she replied.

"They're not gypsies."

"Travelers. But you know what I mean. Hardly a conventional tour of the countryside."

"It's better than all alone."

Miss Finch gave a small gasp, and a sheen of tears glinted in her green eyes.

"What is it?" Jack asked, startled.

"Nothing. I beg your pardon. I don't know why I... I'm not some silly watering pot. It's just that I miss my friends. So very much."

"Which friends are those then?"

"Sarah and Charlotte and Ada. We were in school together and then in London for the season. This is the longest we've been apart in years." She dashed the tears away.

"Ah, I've comrades in Boston I miss as well."

"Do you?"

"Not rogues," added Jack quickly.

Her smile was devastating. Jack felt as if a giant hand had squeezed the breath right out of him. "What are they then?" she asked.

"Roland has a farm west of the city. A big place. You'd call it an estate, perhaps. He does not. Daniel is a lawyer. And Francis is a natural philosopher. Fortunately, his family can afford a dabbler." Jack smiled as he imagined his friend's scowl over this description. "We met in school as well," he said.

"You went to school?"

"I beg your pardon?"

"I just thought…"

"That a rogue would receive his education on the road? Or none at all, perhaps? I went to a good school. My father insisted. It's in Andover, which you've never heard of, have you?"

"I believe there's a town in Hampshire…"

"It was probably called after that one. So much of America is an echo of this place." Jack gestured at the countryside around them. It was still strange to hear names he knew and realize the towns here had existed for centuries longer.

She was frowning at him. "I don't understand you."

"Precisely."

"You sound different."

His father's accent had crept in. It did that when he was angry, which Jack had always found odd. His mother had been far better at slinging curses. On the other hand, his father had been a master of the icy cut. "I run…help run a shipping office in Boston." His position was still there, until and unless he sold it to his partner. Everyone expected him to do that. Much had changed when he was revealed as a British nobleman. His friends had looked at him in a new way. Female acquaintances had grown intensely speculative or suddenly flirtatious.

"You were a shipping clerk?"

And there it was—the incredulity. His great-grandmother had been appalled when she learned of his work. She said the word *tradesman* as if it was shameful. Would it be better or worse to tell Miss Finch he was a co-owner of the company? Lady Wilton had commanded him to hide this dreadful secret. Jack didn't care a fig about her opinion. Miss Finch's, however...

"Shipping," she repeated before he could decide. Her expression grew suspicious. "Do you know my grandfather? Are you...? Did he...?"

"No, no, and no," said Jack. "Never heard of the man until I came here. Still know nothing."

She gazed at him, obviously troubled.

"I had a mind to travel," Jack said, conscious of his evasions again. He'd never been in such a twisty position before, and he didn't like it.

"So you simply left your job and set off." She let out a sigh. "How lucky you are."

He wouldn't put it that way. More in a complicated fix, and growing knottier by the moment. Time to change the subject. "Come and see the camp. I've gotten permission."

She hesitated, and Jack acknowledged he was in a world of trouble. He truly wanted this girl to like him, admire him, perhaps more than that. But what was he willing to do to gain her approval? If he told her he was an earl, she'd change her tune. People did. But he didn't want that kind of reaction. Hot resentment surged through him. Why should a title make a difference in how she saw him? It wasn't anything he'd earned. He didn't know the first thing about how to do it. And *he* didn't want a woman who wanted an earl rather than plain Jack Merrill. Yet the fear she would turn and walk away was a cold grip around his heart.

"All right," said Miss Finch.

The relief was unnerving. Jack walked a little ahead to hide his expression and to wonder what in the world he was going to do.

❦

Harriet strolled along behind him, twirling her parasol in a kind of meditation. Jack Not-Mere was exactly the sort of person her grandfather had forbidden her to meet. Just the sort her mother had married. Well, with the addition of frontier adventures in the wilds of America, which only increased his appeal. If she ran off to Boston with a wandering shipping clerk, her grandfather would be livid with rage. Briefly, she enjoyed imagining his impotent fury.

Not that she would do such a thing. Even if Jack asked her, which, of course, he had not. Her mother would suffer a nervous collapse. Harriet didn't know why the idea had even occurred to her—except nameless Jack was the most interesting man she'd ever met. Just when she thought she'd understood him, he revealed another side and surprised her.

He was more intriguing than all the Corinthians and pinks of the *ton* and suitable gentlemen she'd encountered in London. And when he smiled down at her, with that wicked gleam at the back of his dark eyes, her pulse raced. She'd never met a man who could render her breathless with a glance.

A man who was indulging in a bit of flirtation during his footloose tour of his father's country, a dry inner voice noted. He hadn't even said how long he was staying. He might move on tomorrow. The thought was perilously melancholy. She pushed it aside.

Walking into the Travelers' camp, Harriet felt conspicuous. Her clothes were not like theirs. The parasol felt like an affectation. Her pale skin marked her as an outsider. Murmured phrases as she passed were in a foreign language. The people's expressions were closed. She couldn't tell if they were hostile or merely reserved. If she hadn't been with Jack… But she was. And he seemed entirely at ease. He nodded greetings, scattered smiles, occasionally saluted one of the men. And when a tiny, bright-eyed little girl rushed up and grabbed his hand with a proprietary air, he smiled down at her. "This is Samia," he said. "Samia, meet Miss Finch."

"Hello," said Harriet.

"Hullo," the child replied. Her gaze swept Harriet from top to toe, shrewd beyond her years, and Harriet felt that the value of her ensemble had been thoroughly and expertly cataloged and approved. Her presence at Jack's side had not yet been sanctioned, however. Samia clearly saw her as provisional.

They walked into the center of the camp, an open, grassy

space focused on a large fire. Wagons and brush shelters and tents surrounded it. People watched from all of them. Jack led Harriet across to a fancifully painted caravan, dark blue with a swarm of twining flowers. A wizened old woman sat in the open doorway at the back, under a small, carved over-hang, her feet on the lowest step. A tall staff stood on the ground beside her. A bright kerchief hid her hair and another wrapped her shoulders.

Here was a woman who'd never cared if the sun rough-ened her skin, Harriet noted. She made the parasol feel even sillier. Nor did she seem concerned about the wrinkles that seamed her face. Her dark eyes were penetrating.

"Mistress Elena, may I introduce Miss Harriet Finch," said Jack. "Miss Finch, this is Mistress Elena Lee, who rules the Travelers here."

The old woman snorted. "We have no rulers."

"Only those the people listen to," said Jack, as if this was an exchange they'd had before.

"How do you do," said Harriet. "Thank you for allowing me to visit."

"Jack's a persuasive lad."

The look that came with this seemed like a warning. Harriet couldn't decide whether it was about Jack or her presence in the camp. Both, perhaps.

"Be welcome," Mistress Elena added with an expansive gesture.

And with that, a wave of relaxation passed over the group. Harriet noticed this without knowing how she knew. Perhaps it was the way people stood, or the many who turned back to mundane tasks she hadn't realized they'd abandoned. But certainly, the mood had changed.

Samia darted up to tug at Jack's coat, then led them about the encampment. After Mistress Elena's stamp of approval, Samia treated Harriet like an exotic creature she'd procured to exhibit to her friends. She stopped at intervals to let people stare. Other children tagged along behind them. One boy tried to sell Harriet a handful of hand-carved clothespins and was excoriated by his friends. Harriet gathered that one did not sell to guests in the camp.

Some people said the Travelers were careless and dirty and a blot on the landscape, but Harriet saw no sign of it. The camp was neatly kept. Whatever their sanitary arrangements, they gave off no smell. Instead, savory cooking odors wafted about. The meat might be poached, but she would not speak of that. There was no earl in residence to care for his coveys after all. The ring of the portable smithy followed them about the area. The dogs were wary but polite. The thought of her grandfather's wrath should he ever learn of this visit added spice for Harriet. Here were more of the sorts of people he forbade her to know. Grandfather was so very eager to forbid. And yet quite easily flouted. She reveled in the sensation.

Wherever they went, Jack exchanged bantering conversation with the Travelers. They didn't seem to be friends, precisely, but there was clearly mutual respect. Harriet had passed by Travelers on the road once or twice and seen the contemptuous looks they flung at those outside their circle. She saw nothing like that here. "They accept you," she said.

"Because of my mother," he answered, some sort of challenge in his voice.

"Yes, you said she was a Traveler. What was her name?" Harriet asked.

He blinked as if surprised, then smiled. Oh, that smile! Jack Not-Mere had more charm than any three other men combined. "Calla," he answered. "She had red hair like yours."

The warmth in his eyes seemed to pour over Harriet, like another sun, eluding her parasol, painting her cheeks crimson.

"Are you coming?" called Samia from up ahead. "You haven't seen the *horses*."

"That would be a dire omission," said Jack. There was a laugh in his voice but something more serious in his expression. Unless she was mistaken.

Harriet groped for her customary composure. It was there, a pillar and a refuge. She called upon it when men tried to unsettle her—the insinuating dance master, an oily vicar. But Jack wasn't like them. He was something else entirely. The word *irresistible* floated into Harriet's consciousness. She waved it away.

"What is it?" asked Jack.

She had actually moved her hand! This wouldn't do at all. Harriet suddenly noticed the position of the sun. It couldn't possibly be passing toward the west. The time had gone so swiftly. "I must go."

"The *horses*," called Samia, sounding exasperated.

"You can't miss them." Jack was examining her with… What was it? Surely it could not be tender concern?

"I can only walk alone while no one notices," replied Harriet. "I have been away too long."

He accepted her word at once, without argument. "Miss Finch has to go," Jack told their small escort. "She will see the horses next time."

Samia put her hands on her tiny hips, outraged. "I would have taken her to the horses *first*," she said.

There shouldn't be a next time, Harriet thought. She shouldn't see Jack again. But she thought it very likely that she would.

Three

DINNER AT WINSTEAD HALL THAT EVENING WAS MUCH as usual. Harriet's grandfather preferred a monologue at this heavy, formal meal, punctuated by meek agreements, which her mother provided. He never asked a question or, still less, solicited an opinion. He was the sole source of *those*, reacting to the newspapers or communications from his employees. Now and then, he directed a glare at his companions, emphasizing a point, and every time, Harriet's mother flinched.

Harriet had tried placing herself in the line of fire, so to speak, to shield Mama. But it didn't help. When she spoke, her mother grew even more anxious over what she might say. Harriet had thought this worry would lessen as time passed and they were settled in her grandfather's household. But in fact, it was growing worse. Her mother's fears spread more widely each day. Trivial matters overset her. The lines in her face had deepened; her hands shook. She was no happier than she had been when they were poor, squeezing every penny. Indeed, she was less so. Harriet didn't know what to do. When she tried to speak of it, her mother pretended that none of these signs existed.

"Filthy Travelers," said her grandfather.

Harriet's attention snapped back to him.

"They've camped not far from Ferrington Hall, bold as brass. The thieving scoundrels. Heard the earl was away, I suppose, and rushed in to take advantage. That fellow is shirking his responsibility. But I shall speak to the magistrate and have them driven off." He raked the room with a petulant frown. "On no account are you to go near there."

"Of course not, Papa!" said Harriet's mother.

Harriet made no reply, knowing silence would be taken for obedience. But behind her blank expression, her mind raced. The camp must be warned. Her grandfather would raise a gang of men to harry the Travelers away. She'd heard of that being done, sometimes violently. The thought of Mistress Elena and little Samia and the others being beaten made her cringe inside. "Who is the local magistrate, Grandfather?" she asked.

Brought up short, the old man said, "Eh?"

"He is a great friend of yours, I expect." Harriet made herself smile.

"I am acquainted with him, naturally."

The hint of bluster told Harriet that they were not friends, which was good. "He is one of the neighbors?"

"Sir Hal Wraxton, over at Hentings. It would be the earl, if he was here to fulfill his responsibilities. Don't know what the man means by staying away so long. It's irresponsible!"

"I suppose he has business to attend to." Harriet spoke at random, planning how she would hurry to the camp first thing tomorrow to let them know. It occurred to her that the Travelers might pack up and leave when they learned of this threat. And most likely Jack the Rogue would go with them.

Her heart sank to think she might never see him again. Their brief...idyll was over.

"Business!" The word exploded from her grandfather's lips. "These noblemen know nothing of business. Won't raise a finger in any honest trade. They're happy to spend the money that comes from it though. Runs through their hands like water. Thousands of pounds lost to gambling!" He said the last word like a curse. "Lunacy!"

And yet he insisted that she marry one of these feckless men. Harriet might have pointed out this logical flaw, but she was conscious of her mother's reproachful gaze. She replied with a small shrug. This wasn't her fault. She hadn't meant to set him off.

"Ruling class, indeed. Time to make some changes there." He descended into a mutter.

Power was what he wanted, Harriet realized then. Social climbing was just a stepping-stone on the road to influence and position. She should have seen this, would have, if his schemes hadn't involved her own future happiness. She'd been fixed on the idea of marriage. He had been thinking of extending his financial and political reach, ruthlessly. He would yoke her to a fool, a libertine, a tyrant, if the connection advanced his ambitions. A chill ran through her. Her grandfather wouldn't care how she was treated in such a marriage. She was a pawn to be sacrificed, a mere tool. Remembering his talk of deals, she shivered. He thought he could force her to do as he wished.

Well, she wouldn't, Harriet decided then and there. She would *not* give him what he wanted. Harriet set her jaw and raised her chin, utterly determined. And she found her mother staring at her. Mama had read the resolve in her face, and now she was terrified. Her eyes begged for surrender.

Harriet felt an uncomfortable mix of sympathy and annoyance. It was true that her grandfather could make their life even worse than it had been before he swooped down and lifted them into luxury. If she defied him, he would hound them as he had her father. She didn't see how he could take away the small income Papa had scraped together. But he knew far more about such things than she did. She would have to take care. All right, she would. But she wouldn't be used. Glancing at her grandfather, who was still silently fulminating, she thought she might be smarter than he was, when it came down to it. They would see, when she pitted her wits against his.

Mama was actually wringing her hands. Harriet offered what was meant to be a reassuring smile. It didn't appear to help.

❧

Jack was surprised to see Harriet Finch hurrying into the camp quite early the next morning. She didn't even have her parasol. She rushed over when she saw him, which was pleasant. But her expression was not. She looked worried.

"I've come to warn you," she said, breathless from rushing.

"Come and sit down. There's herbal tea brewing."

"I can't stay. My mother will be looking for me as soon as she wakes. You must listen."

She raised her hands like a supplicant. Jack took them in his own. "And so I shall, to be sure," he replied.

His reaction seemed to startle her. She flushed and gazed up at him with wide eyes. Whatever she saw in his face appeared to calm her a bit. "My grandfather is going to urge the local magistrate to chase you off," she said then.

"Me?" Jack wondered if someone had seen him in the gardens of Winstead Hall. He would have sworn he hadn't been observed.

"The Travelers. The camp."

"Ah."

"He doesn't… He isn't…"

"He thinks Travelers are thieves or worse." He'd heard of such persecutions from his mother. They were probably worse in this stuffy little country.

"Yes."

"Doesn't want them anywhere near you, I suppose."

She brushed this aside as if it was irrelevant. "They will bring men to chase your people off. Samia and everyone."

Jack's brain went to work on the problem. The grandfather seemed unlikely to relent from all he'd heard of the man. "This magistrate? What is he?"

"Magistrates are leading local men who are charged with keeping the peace. His name is Sir Hal Wraxton."

"Lives nearby, does he?"

"Yes, but you can't call on him. He wouldn't… I don't think he would receive you." She looked worried at the possibility, which was gratifying.

"No, I won't do that," Jack replied. A visit would do no

good in his present state. He might be an earl, but he had nothing to prove it. "Tell me where he lives though."

"Why do you want to know?"

She was a stubborn girl. "Matter of information," said Jack. "Lay of the land, so to speak."

Miss Finch frowned over this, as well she might, for the story was thin, but she gave him the magistrate's location. "What are you going to do? I can see you are planning something."

"I'm not certain just yet."

"There is nothing you can do!" she declared, pulling her hands away.

She looked distressed, and Jack dared to hope it was because he was to be run off. "I wouldn't say that."

"You are here without permission." She gestured to include the whole camp.

"Permission?" The word implied a possibility.

"Gypsies, and Travelers, I suppose, can camp if they have permission from a landowner," she added. "He has the say on his own property."

"Ah." Jack seized on this. "And in this case, that would be the Earl of Ferrington?"

"Who is missing. So you can't ask him for permission. Not that he would agree."

"You don't think so?"

"I'm sure he is as snobbish and closed-minded as my grandfather. More so, probably. He won't give a snap of his fingers for anyone else."

"Are you so sure then?"

The lovely Miss Finch glared at him. "That's how they are. You don't seem to be taking this matter seriously. The magistrate will bring a gang of men, and they will *force* the Travelers to move."

"Clubs and horsewhips instead of polite requests," Jack replied. He knew such things happened.

She grimaced. "I hope they would ask first. I don't know this Sir Hal Wraxton at all. I don't think my grandfather does either, which is one good thing."

"I understand," said Jack.

"Good." She let out a sigh and seemed to deflate with the expelled air. "So you will go then."

"That's what you suggest? That I just give up?"

"There's nothing you can do."

"There's always something."

"No, people who have power delight in using it against those who don't." Harriet had seen egregious examples of this during the season in London.

Jack decided that her grandfather must be quite a piece of work. "We shall see," he replied. "Will this scouring of the neighborhood be today, do you think?"

She frowned. "My grandfather is writing to Sir Hal this morning. He will address the complaint in a day or two."

"Right."

She looked around the camp as if bidding the place and its people farewell. "So I won't see you again. This is goodbye."

"I think perhaps you will, Miss Finch."

She didn't seem to hear. "It's not fair," she murmured.

"I would have thought you more of a fighter," said Jack.

Her green eyes flashed up at him, suddenly fierce. "Do you fence, Mr. Whoever You Are?"

This was an odd question. "I never have," he replied.

"But you could learn if you liked."

"I suppose I could."

"Boxing as well. My friend Charlotte's brothers are always talking of tipping someone a leveler. Which means knocking them down with one punch, I believe."

"I know the phrase. But I don't understand..."

"*I* can't learn such things," Miss Finch said. "Any more than I can enter a true profession. I have no way to *fight* unless you imagine that scathing words affect a man like my grandfather."

They were affecting him. He felt beleaguered.

"If you do, you are wrong," she added. "He...squashes opposition. Crushes the least sign of it."

Jack became conscious of a desire to show this man the meaning of defeat.

Miss Finch looked away as if she regretted saying so much. "I must go. Mama is keeping a closer watch on me after this news. She is very...susceptible to worry."

She held out her hand. Again, Jack took it. Her fingers were firm in his. "Goodbye," she said. Did he see a trace of a tear? He thought he did. And that settled it. He had to stay. He squeezed her hand. She returned the pressure, swallowed, and pulled away. It seemed she might say more, but in the end, she simply turned and rushed back the way she'd come.

Jack watched until she disappeared around a bend in the path, acknowledging he was well and truly smitten with this lovely girl. Who despised earls, seemingly. Most of them. He would have to be sure he was an exception.

Returning to the central fire, he gave the Travelers the news and suggested they set a watch. Some wanted to pack up and leave at once, but others were reluctant to abandon such a snug camp. Jack asked for and was granted a day to see what he could do, so long as no threats were spotted. He sat down with a mug of cider and put his mind to the problem.

With more time, he might have tried something elaborate. But in the span available, his thoughts finally narrowed to one possibility. It might well work.

He waited for darkness and then set himself to watch Ferrington Hall. He knew from previous observations that the old couple who took care of the place slept in a room near the kitchen, which was in a wing that jutted out from the rear of the house. Unfortunately, this was on the ground floor. However, it seemed well away from what he judged to be the haunts of their former master.

He saw the light in their bedroom extinguished. Unmoving, he let an hour pass. When he was reasonably certain they were asleep, he approached the house from the other side, aiming for a door that led out into a walled garden. He carried a small, dark lantern, which had been easily available at the camp. Suspiciously so, perhaps. Jack hadn't asked.

The wall was no serious obstacle, and Jack knew how to pick a lock. A disreputable friend of his father had taught him when he was ten years old. The men had roared with laughter over it. Until his mother had looked in, and they'd gone sheepishly silent. He didn't think any of them had told her of her son's new skill. He'd certainly known better than to confess it.

The lock was old and not complicated. Jack focused a narrow beam from the lantern on it, and soon he had it undone. He eased the door open. The hinges creaked, sounding loud in the quiet night. Jack closed the lantern and froze, listening with all his might. Minutes ticked past. At last, hearing no reaction, he slipped inside.

He had to dare the lantern again, to avoid colliding with ghostly sheeted furnishings, but he used the smallest possible beam as he made his way to the room he had recognized as a study from the outside.

Once there, he closed the door and unlatched a window, in case he had to run. Then he pulled off the sheet covering the desk. None of the drawers were locked, and in the third he tried, he found some crested stationery featuring the coat of arms of the Earl of Ferrington. He lifted out a few sheets, found a quill, and uncorked an inkwell, fortunately not dried out. Jack wasn't certain what he would have done if it was.

After listening again and hearing no sounds, he sat down at the desk and began to write a letter. Having thought about it all day, he had the words ready in his head. He wrote quickly, signed the unfamiliar name with a flourish, and then produced a second exact copy. One would go to this magistrate, and the other would be entrusted to Mistress Elena for safety's sake.

Jack found a stick of wax and a seal in another drawer. He softened the wax with the flame of his lantern and sealed one of the notes. This one would be delivered to the magistrate's house first thing tomorrow by a Traveler lad who had assured Jack he knew how to drop off a packet without being noticed.

Returning everything to its previous state, Jack latched the window and slipped out the way he'd come, relocking the door behind him. Then he was over the wall and away into the quiet darkness.

❧

Harriet sat with her mother in the small parlor Mama liked to use at one end of Winstead Hall, well away from the din of construction on the new wing. Late-afternoon sunlight poured through the tall windows like golden honey, illuminating the flowered wallpaper and comfortable furnishings. This space was less crammed with opulent objects than the rooms her grandfather frequented, which was restful. Sweet scents from the garden and the twitter of birds drifted in. Altogether a peaceful scene, with no reason for melancholy, and yet Harriet's spirits were low. She imagined the Travelers packed up by now and moving along the road away from here, Jack among them. When she walked that way again, the field would be empty, crushed grass and fire-blackened stones the only signs of their lively presence. She would never see him again. She wished she had done…something more during their brief acquaintance. She might have kissed him. Harriet blinked, startled by this unprecedented idea. Why was she thinking of kisses? She didn't do that—either the thinking or the kissing.

For that matter, asserted this errant part of her mind

with blithe disregard, he might have kissed her. But no, he wouldn't have presumed. He was a gentleman. Despite his vagabond state, she was certain of that. He would never take her in his arms and capture her lips and send her dizzy with desire. Unless he was encouraged, of course. Which she could not do. Because he was gone. And because, of course, she did *not* do such things. And never would. Harriet put a hand to her burning cheek, wondering if she had gone slightly mad.

"What is that noise?" asked her mother.

Harriet became conscious of a sound echoing down the corridor. It was her grandfather's voice, roaring in the distance.

"Oh dear," said her mother. "I wonder what has happened now."

"Some news from London, I expect," replied Harriet. Her grandfather often railed at the young men who traveled up from town with reports on his business.

But the sounds were rising in volume.

"He's coming this way," said her mother. "He doesn't come here." She shrank back in her chair even as she gazed at the window as if she might climb through it and escape.

Harriet rose. "I will go and see." She didn't enjoy her grandfather's temper tantrums. But they didn't frighten her as they did Mama.

"No, no. Let it be. Don't annoy him."

"Clearly, he is already annoyed, Mama. And coming to tell us why. I will try to stop him." Harriet went out into the hallway and intercepted her grandfather before he reached the parlor. He was red-faced and glowering. "What has happened?" she asked.

"The earl has given permission for those wretched Travelers to camp on his land," he answered. "It is an outrage."

"What?"

"Sir Hal received a letter from him, saying as much. Nothing he can do, he says, if a landowner approves. Not that he seemed to care very much, the dolt. He thinks 'the Travelers rarely do any harm.'" The old man shook a sheet of paper in his hand. His cheeks trembled with rage. "He writes that I shouldn't worry. The man is an imbecile."

Harriet realized that her mouth was hanging open. She closed it. "I...I thought the earl was missing. Has he come home?"

"He has not! I sent someone over there as soon as I got this ridiculous note. The idiots at Ferrington Hall know nothing about the matter. They claimed they didn't even know the Travelers were there. Which is impossible, of course. No one is that stupid."

Harriet's mind filled with questions. How had the earl learned about the camp? Or the complaint about it? Where had he written from? Who had brought the letter? Were they certain of its authorship? She asked none of these, because she didn't want her grandfather to begin wondering about the letter's origins. As she was. With a growing sense of horror and a touch of admiration, she suspected that any investigation would lead straight to Jack the Rogue. "How...odd," she said.

"Odd? It's unconscionable. The end of the matter, Sir Hal says. Letter on the earl's special, crested notepaper. Hopes the fellow will return home soon. Blast them! They think themselves above us all."

Harriet wisely held her tongue.

"You are not to go beyond the gardens, Harriet. Not with a pack of tramps given free rein to roam the countryside." He stomped away without requiring her promise, which was a relief since Harriet did not like to lie. She *would have*, but it was good not to need to. Her mother called anxiously from the parlor, wanting to know what was amiss, and Harriet had to go to her rather than rushing over to the camp as she really wished to do.

In fact, Harriet could not get away until early the following morning. Her grandfather was with his London messenger in his study, and her mother lay abed late. She evaded the eyes of several servants and a trio of workmen carrying planks from a wagon, slipped out through the shrubbery, and nearly ran across the woods to the camp.

They were all still there—the wagons and tents and brush shelters. The scent of woodsmoke wafted over them. People went about their daily tasks with no sign of concern. Harriet scanned the peaceful scene, spotted Jack setting down a load of wood near the central fire, and hurried over to him. "What did you do?"

"How splendid to see you," he replied. "And that we did not have to say goodbye after all."

"You forged a letter from the Earl of Ferrington," Harriet accused. He must see it had been a dangerous thing to do.

"I did not. I give you my solemn word."

She was brought up short. She heard truth in his voice. But believing him would bring down the whole edifice of her explanation. "You know that the magistrate received a letter of permission from the earl?"

"So we heard. Good news, eh? Perhaps they're friends, and this magistrate asked him about it."

"No one knows where the earl is," Harriet pointed out.

"Someone must."

Harriet brushed this diversion aside. "And how could *he* know the camp was here? Since he is not."

"Perhaps he keeps tabs on the place."

"From quite nearby?" Harriet asked sarcastically. "Close enough to send a letter on the heels of my grandfather's complaint?"

"That's it."

"Why would the earl stay near Ferrington Hall but not *in* it?"

"Some of these noblemen are eccentric, are they not? I've heard they are."

"Do you imagine they hide in caves like ancient hermits? From which they can nonetheless send letters on crested notepaper?"

"Are there caves hereabouts?" he asked with what seemed genuine interest.

"No, of course there aren't! The countryside is quite flat."

Jack burst out laughing, and Harriet was tempted to join him. But the mystery nagged at her. "I don't see how this came about."

"It was just a matter of good luck, it seems," he said.

Jack smiled down at her. Harriet refused to melt. "No, I don't believe that. I am convinced you wrote that letter."

"Well, perhaps I am the earl," he said.

She snorted. "And I am the princess royal."

"You are to me."

"Will you be serious?"

"I could be the earl," he answered. "Journeying incognito."

"With a troop of Travelers? Don't be ridiculous."

"If I were…"

"You are not!" Harriet exclaimed. "Fortunately, you are nothing whatsoever like an earl."

He flinched as if something had hit him. Harriet actually looked over her shoulder to see what the threat might be, but there was nothing there. When she turned back, Jack the Rogue seemed rueful and perhaps sad.

For the first time in their acquaintance, Harriet felt uneasy. Jack was always so lighthearted. He'd given no sign of caring about rank, and he'd appeared impervious to insults. Not that she'd meant to insult him. Nearly all the noblemen she'd met were arrogant and vain, and some were positively despicable. The few exceptions merely showed up the others. She should tell him her remark had been a compliment.

"Look at that then," he said before she could speak. He pointed.

Harriet turned, becoming aware of the others around them. All around. Their conversation had certainly been overheard by a number of Travelers.

"There," said Jack.

Following the direction of his arm, Harriet saw Samia sitting beside Mistress Elena on the steps of the old woman's caravan. The little girl threw back her head and loosed a peal of youthful laughter.

"Mistress Elena is finally teaching Samia palm reading," Jack explained. "Samia's nagged the life out of her to learn."

Harriet looked up. He was smiling now. There was no trace of sadness in his expression. She must have imagined it. Jack the Rogue could not be dejected.

"Come and see," he added.

Harriet wanted to say something more, but she couldn't decide what exactly. And then he had walked away. She followed him to the caravan.

"Just what we need," said Mistress Elena when Harriet reached them. "Samia will look at your hand." Her dark eyes gleamed with humor. "Mine has too many wrinkles." She made an imperious gesture. "Rolf, bring a chair."

A boy went to the central fire circle, turned a bit of log on its side, and rolled it close. He set it upright in front of Mistress Elena and plopped a cushion on top with a flourish. "My ladies," he said. Samia giggled.

"Sit, sit," said Mistress Elena.

Harriet sat.

"Give Samia your hand. The one you write with."

Harriet obeyed, and the little girl bent over her open palm, earnest and yet also ready to laugh. "This is your Life line," she said, tracing a crease that ran diagonally down Harriet's hand. "And this is your Heart line." She indicated a more horizontal mark with a twinkling glance.

"What do you see?" asked Mistress Elena.

Samia bit her lower lip. "There's a kind of wiggle here near the beginning. A big change in her life maybe?"

The old woman bent to look, nodded. "Remember what I said."

"Watch their eyes when you speak, but don't let them

notice," Samia replied. "You will see when you have hit upon a true thing. I forgot."

"And Miss Finch has had a change, I think." Mistress Elena's smile was sly.

"You saw that in my eyes?" asked Harriet.

The old woman's smile broadened.

"Or I just told you so." Harriet shook her head. "Do you just make it up?"

"We find a story together, engraved in the hand."

"Isn't that fooling people?" Harriet didn't believe in fortune-telling, but she had thought those who did it would pretend to, at least.

"It is not," replied Mistress Elena crisply. "Many people have no one who pays close attention to them. Not a single comrade. I watch and listen and encourage their thoughts. They can learn much, if they wish to."

For some reason, Harriet thought of her mother. But that was silly. She did listen to her.

"Your Heart line is very strong," said Samia. "It goes all across your hand. And look here, near the beginning, it crosses your Life line. Some great thing *did* happen then."

When her father had died, and she thought her heart would break. Harriet shook her head. They were simply playing on her imagination. "I must go back," she said. If she was caught outside the gardens, her grandfather would prevent her from ever returning.

Samia gave up her hand reluctantly.

Jack walked with her toward the path to Winstead Hall. She thought of questioning him further about the letter, but somehow her thoughts drifted back to the idea of kissing him. He was right here, at her side. They'd come under the trees, so no one could see. But how did one go about it? One didn't simply throw oneself into a man's arms. What if she tripped? He would catch her. And then... But what if he didn't wish to kiss her? The possibility made her cheeks burn.

Jack put a hand on her arm, making her jump. Had he read her thoughts somehow?

"Your grandfather has set watchers," he said.

She hadn't been paying attention. Without Jack, she would have walked right into the man posted on the border with the Ferrington lands—one of the Winstead Hall gardeners, she thought. On the other hand, if Jack hadn't been there to distract her, she would have seen him. She was usually quite observant!

"This way," he murmured.

He showed her a way to evade the patrol, through a thicket that had an open space down the center. It was perhaps better than the hidden route Harriet would have taken on her own. A little.

When they paused at the end of the bushes to make certain the way was clear, he said, "Could you come back tonight? There's to be a bit of a festival."

"After dark?"

"I would wait in that shrubbery by the house to escort you. And bring you back as well, of course. Not too late. It will be a fine evening."

An automatic refusal rose to Harriet's lips, born from a lifetime of genteel poverty and its precarious social position.

She'd always known that the least breath of scandal would ruin her, as it would not a better-placed young lady. She could make no missteps, even as a certain sort of man saw her as an easy mark. She'd built up a wall of cool distance to fend them off, and her defenses had served her well until a few months ago at the start of the London season. Then, suddenly, Harriet was expected to welcome the attentions of a host of young men. She was to be flattered and sweetly accessible. Even her best friends hadn't understood how difficult she'd found this. Some nights Harriet had seen her suitors as a kind of ravening horde vying for—not her, but her grandfather's money. At those moments, she'd simply wanted to run.

"Miss Finch?" said her companion.

This thicket in the woods wasn't society. This politely charming rogue knew nothing of her dowry and cared less. No one would know what she did in the Travelers' camp. "I will try to come after dinner," she heard herself saying. "I can't be sure I will be able to get away."

"I'll wait for you where the path forks into three."

He said it as if he meant he would wait forever. Speechless, Harriet raised her hand in a half wave and hurried away.

She made it into the garden and then inside, finding no sign her absence had been noticed. It would be harder tonight, but Harriet made up her mind to find a way.

❧

Hours later, Jack waited in the shrubbery of the Winstead Hall garden and hoped. At one moment, he thought she would come. In the next, he doubted. This wasn't the sort of invitation that a high stickler like Lady Wilton, for example, would approve. But Harriet Finch was nothing like that crotchety old lady. She'd shown him that. Hadn't she?

Jack had glimpsed her family at the dinner table before the servants pulled the curtains closed. The meal hadn't looked like a happy occasion. The fat old man who faced the window had looked like an evil-tempered tortoise. He'd appeared to be holding forth on some unpleasant topic. Miss Finch, on the fellow's left, was stiff and solemn. The small lady opposite, surely Miss Finch's mother, had been plucking at her napkin in what looked to Jack like nervous terror. If that had not been so unlikely. Nobody was smiling.

It had been some time since then. Dinner was surely over, but he had no idea what they did afterward. The festivities at the camp had certainly begun, but he didn't care much about them without her. And so he waited.

Finally, after what seemed an eternity, Jack heard footsteps approaching. Surely this could only be Miss Finch at this time and place. Still, he didn't take a chance but stood still and silent in concealment.

"Are you there?" came a murmur. Her voice.

His heart leaped. He couldn't remember ever being so glad to see someone. "Here," he replied, stepping out of the interlacing branches.

She started, a dim figure in a hooded cloak. "It's so dark."

"It's nearly moonrise. Take my arm."

She did, and he led her along the twisting path to the edge of the garden and on toward the camp.

"The watchers," she whispered.

"They went home with the sunset," Jack replied. He'd observed their restlessness as the day waned, a muttered conference, and their somewhat furtive departure.

"What? They only patrol in daylight? That's silly."

"I think many of them find the task silly." It certainly was. The Travelers were no threat to Winstead's large, prosperous holding. He'd told them of the man's hostility, and everyone was staying well away. And if they had wanted to get close, the patrols were ridiculously simple to evade.

Jack had continued his wandering around the neighborhood, talking to people of varying degree, trying to learn his new terrain. He'd found that the poor opinion of Mr. Winstead was widespread. He wasn't much liked or respected. His quick temper had roused resentment. On the other hand, his money and the work he brought were appreciated. He made hard bargains, but he paid his bills in full and on time. It seemed the late Earl of Ferrington was far more erratic about such matters, particularly when he'd been drinking. As he quite often had been, apparently. And yet the earl was remembered with fondness. Generally, the neighborhood was eager for his replacement to arrive. Jack didn't completely understand these sentiments. The mere fact of an earl seemed to matter to people. They desired such a figure in their midst. An earl's individual qualities were as unpredictable as the weather and treated rather the same, as far as Jack could make out. Constantly talked of and accepted as beyond anyone's control.

"How can you find your way?" whispered Miss Finch. Her hand was warm in the crook of his arm.

"My eyes have become accustomed to the dark." The path was just visible in the starlight. It was fortunate they didn't have to slip through the thicket, however.

They passed into the band of woodland, where it was dimmer, and had to walk more slowly. But as they neared the Travelers' camp, light from a great fire in the center painted the trees. Lively music rose ahead. Jack pulled his prize into the open and enjoyed the look on Miss Finch's face as she took in the scene.

Three of the Travelers sat atop one of the caravans and played a violin, a flute, and a small drum. They were skilled, and the music made one want to move. Below them, circling the fire, the camp danced. Couples, children, oldsters revolved about the flames. Tossing heads, upflung arms, a rainbow of fluttering scarves, and stamping feet blended into a thrilling picture. Off to the side, there was a large keg of cider with mugs ready to be drawn.

Jack was glad to see Miss Finch greeted with nods if not smiles. He took her cloak, laid it aside, and offered a hand. "Come and dance," he said.

"I don't know the steps."

"You are free to make up your own."

Harriet saw he was right. Some pairs seemed to be executing a stamping, bowing pattern, but others were twirling, romping, hopping, apparently improvising according to their temperaments and abilities. Harriet spotted Samia capering like a wild elf and Mistress Elena gesturing and swaying at the far edge of the circle. She couldn't resist. She let Jack the Rogue pull her into the melee and gave herself up to a dance that couldn't have been less like a society ball.

He held her as if they were waltzing, one hand warm at her waist, the other pressing her fingers. But they moved far faster than any waltz, skipping and spinning and sliding until her head swam.

Then, suddenly, the violin and flute fell silent. The drum boomed out a staccato rhythm, and there was a general shout of, "hey!" Jack lifted her off her feet, swung her around in a dizzying arc, and set her down facing the opposite direction. Harriet nearly tripped as she lit, but he caught her. Pressed close against him, she looked up. His dark eyes held their own fires. His smile flashed white, and elation shot through Harriet. She was drawn to him as she'd never been to anyone. She longed to throw her arms around his neck and give in to the attraction that shook her.

The music started up again, and the dance went on with the direction of the circle reversed.

Harriet moved to the music. A heady sense of freedom ran through her veins, more intoxicating than any glass of champagne. In that moment, she thought people should always dance under the stars rather than in stuffy ballrooms. And when the music paused and the drum called and Jack swung her through the air, the feeling was glorious.

After a time, the musicians took a rest. Harriet thirstily drank down a mug of cider and then blinked at its strength. The Travelers around her spoke to each other in their own language, which she couldn't understand, but she joined in the laughter that rose with the sparks from the fire. Then, the dancing resumed, and she threw herself into its pulsing rhythm with an unfamiliar joy.

It seemed only a little time had passed when Jack the Rogue said, "I should take you back now."

"Is it midnight?" Harriet asked, feeling like Cinderella, the magic that had buoyed her about to dissolve.

"Well past that, I would think."

"Oh." Of course she had to go. She'd sent Slade to bed early, so there would be no one waiting. She'd purloined a key to a side door. But her time was still limited. She'd had her escape. Now she must return to what had begun to feel like a kind of prison.

Melancholy built with each step back toward her grand-father's house. In the garden, with the darkened pile ahead of them, Harriet paused and gazed up at her escort. She couldn't really see his expression in the dimness. Did he regret the end of their escapade as much as she did?

Harriet moved closer to him, breathing in his masculine scent along with the sweetness of flowers. She raised her chin. Surely he would kiss her now, after the way they had danced. The whole evening had led up to this moment. He bent his head. Her lips parted, awaiting the touch of his. The world seemed to teeter in the balance.

But then he stepped away. "Good night, Miss Finch," he murmured. He moved farther off, nearly disappearing into the darkness of the shrubbery.

One of Harriet's hands rose in unconscious supplication. She snatched it back. She would not beg! Bitter with disappointment, Harriet fled to the building that was not her home.

Four

MISS FINCH DID NOT VISIT THE CAMP THE FOLLOWING day, but Jack hadn't expected her. She'd taken a risk coming out last night and might well feel she must draw back. He didn't think she'd been caught. The silent darkness of Winstead Hall as she slipped in had promised safety.

Jack paused in his circuit of the rabbit snares. That last moment, before she'd gone inside, burned in his memory. After an evening of holding her in his arms as they danced, he'd been desperate to kiss her. And he dared to think she'd wanted the same. The yearning had vibrated between them there in the fragrant dimness. It set him afire even now. Stepping back had taken every bit of his honor and resolution.

The problem was: He wasn't who she thought he was.

Jack moved on through the meadow. As they grew closer, it became more important that he tell her the truth. But whenever he came near to confessing, he heard her declaring he was nothing whatsoever like an earl. Approvingly. Happily. The phrase, and the tone, had been nothing like his great-grandmother's sour judgment. The girl he…greatly admired was delighted that he was *not* the titled nobleman he actually *was*. In name, if not essence.

If ever a fellow was in a cleft stick.

He needed to tell Miss Harriet Finch the truth before things went any further. And he did wish to go further. How far, he wasn't yet certain. But what would she think of him when she knew? Would her attitude change? She spoke of the nobility with such contempt. Worse, the truth would spread. There'd be no hiding once he spoke, and very likely, Lady Wilton would rush up here to "lick him into shape" and push him into the society he was assured would disdain him. That prospect made him shudder. He'd gone to great lengths, literally, to escape his great-grandmother.

And then, on the other side, there was Miss Finch's grandfather. From all Jack had gathered, it seemed the old man would grasp at any sort of earl at all. He wouldn't care if Jack had two heads or been born in a back slum as long as he held the title. He'd want to... What, be friends? Throw his granddaughter at Jack's head, whether she wished it or not?

The two old frights would push at them from their different directions and wreck everything. Insofar as there was an everything—which was not far yet.

Jack rubbed his forehead, where a headache threatened. He supposed he *was* nothing like an earl and never would be, but he was one. With a house next to Winstead's. Neighbors for good or ill. At some point, he would have to take up the position or continue to run. Neither choice appealed. He didn't want to leave Miss Harriet Finch. He certainly didn't want to stay and lose her. There must be a way out, but he couldn't see it just now. Not for the life of him.

That day passed, and another. Jack wandered the landscape between Winstead Hall and his ancestral home, evading the guards, hoping to glimpse Miss Finch, racking his brain for a plan. He failed in all but the first effort, but his rambles did mean that he was nearby when a great bustle of activity was reported at Ferrington Hall. Samia and her mob said several carriages had arrived and a crowd of people had moved in. They assumed this was the earl finally making an appearance.

For a moment, Jack did too. Then he remembered it could not be, because he was the earl. Had an impostor shown up to claim the position? The idea almost made him laugh, despite the tangle such a development would create. But all humor drained away when it occurred to him that the visitor might well be Lady Wilton, come to hunt him down in person. She would recognize him, and all his choices would be taken away.

He had hidden spots from which to watch the house, and it was simple to observe the coming and going of new servants and delivery of supplies. The arrivals had clearly thrown the elderly caretakers into a frenzy. They buzzed about like bees disturbed in their hive.

Eventually, Jack saw the owners of the carriages as well—a sleek, young couple. The man had black hair, an athletic figure, and an annoyingly handsome face. Even to one who knew very little of fashionable dress, his clothes looked superior. He strolled about as if he owned the place, his manner imperious even from a distance.

His companion—wife, if their behavior was any gauge—was beautiful and even better dressed than Miss Finch. She had golden hair and the face of a renaissance angel. She also had a ringing laugh her husband seemed to delight in evoking. Jack liked that about them. Still, they were the sort of polished, sophisticated creatures who made him feel awkward and foreign. But at least they were not Lady Wilton.

Word filtered out into the neighborhood that the visitors were a duke and his duchess. Jack did wonder at first if this was some sort of ruse. But they'd brought so many servants, and the caretakers had accepted them without a murmur. On the second evening, he eeled his way through the overgrown garden and crouched below an open window to listen to their dinner conversation. In the midst of other talk, Lady Wilton was mentioned, as if she was the reason they were here. Jack felt a brush of annoyance. The old lady had no right to invite people to... He stopped, realizing that some part of him had begun to think of Ferrington Hall as *his* house. He frowned. They could hardly usurp what he refused to claim, but he resented it nonetheless.

He slid back into the shrubbery. Friends of his great-grandmother could not be good news. And they were likely to ruin his chances of seeing Harriet Finch any time soon. It seemed all circumstances conspired against him.

❧

Harriet wondered if this was what it felt like to go mad. She was trapped in her mother's small parlor for another afternoon. Any move to escape brought plaintive reproaches, grasping hands, and even tears—all far beyond any behavior Mama had exhibited before. Harriet was certain her mother did not know of her recent adventure. She would have spoken of it if she did. *Spoken* being a vast understatement. The thought of the scene that would be played out made Harriet wince. But Mama did seem to sense something—a change in the atmosphere—and she'd reacted at full bore. It felt like being wrapped in cotton wool until one was ready to choke.

Mama could not trap her mind, however. Harriet let her thoughts drift back to that night, when she'd danced in Jack the Rogue's arms and whirled wildly around the fire. When she'd downed a mug of fiery cider without a moment's worry about how it might look. She'd felt so free. The constraints of so-called polite society and the perils of losing one's position in it had been…simply irrelevant, less than a distant memory. No one there had cared.

Of course, such things could not last. Harriet was well aware of that. She would never join a Travelers' camp, even if they allowed it. Which they would not. But that giddy sense of freedom had made her wonder about other possibilities. She began to weave a vision of a different sort of life. Far from the *haut ton*, from the irritating demands of propriety and the dark undercurrents they concealed. In another country, perhaps. Where expectations were looser and opportunities wider.

Which brought her around to Jack the Rogue. He had made her think of these things, and he featured in the pictures she evoked. She felt again his hands at her waist, the elation as he lifted and spun her. She knew he'd so nearly kissed her in the garden at the end. So nearly! He'd behaved like a gentleman, not a rogue. Partly she was glad of that, and partly she regretted it. If she ever got another chance, she was going to kiss *him*.

At the moment, however, that possibility looked remote. Harriet ground her teeth in frustration. "I believe I will go out and take some air in the garden."

"Oh no. It is so sultry. I expect it will rain at any moment."

Harriet stared out the window. She didn't see any sign of rain. Not that she cared. She would happily stand in a downpour if she could just get away for a little while. "I don't think it will, Mama. I wouldn't be long."

"But I need you to help me sort my embroidery silks," was the plaintive reply. "You have such a splendid eye for color. I wonder that you never do any fancywork yourself."

Harriet did not say, *Because inscribing tiny flowers onto a cloth is tedious beyond belief.* She had once, long ago. Her mother had laughed then. She was unlikely to do so today.

The closed door of the parlor rattled, and Harriet's grandfather burst in like a charging bull. Harriet's mother started and yelped. She'd pricked her finger. A spot of red appeared on her embroidery.

Grandfather didn't notice. His smile was the one he used when he'd put one over on a competitor, showing plenty of teeth. "The Duke and Duchess of Tereford have come to Ferrington Hall," he declared.

"What?" Harriet stared up at him. "Why?"

"I have no notion, but I know you are well acquainted with them." He rubbed his hands together. "We must call at once. Let my neighbors see that! *They* won't know them. Sir Hal may wish to change his tune when he realizes I have such high-ranking friends."

Harriet could not deny that she—and *not* her

grandfather—had become friends with the Duchess of Tereford during the season in London. Or with Cecelia Vainsmede, as she'd been before she married. Harriet glanced at her mother. Mama had known Miss Vainsmede's mother at school, and she'd written Cecelia asking for advice and aid with Harriet's debut. This was back when Mama still showed some spirit and initiative. Cecelia had agreed to help apply a bit of town polish, and Harriet had found she liked her. She'd expected to disdain the leaders of society, the sort of people who had scorned her until she became an heiress and fawned over her once she had. And she had disliked many of them. Cecelia was one of the exceptions. Harriet didn't know the duke nearly as well. But her grandfather had pushed in at one evening party, and she'd been forced to introduce him to them both.

"Get up, girl," he said to her now. "Change your dress. You too, Linny. You look like a sloven."

Harriet hated the way he spoke to her mother, with a dismissive nickname as if she was a dim child. This had grown far worse now that they were alone with him in his own house. She had to fight down icy rage before she could say, "You wish to go now?"

"Of course. The sooner, the better."

"It's not the right time of day for a call. We had better go tomorrow morning."

"Now would be improper?" her grandfather asked.

"Yes," Harriet lied. She would not descend on Ferrington Hall without preparation, of various sorts.

"Very well. Midmorning?"

He was actually deferring to her. Harriet agreed.

"I'll see about something to take them. From the Indies, perhaps." He nodded. "Yes. That will be a novelty."

"Gifts aren't necessary," replied Harriet.

"Nonsense. We want to impress them."

He would offer something ostentatious and most likely inappropriate. But there was no stopping him. He wielded his wealth like a bludgeon and then couldn't understand when people resented the blow. He bustled out, rubbing his hands together in satisfaction once again.

"I hope the duke doesn't snub him," said her mother when he was gone. "He will be so angry."

"Cecelia is my friend," Harriet replied. She didn't fear rejection from the Terefords. She did wonder why they were here in a house not their own. The duke certainly had plenty of properties they might visit.

Harriet dispatched a note to Ferrington Hall declaring their intention to call. It was cordially acknowledged, and this made her grandfather affable enough to placate her mother. Harriet managed to convince Mama to lie down for a bit before dinner, which gave her a sliver of time to slip out and make her way to the Travelers' camp.

Her heart sang as she threaded her way through the middle of a dense thicket. It had become an odd habit, rushing along this path through the woods, anticipating the sight of one particular gentleman who affected her as no other ever had.

She found Jack the Rogue chopping wood not far from the camp's central fire. He wore no coat and had rolled up the sleeves of his shirt. Muscles flexed in his arms as he raised the ax and let it fall. His skin was bronzed by the sun and sheened with perspiration. His movements were deft and precise. Not so long ago, Harriet had felt that strength sweeping her away in the dance. What would it be like to run her fingers over his heated skin? She found herself transfixed by the question.

He seemed to sense her gaze. After the next fall of the ax, he turned to look and spotted her. He stopped at once and smiled so sweetly that her heart contracted. "Miss Finch," he said. His voice seemed to reach out and caress her.

Harriet felt her cheeks burn. If he had any idea what she'd been thinking... But, of course, he did not. "Ah." She had to clear her throat. "You should stay away from the hall," she said. "Some visitors have arrived."

"I know." He set the ax aside and moved toward her.

Of course he knew. He noticed everything. There had been no need for a warning. She'd wanted an excuse to see him.

"Friends of this Lady Wilton, I hear," he added.

Where had he heard anything like that? Harriet was surprised he remembered the old lady's name. "Not so much friends as relations," she answered. "Lady Wilton is Tereford's grandmother."

"Tereford?"

"The Duke of Tereford. He and his wife, Cecelia, have come."

"You know them?" His smile had gone. "Are they relations of the earl then?"

"Yes." Harriet frowned. "The duke is some sort of

cousin? But it is strange for them to be here. I don't understand it."

"Sent to look things over?"

"I can't imagine Tereford allowing himself to be sent."

"Him being a duke and all," Jack said.

"Yes. I wonder if…" Harriet became conscious of a
murmur rising in the camp.

Samia ran by with a group of her friends. "That man is
coming," she called.

"What man?" asked Jack.

"The one who moved into the house." The little girl
threw the answer over her shoulder as she ran on.

"Oh no." Harriet turned. She could see a stir of movement approaching. "I must go." She stepped toward the path
back. "He mustn't see me."

"He will if you go that way," said Jack. His face had gone
wooden.

There was a stretch of empty field between her and the
woods. "I can't be caught here. The duke will remark on it,
and if he tells my grandfather…"

Jack the Rogue looked around. Shielding her from the
approaching hubbub, he herded her toward a caravan near
the woodpile and opened the door. "Get in," he said.

"I couldn't intrude," Harriet began.

"It's that or be seen," he said. "Gina won't mind."

Harriet hesitated one moment more, then stepped up
and in. Jack shut the door behind her, and she was enclosed
in a marvel of neat, wooden drawers and compartments,
from sizable to tiny. There was a little stove on a metal base,

unlit right now, and a bed at the front covered in a gorgeously colorful cloth. Small windows around a sort of flat turret at the top were propped open, letting her hear but not see the outside.

❧

Jack moved back toward the woodpile as he watched the disturbance come nearer. He strongly resented the appearance of this duke, who made Miss Finch ashamed to be seen with him. He wanted no connections of Lady Wilton barging in with their high-nosed opinions and possibly exposing his identity before he could do so on his own terms. He picked up the ax—not as a threat but as a potential distraction. He had to put this intruder off.

A loose circle of male Travelers surrounded the visitor, who was the polished man Jack had observed at Ferrington Hall. The fellow—the duke—looked like a peacock among the pigeons, and he did not seem the least intimidated by the clear lack of welcome. Jack began chopping wood again, hoping he and his watchful entourage would walk on by.

Of course, the man stopped, as if he had some malign instinct. Jack could feel his judgmental gaze. Doggedly, he kept working.

"That looks like hot work," said this duke.

As if he had ever done a day's labor in his life. A sharp current of annoyance ran through Jack. He hated being pushed. Letting the ax blade drop, he wiped his forehead with one arm and gazed at this polished product of Lady Wilton's precious society. The duke looked primed for disdain. Rebelliously, Jack put on the thickest accent he could produce, taking cues from his mother and these people he'd been living among. "Na so vairy bad," he answered. "Ah'm used to it." As you are not, he didn't add. He could see amusement gleaming in the eyes of the Travelers at his rustic speech, though he didn't think a stranger would notice.

"Indeed." The duke looked around at his escorts. "Have you seen anyone about Ferrington Hall? Before we arrived, I mean."

He received no answers. Jack shrugged, feigning blank incomprehension.

"No?"

Jack caught an ironic glint in the man's piercing blue eyes. This duke might be a pompous ass, but he wasn't gullible.

"I understand you have permission to camp here," he went on. "From the Earl of Ferrington."

A murmur answered him. Many of the Travelers had gathered in a wider circle. They hoped to chase off the visitor with silent hostility, as was their practice. Jack saw no sign this was succeeding. "Best ask Mistress Elena," he said. "She's got the letter and all."

"I should be interested to see it," answered the duke.

"Only she's gone off." Jack didn't know where she actually was, but he was certain word would spread from the outer edges of the circle and she'd be out of the way when looked for.

"Off? Like spoiled cream?"

The damned fellow thought he could amuse himself at their expense. Jack wished for an excuse to punch him.

But instead, he said, "Picking of 'erbs in the forest, belike." Where had he heard the word *belike*? He had no idea or whether it fit with the accent he'd cobbled together. It sounded idiotic from his lips. In that moment, Jack remembered Miss Finch was overhearing his performance as a dim-witted yokel. How had he forgotten? His cheeks heated with mortification.

"Taking this letter along with her?" asked the duke. He looked entertained. This man was dangerous.

"Don't do to leave it lying about," muttered Jack.

"Of course. One never knows when someone might… inquire."

Jack began to have a bad feeling about the situation. Why was this duke addressing him rather than some of the others? What had Lady Wilton told him?

"Perhaps you would tell her that I wish to see it?" the intruder added. "I am Tereford, by the way."

"Tereford," Jack repeated. Were dukes above normal names? And did the man think this label would tell the Travelers anything? He couldn't stop himself. "My Lord Tereford, would that be?"

"Not necessarily," the duke said. "And you are?"

"Calls me Jack the Rogue, they does." He heard a sound from the caravan, to go with the bitten-off grins from the Travelers. The word *debacle* floated into his brain.

"Does…they?" The fellow was smiling, damn him. "*They* appear to have vivid imaginations."

His gaze was exceedingly sharp. Jack realized he should have pretended to be mute. He certainly should have resisted that last remark. Too late now. He was groping for a way to save the situation when the duke turned away. "Don't forget to give Mistress Elena my message," he said over his shoulder.

Jack nodded. Not subserviently, he was aware. It was the best he could manage.

He waited. The duke strolled out of sight. When one of the Travelers signaled from the edge of camp that he had really gone, Jack opened the caravan door.

Miss Finch surged out. "What in the world were you playing at?" she demanded. "You sounded like one of the clowns from Shakespeare. Done by a dreadful actor."

"Misdirection," he muttered.

"From what to what?" She looked at the lowering sun. "Oh no, I shall be late." She turned and ran for the path home. For once, Jack did not go with her.

❧

When Harriet rushed into her bedchamber twenty minutes later, she nearly ran into Slade, who stood just inside the door. The thin, upright abigail did not shift as Harriet lurched to the side to avoid a collision. Only her blue eyes moved, cataloging her charge's disheveled state. Harriet was breathless. A grasping branch had caught her bonnet and pulled it awry, along with a spray of red curls. Her shoes were dusty. She'd gone out so quickly that she'd forgotten her gloves. She could see Slade deploring that lapse.

"I informed your mother, when she came to inquire, that

you were in the garden," the woman said. "I believe she went out to look for you. She was most distressed when you could not be found."

"Did she tell Grandfather?" burst out before Harriet could stop it.

"No. Miss Dorn persuaded her that she must have missed you in the shrubbery."

That was a relief. Mama's maid was also a new addition, and Harriet had no reason to count on her, though she did seem eager to soothe Mama's anxiety. "I was...I was..." Harriet hadn't prepared a tale for the very superior lady's maid her grandfather had hired to dress her.

"You *are* expected at dinner," the woman added. "Which is in ten minutes."

Slade looked just as she always did, blandly professional. Harriet untied the ribbons of her bonnet, pulled it off, and threw it on the bed, where one of her evening dresses was laid out and ready. A pair of matching shoes sat beneath it, lined up in Slade's precise way. The necklace and earrings that completed the ensemble waited on the dressing table beside the hairbrush. The neatness seemed like a reprimand. "I haven't done anything wrong," Harriet said. It was very nearly true. She had disobeyed her grandfather's orders, but she hadn't promised to obey him.

The abigail made no reply. She simply moved forward to unfasten the buttons down the back of Harriet's gown, working deftly and quickly. When the garment was off, she indicated the basin of hot water on the washstand. Harriet made use of it before slipping into the evening dress and shoes. She sat so Slade could deal with her hair, fastening the ornaments as the woman worked.

"Mr. Winstead asked me to watch you and report on your conduct," Slade said.

Harriet started to turn. The comb caught painfully in her hair. "What?"

"Please do not move." Slade eased her head back toward the mirror and inserted the last few hairpins. "I made no reply. I believe he took this for agreement."

"He is…" Harriet was too angry to find the words.

"It was not," the abigail continued. "I do not consider spying to be part of my responsibilities. Should he inquire, I shall say I have noticed nothing unusual."

"Thank you," Harriet began.

"However." Slade examined Harriet's reflection, nodded her satisfaction with her work, and stepped back. "One's definition of *usual* can only be stretched so far," she finished.

"I understand you," said Harriet. She couldn't expect Slade to take risks for her. Why should she? Theirs was not a family with long-time retainers. Harriet and her mother had not been able to afford much help at all until recently. And her grandfather treated his staff like employees, not part of the family. "I was walking in the woodland, and…"

"You had best go down," Slade interrupted, with the air of one who didn't really want to know. "Mrs. Finch remains quite anxious to find you."

"Yes." Mama's only mood was fearful these days. Harriet walked slowly downstairs, taking calming breaths, wrestling with her anger at her grandfather, tamping it down so she could keep her temper through the meal.

Fortunately, her grandfather was in a jovial mood, full of his plans to call on the duke, and he required little in the way of responses to his monologue. His good mood lasted into the following morning when they set off in his carriage to call at Ferrington Hall. Harriet made no comment about the small casket he held in his lap. The Terefords would find it odd to be brought a gift by a man they'd barely met, particularly one that glittered with what seemed to be jewels. But they would be polite.

It was strange to drive up to the house openly after she'd lurked about it and peered inside. The place was greatly improved already. The front garden had been tidied, and the windows shone. They were admitted by an elegant manservant and taken to the largest reception room. Along the way, Harriet saw the covers had come off the furniture and polish had been liberally applied. Cecelia must have found staff in the neighborhood to augment those she'd brought. The air smelled of beeswax and lemon.

The duke and duchess rose to greet them as they entered, as handsome and fashionable a couple as one could well imagine. Harriet was glad to see her friend Cecelia looking happy.

Her grandfather surged ahead, holding out his gift like an offering. "Thought you might like to have this," he said. "It's Arabian. I've forgotten the name of the place. One of my ships brought it back in ninety-eight." He thrust it at the duke.

Tereford showed fleeting surprise, but he took the little casket. "Ah, thank you, Mr. Winstead."

"How interesting," said Cecelia. "Very beautiful work."

"Worth a good few hundreds," replied Harriet's grandfather, mortifyingly. "I had it looked over, and those jewels are real. My agent paid next to nothing for it, of course."

"Ah," said the duke again.

His wife took the item from him and set it on the mantel above the fireplace. "How kind of you to think of us, Mr. Winstead." She did not look at Harriet or show any sign of disapproval, because she was a kind friend.

They sat down. Refreshments were brought. The duke civilly inquired about Mr. Winstead's health and current activities, and Harriet's grandfather happily held forth.

"You must be wondering why we've come here," Cecelia said from her place at Harriet's side.

Harriet nodded.

"Lady Wilton nagged until we agreed. Perhaps you've heard there has been some sign of her great-grandson the earl?"

"Sign?" asked Harriet, though she was afraid she knew what her friend meant.

"He sent a letter, giving a group of Travelers permission to camp on the estate," Cecelia answered. "The Rileys—the caretakers here—informed Lady Wilton at once."

Fortunately, she had a soft voice. Harriet glanced at her grandfather. He hadn't heard the word *Travelers*, which would certainly provoke a tirade.

"It was very odd, of course," her friend added. "No one seems to know where the letter originated. Or how he might have known to send it."

Harriet nodded again, feeling more and more uneasy.

Jack had sworn he hadn't written that letter, but she hadn't quite been able to believe him.

"So we've come up to investigate." Cecelia smiled at her and waited.

After a moment, Harriet realized Cecelia expected her to react to that last word. Harriet and her school friends prided themselves on solving mysteries. She ought to be eager to help. She would have been, if not for her worry over Jack the Rogue, who had behaved so very strangely in his encounter with the duke. Harriet had the sense of events running away with her. "What are you going to do?" she managed.

"We will begin with first principles," said Cecelia with a smile.

Harriet remembered saying something similar in easier times.

"Lady Wilton gave James a note the earl wrote to her," continued the duchess. "We will compare it to the letter sent to the magistrate to see if the handwriting looks the same. James means to ride over tomorrow and procure the letter."

"Oh. That's…a good idea."

Cecelia was obviously disappointed in her reaction. She began to look puzzled. "We also have a description of the earl. But Lady Wilton was not able to supply much detail. Anyone might have dark hair and eyes and a 'commonplace face.' It's not as if he has a scar or some other distinguishing mark."

Harriet nodded, her mind filled with the idea that she must tell Jack about this plan. If he had written that letter, this was bound to catch him. He'd given her his word, but… he *was* a rogue. Rogues played confidence tricks.

"Are you all right, Harriet?" asked Cecelia. "I thought you would be pleased with our cleverness. And have all sorts of suggestions of your own."

"I…ah… Of course I am." She was not behaving like herself. Or perhaps she was. She was simply less focused on the mystery to be solved than on a…a friend to be saved. She searched for words.

"Travelers," exploded her grandfather. Harriet's mother shrank back in her chair and looked even more cowed than she had for the entire visit. "Filthy, thieving rabble!"

Harriet made a small gesture, encompassing the scene—her grandfather's intemperate rage, Mama's fear, the constant, dreadful disharmony of their household. Cecelia looked, assimilated, and seemed to accept this as an excuse for Harriet's responses.

"I tell you what we should do," her grandfather continued. "Gather some men and chase them off." He leaned forward, fixing the duke with a fierce stare.

Her grandfather knew he didn't have the authority to carry this off on his own, Harriet realized. If the duke joined him, however, objections would be muted.

"I understood they had permission from the landowner," Tereford said.

The older man brushed this aside. "Once they're gone, everyone will be glad. An apology is always easier than permission." He smiled. He meant to be ingratiating, Harriet thought, but he only managed to look predatory.

"I think the matter must be left to the local magistrate," said the duke.

"That fool! You cannot side with *him*."

This was a step too far. The duke raised one black eyebrow. His blue eyes grew cold. "I beg your pardon?"

Her grandfather's face went even redder. Harriet's mother looked terrified. An intemperate insult, followed by a definitive setdown, loomed. And after that, disaster. Harriet sprang up. "We should be going," she said.

Cecelia popped up at her side. "It was so kind of you to call."

"It was delightful to see you again."

"Indeed, I am glad we are to be temporary neighbors."

"Are you ready, Mama?" asked Harriet. She tried to bring her mother to her feet by sheer mental influence. Unfortunately, Mama cowered backward, as if she hoped for invisibility.

Cecelia moved to take her hand. "It was so pleasant to see you, Mrs. Finch."

Harriet saw her practically drag Mama up from the sofa.

The duke rose as well. He had begun to look amused rather than haughty, which was good.

"You have someone coming up from London to see you, don't you, Grandpapa?" Harriet asked.

The old man glowered at her. "He can wait."

"You said it was very important business, I believe." He hadn't, but he liked all his affairs to be treated so. Harriet made herself smile at him, though it felt more like gritting her teeth.

"As if you understood anything about it," he growled. But he stood. Perhaps it had penetrated that he didn't want to offend the one duke he'd managed to meet.

"We will see you again soon, I hope," said Harriet to the Terefords. She herded her family toward the door.

"Perhaps your mother will spare you to me one afternoon," answered Cecelia. "I would enjoy your company."

Harriet nodded. She would be glad to spend time with her friend. And then she realized Cecelia gave her a perfect excuse to visit Ferrington Hall's environs any time she liked. She would make certain those visits included Jack, she vowed as they went out to the carriage.

∽

Left alone in the reception room, the Duke and Duchess of Tereford sat down side by side on an aged sofa. He put an arm around her. She smiled up at him. "Why did I allow my grandmother to harass us into coming here?" wondered the duke. "I really cannot remember."

"Lady Wilton can be quite persuasive," said his wife.

"No, she cannot. Demanding, dictatorial, even threatening, yes. But she does not try to persuade. And I've never liked being ordered about."

"You would rather be cajoled," she suggested.

He laughed down at her, his deep-blue eyes warm with affection. "As if you have ever done so."

"I have! Dozens of times."

"Name one."

The duchess considered. "When you decided to set up a racing stable."

Tereford, often called the handsomest man in London,

grew reminiscent. "You presented me with a chart of likely costs and 'inevitable' losses. The thing covered half the dining table and was as complex as a plan of attack for Waterloo."

His wife nodded. "What a lot of work it was."

"You call that cajoling?"

"One can cajole with mathematics," she replied.

"I don't think one can, really, Cecelia." He shook his head. "Or perhaps only you can. You were all of thirteen, I suppose. Solemn as a lowly church bishop."

"Fortunately, for your sake. If your affairs had been left to you and Papa..."

"We would have murdered each other, I suppose. No, I would have murdered *him* and been hanged for killing my trustee."

"Don't be silly."

"I think that is what you said the day you marched into your father's library and ordered us to stop arguing. A small, blond Valkyrie of nine." He gazed at her fondly.

She giggled. "Papa was so grateful."

"I was, too, eventually."

"After a good number of *years*," she replied.

"I admit I was slow to recognize your genius. But I am fully appreciative *now*." He punctuated this assurance with a kiss.

She returned it with equal enthusiasm, and conversation lapsed for a delightful interval.

"One of the servants may come in," the duchess said then, catching a hairpin as it fell from her golden locks.

"They must be accustomed to our scandalous behavior by this time."

"Not the new ones."

"Who are not our employees, strictly speaking, Cecelia. They belong to the elusive earl. Or will do so when he turns up and takes the reins." The duke sighed. "Why did we leave London?"

"We decided we should make the rounds of all the ducal properties and put them in order while the workmen restore the London house."

"We? That is not precisely the way I remember it. Was there cajoling involved?"

She smiled at him. As always, the effect was glorious. "You agreed with me."

"As I inevitably do. But I must point out that Ferrington Hall is *not* a ducal property and is quite out of the way on that round."

"It is. Lady Wilton's nagging grew insupportable. But now that we are here, I'm glad."

"Indeed?" The duke looked mystified.

"There's something odd about Harriet."

"She seemed much the same to me."

The duchess shook her head. "No, she's…softer and… brighter. But at the same time, wound very tight. Something has happened to her."

"Surely this is just fantasy? Miss Finch appeared cool and collected, as usual."

"You don't know her as well as I do."

"True."

"Living with her grandfather must be hard," the duchess said.

Her husband conceded this with a shrug.

"I shall find out." She cocked her head. "You will enjoy finding Ferrington," she added, as if offering a rare treat.

The duke acknowledged her teasing with a smile. "If I do. I have a great deal of sympathy for the fellow. I'd hide from Grandmama if I could."

"She said she wouldn't come here."

"We are off at once if she does."

"Agreed." She nestled close and raised her face for another kiss to seal their pact.

Five

WHEN JACK LOOKED UP THE NEXT MORNING AND SAW Harriet Finch hurrying toward him across the field, he felt a rush of delight. She looked so lovely in a dress of white muslin sprinkled with tiny blue flowers. She carried no parasol today, but a broad-brimmed straw hat shaded her face and hid her ruddy hair. Which was a shame. He had often imagined it tumbling over her shoulders, a glory of curls.

So many of his thoughts now centered on this girl, a new piece to the puzzle that was his life. Jack felt that circumstances were closing in on what had started as a pleasant summer escape. He'd run impulsively from London, but he had to make a decision about his future soon. And he was more and more certain that Miss Finch must be a part of it.

He went to meet her and turned her back toward the trees.

"I had to see you," she said.

He was delighted to hear it, because increasingly he had to see her as well. A day when he didn't felt melancholy and empty. He took her arm and led her to a little clearing near the edge of the wood, a more private place with a large, dry log to sit on. He handed her to it, daring to drop a kiss on her hand as he let it go.

Her green eyes flashed up at him and dropped. A flush warmed her cheeks. "I have something important to tell you," she said.

He was glad she looked for an excuse. He was happy to see her whenever he could.

"We visited Ferrington Hall yesterday," she went on.

Jack knew this, of course. He'd seen the carriage arrive and her party enter. He'd felt jealous and excluded as she disappeared inside. Into *his* house! Now occupied by agents of his poisonous great-grandmother.

"The duke has a letter written by the Earl of Ferrington, and he is going to compare the writing with the one received by the magistrate here," she blurted out.

"Is he?" The duke was an interfering busybody, apparently. Why did he have to stick his nose in?

"You swore to me that you didn't write to Sir Hal."

"I said I didn't forge any letter." Jack was aware this was deceptive. He had to tell her the truth. But he hated being forced by his great-grandmother's minions. "I didn't," he repeated. "Because…" Remembering she despised all earls, he couldn't go on.

Miss Finch examined his face. She looked worried. About him. That meant she cared, did it not? He wished he knew. There was such a tangle to undo. Of his own making, he admitted.

"I'm glad you didn't," she said, rising. "I must go. I'm on my way to visit my friend Cecelia."

"Cecelia?"

"The duchess." She gestured in the direction of the hall.

"Ah." Jack heard the sourness in his voice.

"She is very kind, not at all grand."

Jack doubted this. Or rather, he believed the duchess was kind to Harriet Finch, the rich society girl. She would probably see *him* much as his great-grandmother did. Would she convince Miss Finch to share her opinion?

"I can call on Cecelia often," this young lady added, looking suddenly shy. "Grandfather wants to cultivate the connection. I can stop here on the way. No one will question her on the exact times of her callers."

"You want to come here?" Jack asked.

"Yes," she murmured, eyes on the leaf-covered ground.

"To see me?"

She looked up and met his gaze squarely. "Yes."

Jack thrilled at the shy longing he saw in her expression.

"This is where you say you are glad of that and want me to come," she said.

Jack stood and stepped toward her. "I am tremendously glad and want you with all my heart."

The flush was very visible on her pale skin. Her smile was warmly glorious.

Jack held out a hand. She took it and then, startling him, moved close and leaned in. Their lips met in a kiss of such sweetness that Jack was stunned. All the kisses of his life paled in comparison. The tumultuous splendor of it washed over him—tenderness, arousal, amazement. His head spun. She slid her arms around him and held him tight, as if she too hoped the kiss would never end. For an ecstatic, reeling time, it seemed it would not. But, of course, it did. They drew back. She gazed up at him with green eyes softened by desire.

She was his. She was the answer to all his questions about the future. "I must tell you something," he began.

"Yes?" she breathed.

"When I said I had not..."

The clearing erupted with laughing children, dancing around them, led by Samia. "You were kissing!" she exclaimed.

Harriet pulled away.

The children swirled and capered around them. "We saw you!" Samia said. "Kissing. Kissing."

They made it a chant. Jack batted at the children as if they were swarming gnats. "Go away! Shoo!"

"Kissing, kissing," they sang.

Scarlet with embarrassment but laughing, Harriet moved farther away from him.

"Don't go," called Jack. But he was engulfed by giggling children, and she shook her head.

"I will come again," she said. And slipped away into the trees.

"For more kissing," called Samia, her face alight with laughter.

"You and your friends are a pestilential nuisance," Jack declared.

Samia cackled at the label. "You're in our dancing place," she retorted.

He hadn't realized the Traveler children had claimed this little clearing. He needed to find a private spot where he could talk to Harriet Finch, tell her his true story, and ask her to marry him. With many more kisses involved, he hoped. Had things been different, he would have gone at once to Winstead Hall and made a formal offer. But they were not. If the aristocratic strangers hadn't appropriated Ferrington Hall, he might have revealed himself and moved in there. But they had. Circumstances kept overtaking him. Ever since the stuffy Englishman had arrived in Boston to fetch him, he'd floundered behind events. It was time to take control. He left the dancing children and headed for the camp.

∽

Harriet moved toward Ferrington Hall on a cloud of desire. No wonder young ladies were taught to avoid kisses, particularly girls with no prospects in the world and no one to protect them. She saw now how one could be swept away into acts that led to social disaster.

She'd taken care, when poor, never to make a single misstep. Then, as a sudden heiress, she'd been repelled by the young men with avid eyes who wanted her fortune far more than her person.

Now, here was Jack the Rogue, who had nothing to do with the marriage mart and was utterly unacceptable in every way except the most important. She loved him. She'd flung caution to the winds with Jack, and she wasn't sorry. Her body and spirit still rang from that kiss! He'd opened a whole new landscape to her, a vision of a different kind of life far away from the stuffy confines of English society. That life did not depend on her grandfather's fortune, which would be whisked away the moment he learned of her choice. They could leave Grandfather behind, go thousands of miles beyond his sphere of influence. Harriet felt as if vistas had opened at her feet and bonds she hadn't even been aware of were falling away. She didn't have to care about the proprieties that had been drilled into her. There was a larger world out there.

Except. Harriet was brought up short by thoughts of her mother. If she defied her grandfather's wishes, stepped into that freedom, Mama would collapse. Harriet had no doubt about that. And she would have to support her, drawn back into the social snares her mother espoused. It wasn't fair! Yet she couldn't desert Mama. Leaving her to Grandfather's revenge would be an unimaginable cruelty. Harriet's spirits began to sink.

But Jack was…ingenious. He lived to scheme. He flung himself into pranks and adventures. Harriet remembered his ludicrous teasing of the duke at the camp and laughed as she walked. Jack had no instinct to defer or be overawed by a title. Indeed, he despised society as much as she did. He would help with Mama. Together, they would find a way out of the toils that had bound her all her life. Harriet skipped a few steps as she entered the Ferrington Hall gardens. Her faith in her roguish love was deep.

Harriet's arrival coincided with the return of the duke. He was walking up from the stables as she crossed the garden. "I convinced the local magistrate to give me that letter," he said, holding up a folded sheet of paper.

"Oh…good." There was no reason to worry, Harriet told herself. Jack had said he hadn't written it. And even if the letter was shown to be false, there was no reason to connect it with him.

They found Cecelia in a smaller reception room, which had become a cozy, flower-filled place since she took charge. The duke took the letter over to a writing desk, unfolded it, and set it beside another sheet of paper that lay there. He looked back and forth between the two missives.

Harriet braced herself. What should she say if they…?

"The writing seems the same to me," Tereford said. "What do you think?"

Cecelia stepped up to look. Harriet followed her.

"I agree," said Cecelia. "See the flourish on the *t* there and the way the *a*'s are not quite closed."

It was true. Harriet stared at the two pages. The note to Lady Wilton was a few lines with no signature, and the permission letter was a formal document on engraved letterhead, but the hand was the same. Harriet was astonished and then filled with joy. She had doubted. She admitted it. Jack was, after all, a rogue. But he had not lied to her. The relief of that was more intense than she'd expected.

"Are you all right?" Cecelia asked her.

Also, Jack was not in jeopardy, Harriet thought. That was wonderful, too.

"Harriet? Is something wrong?"

She gathered her scattered faculties. "No. Nothing."

"But you seem to be…trembling?" The duchess frowned at her.

"I'm fine." Harriet pushed down her emotions, as she had a lifetime of practice in doing. She did not intend to tell Cecelia about Jack. Cecelia was a delightful person, a good friend, but she was not unconventional. The perfect duchess, she wouldn't understand, or approve of, Harriet's choice. Harriet feared even her best friends would have doubts. She could hear Charlotte's sharp questions and Sarah's softer doubts. Ada had married another duke. She'd had no longing for escape. But none of them had grown up on the margins of society or been a victim of its looming threats and petty spite.

Briefly, Harriet worried that her long, precious friendships would not endure. Must she be ready to lose all she knew if she allied herself with Jack the Rogue? No, they would stand by her. They'd been through so much together, including a shocking glimpse into the darker side of society last season.

"Harriet?" said Cecelia again.

She shook off her doubts. The future would have to take care of itself. "Yes. So now we must wonder how this letter came to be," she said. Harriet's zest for investigation could surface now that she didn't have to worry about Jack. "Where it came from and how the earl learned of the camp on his land," she added.

"All those things," the duke agreed with a smile.

Cecelia looked reassured by Harriet's spate of questions. "Do we know how it was delivered?" she asked.

"A boy on horseback brought it," her husband replied. "Perhaps a groom. No one in Sir Hal's household remembered anything else about him."

"That sounds like someone coming from nearby," Harriet said. "But where?"

"Not this house or Winstead Hall," Cecelia answered. "And not Sir Hal's estate either, obviously. That appears to account for the large places in this neighborhood."

"An inn?" Harriet wondered.

Tereford was frowning. "From what Lady Wilton told us about the new earl's mother…"

"In strictest confidence," Cecelia interrupted. "She was most insistent about that."

"Yes," answered the duke dryly.

Their eyes met. Clearly a good deal of information passed in that glance. Harriet was not party to any of it, and she felt a wisp of envy. These two had a true partnership.

"We must continue our inquiries," he added. "I will do so."

In other circumstances, Harriet would have pushed for a role in the search. But now she simply longed to run and talk over this news with Jack. Everything that happened these days made her want to hurry and tell Jack. A good sign, she decided. Of course, she wouldn't mention that she was delighted he hadn't lied to her.

Tereford bade them farewell and went out.

"Come and sit," Cecelia said, going to the sofa.

She expected a quiet, cozy talk. Harriet went to join her.

"I had a letter from Ada," Cecelia added. "She is in transports over her stonemasons."

"I heard that, too," Harriet responded with a smile. Her old school friend and newly minted duchess was deep in the restoration of a half-ruined castle.

"She hoped I could recommend a seller of paving tiles. I don't know why."

"Because you have been managing estates since you were in pigtails," Harriet answered.

Cecelia burst out laughing. "Not quite that long."

It had been almost that long, Harriet knew. She'd met Cecelia's feckless father. "Is all going well with the Tereford properties?"

"The London house is nearly cleared. A small army of cleaners has gone to work there, and the workmen will follow."

The recently deceased Duke of Tereford, great-uncle of the current one, had piled up goods like a dragon of legend. Only his hoard had consisted of broken-down furnishings and ornaments stuffed into every nook and cranny of a sizable mansion.

"I was just getting started on the rest before we came here," Cecelia said.

"The rest?"

"James's great-uncle neglected all the ducal estates. There's a great deal to be done."

"They're not all like the London house!" Harriet couldn't imagine that number of *things*.

"No." Cecelia gave a small shudder. "I sent inquiries. There's nothing else like that. But there is much disrepair and…unusual tenancies."

"The duke is very lucky to have you."

"He is aware." The duchess's small, secret smile affirmed this marriage was going well. "But how are you? Have you… settled in?"

Harriet shrugged. Her friends knew some of her difficult history with her grandfather. And they'd met him, of course. Grandfather did not make a pleasant impression.

"I wish I might invite you for a visit," Cecelia responded. "But I have no place for house parties this summer."

"My grandfather would probably refuse permission. He likes to keep us under his thumb." Harriet had not been allowed to accompany her friend Charlotte home. But if she had gone there, she realized, she wouldn't have met Jack. So she had her grandfather to thank for her new vision of life. Perhaps she would tell him someday. How he would hate that!

The sound of hoofbeats drifted in through the open window. The crunch of wheels and jingle of harness heralded a carriage.

"I wonder who that can be?" said Cecelia.

A moment later, Harriet's mother rushed into the room. She headed directly for Harriet, scarcely seeming to notice Cecelia's presence. "There you are!" She grasped Harriet's hands and held on so tight, her fingers were crushed.

"What's wrong?" asked Harriet, fearing some upheaval or accident.

"I couldn't find you!" Her mother's face was creased with distress.

Was it no more than that? "But you did find me, Mama," Harriet replied. "Here I am. I left word I was coming to visit Cecelia." She pulled her hands free and gestured toward their hostess.

"Oh. Yes." Her mother managed a tremulous smile. "Good day, Your Grace."

"Mrs. Finch, how nice to see you." Cecelia met Harriet's eyes, a question in her own. Harriet didn't know how to answer it. "Won't you sit down?" Cecelia added.

"No, I...I said I was going for a drive. He might ask... Harriet, you must come with me!" She grabbed Harriet's hands once again. Hers were trembling violently.

"Has something happened?" Harriet asked her.

"Everything is fine."

It obviously wasn't. "Wouldn't you like to stay for a while?" Harriet asked, pulling her mother toward the sofa. Surely she would calm down if she sat quietly with them. "Have you eaten?" Mama had been picking at her food lately.

"No, no! I must go for a drive. And then back home." Her mother's voice had risen to a frantic level.

"Very well, Mama. That is what we will do." Harriet exchanged another perplexed look with Cecelia as her mother tugged at her arm. There was nothing to do but go. When Mama grew so agitated, she required time and a great deal of soothing to regain her equilibrium. Cecelia would understand, as far as anyone could.

Harriet didn't know why her mother was increasingly fragile. Grandfather was a trial, but his ill temper didn't explain why Mama was growing worse. He'd been just as unpleasant in London. She would not see this as a burden, Harriet told herself as they went out to the waiting carriage. Even though it tugged her back just when she had been feeling so free. She would find a way to help.

❧

"That man is in the camp again," Samia told Jack as the sun was lowering late that afternoon.

"What man?"

"The handsome one."

"Handsome? Isn't that me then?"

"He's handsomer than you."

Jack put his hand to his heart, pretending to be wounded.

"The one you tried to fool by talking silly," Samia added.

He noticed the *tried*.

"He asked about you," Samia added.

Of course he had, just when things had begun to go well with Harriet Finch but before he'd had the chance to settle things with her. Jack considered fading into the forest until the irritating duke had gone, but who knew what the man would do if he couldn't be satisfied. Jack couldn't leave the Travelers at his mercy. He straightened his less-than-fashionable coat and went to find the man.

Once again, a wide circle of male Travelers surrounded the fellow. The duke seemed as unaffected as ever. He looked about as if he had every right to walk among them. Discouraging stares had no effect. Jack crossed his arms, took up a post near the central fire, and waited.

"Ah, there you are," the duke said, stopping a short distance away.

"Here I ahm."

"I was able to examine that letter from the earl."

"Were you and all?"

"Sir Hal Wraxton lent me his copy. It appears valid."

"That's good then."

"Very fortunate for you." The man included the whole group in his glance. "But I find it strange that the earl, who remains missing, knew to write it. How did he learn of your situation?"

Jack went so far as to scratch his head and say, "Huh."

The damned duke laughed. "You said you were called Jack the Rogue."

"Aye."

"Jack is sometimes used as a diminutive for Jonathan, is it not?"

"Dim…what? That's a great long word, that is. Yer Honor."

One of the Travelers snickered, which didn't help matters. This duke threw him a sardonic glance. He was not behaving as Jack expected.

"You don't quite fit here, do you?"

Exasperation threatened to divert Jack. These English were so obsessed with fitting in—dressing a certain way, speaking in the right accent, behaving along rigid lines. They tried to define a man by externals, even if those had nothing to do with him.

"The Travelers have a kind of family resemblance," the duke went on. "Which you don't really share."

In other words, he belonged nowhere, Jack thought. He knew that. He didn't need to be told.

"And your accent is…unreliable."

"I speak as I can. Yer Honor."

"Or perhaps I should say *creative*," the duke continued. "It wavers, creatively, from country to country and into the realms of fiction."

"I don't know what Your Honor means by that." Jack struggled with his temper. He longed to wipe the smug arrogance off the fellow's face with a solid punch.

"I mean that you are not the dolt you pretend to be," answered the duke crisply.

"Dolt, is it? Eh, that's not kind."

"I said *not*." The intruder raked him with a look. "What is your surname, Jack the Rogue?"

"Surname?" Jack needed a way to put him off once and for all. But he came up with none. "That would be…"

"The family name you were born with."

"Oh, that was long ago."

"Twenty-four years, perhaps? I suspect it is Merrill and that you are the 'missing' Earl of Ferrington."

"Why would you think such a daft thing as that?"

The duke began to tick off points on his aristocratic fingers. "You are not a true member of this camp. There is a whole different feel about you. You match the description I was given of the earl, though I admit it was vague. Your accent and rustic act are very unconvincing. You are perfectly placed to have written that letter of permission. And finally, I am aware the missing earl's mother was connected with the Travelers, so he—you—might well be accepted here."

Jack gritted his teeth. That last bit of knowledge had no doubt come from his great-grandmother and been put in the worst possible light. As if he would ever be ashamed of his mother!

"Do you swear to me that you are *not* Jonathan Frederick Merrill?" the duke asked.

Jack was tempted. He owed this arrogant nobleman nothing.

"If you give me your word of honor, of course, I will accept that," the man added.

He spoke without condescension, as if honor was a concept that applied to them both equally. Which made it impossible for Jack to lie. "Damn you," he said.

"You *are* the earl."

Jack knew his nod was sullen. Why shouldn't it be? The man was an interfering ass.

Murmurs rose around them, and Jack saw his mistake. He should have taken the duke aside for this talk, though he hadn't known how it would go, of course. Now the man had ruined the camp for Jack. The Travelers would treat him differently, see him as more alien than he'd already been. They might not throw him out, but their easy comradeship was ended. Had the duke known that would happen? Or was he simply too pleased with his own cleverness to notice?

Jack moved away from the group. No need for them to hear more. The duke followed him. "I won't go back to London to be schooled by Lady Wilton," Jack said, dropping all pretense of an accent.

"I can't imagine anyone who would want to do that."

His tone was understanding. Jack gave him a closer look.

"But it does seem time to take up your proper position," the duke added.

"Proper!" Jack spat the syllables. "That word seems to cover a vast deal of judgment and spite. I've been told I am entirely *improper*, and I don't see why I should 'take up' anything at all." In fact, he wasn't sure what his "position" meant, beyond Lady Wilton's wish to change everything about his appearance and manner.

"It is a matter of duty," said the other man. "A great estate, and title, brings responsibility for many other people." His expression grew wry. "As I have had cause to learn."

"This is what you have been taught and trained to accept," Jack pointed out.

The duke nodded.

"*My* father was thrown away by your proper society. As if he was worthless. I think it broke him." He hadn't really understood his father's history until he came here. The bare outline didn't convey what his father must have felt, tossed from a place like Ferrington Hall into a solitary scramble for survival. Papa hadn't been able to rise to the challenge, true. But it was a greater one than Jack had realized.

"That was unconscionable," said the duke. He sounded truly outraged.

Jack searched for insincerity in the fellow's handsome face.

"It is too bad his family cannot make it up to him," he went on. "Perhaps we may do so to you."

The only family Jack had known of was Lady Wilton. Was this duke putting himself in the same category? He was some sort of distant cousin, Miss Finch had said. Did that really mean anything? He shrugged.

"Do you intend to run away again?" There seemed to be sympathetic curiosity in the man's cool, blue gaze.

At one time, he had. But now there was something keeping him here. Jack hesitated.

The duke took this as encouragement. "I suggest we stage your official 'arrival' at Ferrington Hall in a day or so. I can set the thing up, with a carriage and so on. You move in and set up as the earl. We'll welcome you. Grandmama can't complain about that."

"Grandmama?"

"I beg your pardon. I thought you knew. Lady Wilton is my grandmother."

This made Jack frown. He couldn't imagine calling that harridan *Grandmama*. Or anything else, actually. Also, the duke looked about his own age. Or just a few years older. "Great-grandmother, you mean?"

The man shook his head. "My father married late. He was well past thirty. His sister—your grandmother—seems to have been married right out of the schoolroom."

"Made to, most likely," said Jack, thinking of the autocratic Lady Wilton.

"I expect so. A seventeen-year-old girl would find it difficult to resist. If she wished to."

"She died young, my father said." Jack's curiosity about his family battled his determination to remain aloof. He'd hoarded every crumb of history his father let fall when he was into the brandy. It added up to very little.

The duke nodded. "I never knew her."

"And then Lady Wilton sent my father across the sea when he was barely out of school."

"So I understand."

"A fine sort of family," said Jack bitterly.

"Reprehensible," the duke replied.

"And yet you're here doing her bidding."

"That is not what I'm doing." His tone was sharp.

"What do you call it then?"

The other man considered a moment, then made a wry face. "I did give in to Grandmama's nagging. I admit it. She is relentless."

Jack could vouch for that.

"My wife convinced me we should…take the path of least resistance."

This was the woman Harriet Finch called a friend. What was she after? Was she another virago, issuing orders to dukes? Jack felt as if a net was closing on him.

"Grandmama has no real power over you, you know," the duke added.

"Beyond nagging me to death with her criticisms."

"Beyond that, yes." The dashed duke smiled at him.

"Nor do you," replied Jack grumpily. "I could throw you out of my house."

"You could indeed. I almost wish you would. But Cecelia wouldn't like it."

"Why not?"

"She wants to help."

Help who, to do what? Jack wondered.

"I assume your Traveler friends will keep quiet about your stay with them?"

"If I ask them to. And who would they tell?"

"Indeed. And no one else in the neighborhood knows you. So you can appear at your new home without awkward questions."

No one except Harriet Finch. He wouldn't be telling this duke about their meetings. He had no reason to trust him. And he could make no move without speaking to her. "I haven't said I would," he answered.

"I really think this is best," the man said.

That might be kindness in his eyes. Jack didn't know him well enough to be sure. "I don't know."

The duke waited.

"I'll think about it."

The visitor seemed about to say more, then he shrugged. "Very well. It is your choice."

That was a fresh attitude. "I don't suppose you would just go back to London and tell Lady Wilton you couldn't find me?" Jack asked as a last hope.

"I might, but she would send someone else. Or come up here herself to wreak havoc."

Jack shuddered.

"If I begin to set things in train, we could stage your 'appearance' tomorrow."

"Not so fast. I haven't agreed." Perhaps there was some other way out? But whether there was or no, he had to get to Miss Finch.

The duke nodded. "You need only send word when you are ready."

He assumed Jack would give in. Perhaps they always did when he commanded. And people here couldn't believe a man would refuse to be an earl.

"If there's anything you need…"

"Nothing." Thinking only of Harriet Finch, Jack made

cursory farewells. And as soon as the duke had gone, he rushed through the woods toward Winstead Hall. Jack was so distracted that he nearly ran afoul of one of the watchers at the border. He evaded him at the last moment and eeled his way into the gardens surrounding the house.

The day was waning. Lights had begun to show in the windows. There was no one about. He thought of knocking at the kitchen door and asking for Miss Finch. But that would rouse questions and perhaps a great furor. Her grandfather might have him tossed out.

Nearly overcome with frustration, Jack realized the Earl of Ferrington would be in a totally different position when he came to this house. *He* wouldn't have to fight his way in. *He* would be welcome. *He* could walk in and see Miss Finch any time he liked. His proposal of marriage would delight her family. No one would snub *him*. Jack rather liked that notion, even as he—ridiculously—resented this carefree earl. But perhaps change was for the best, and he should become that man. As soon as he reached Miss Finch and prepared her. He must talk to her alone, not in a crowd of people fawning over the newfound earl. Not before he figured out how to *be* that nobleman.

He turned away. He would write a note. Surely there was paper and pen somewhere about the camp. He would ask Miss Finch to meet him. Urgently. He could slip it under the front door and let a servant find it.

⌘

"I've done it," the Duke of Tereford told his wife when he returned to Ferrington Hall.

"It?"

"I found the earl."

"In the Travelers' camp?"

He gazed at her with fond exasperation. "Must you always be a step ahead of me, Cecelia?"

She spread her hands. "Knowing about his mother, the coincidence was too great."

"Yes, but you might have pretended to be surprised and impressed."

The duchess smiled. She clasped her hands and offered him a wide-eyed gaze. "Oh, James, how clever you are!"

"Unconvincing," he replied. His lips twitched, but he resisted the smile.

"Well, you wouldn't wish me to pretend admiration."

"Wouldn't I?" He shrugged. "Not when you don't feel it," he conceded.

"You know very well how I feel about you. I love you with all my heart."

He met her steady gaze and held it for a long moment. "Likewise."

The duchess smiled. "Likewise? Is that the best you can do?"

"Oh, I can do better. I will show you later on."

Her cheeks reddened. "I merely gave you credit for being as intelligent as I am," she added.

"Now there is a compliment!"

"And thus, I assumed you had drawn similar conclusions."

"How can it be so enflaming when you say *thus*?"

"I suppose it is one of my special talents."

"You have so many of those."

Her flush deepened.

Six

HARRIET SAT BESIDE HER MOTHER'S BED, HOLDING HER hand as Mama tossed and fretted. She'd refused to let Harriet out of her sight when they returned from the brief carriage ride. "Please tell me what's gone wrong, Mama," she said. Again.

"Nothing! I already said—nothing."

This was clearly not true. But Harriet didn't know whether there had been some new misfortune or if this was baseless anxiety. She could only hope Mama would calm down, given time. She'd ask Slade if she'd heard of any disturbances. Her grandfather often shouted his complaints.

Her mother pulled her hand away and sat suddenly upright. "What is the time? We must dress for dinner. We will be late."

"Wouldn't you like to stay here and have a tray?" Harriet asked. "I could join you." And then neither of them would have to dine with her grandfather. That would be a relief.

"No! We must go down. Papa expects us."

"I can tell him you're feeling ill."

"I am not ill! You know how he despises weakness."

"Unless it is some little malady of his own, which must be catered to by the whole household."

"You mustn't say such things! Promise you won't argue with him."

Harriet looked into her mother's strained blue eyes. It was ironic that Mama resembled Grandfather, as Harriet did not. And she looked even more like him since they'd come to live with Grandfather in the country. So much older and more tired, her round face creased with worry. She'd grown thinner, too. Once upon a time, Mama had relished her food, particularly sweets. Now it was hard to tempt her even with rich confections. "You know I try to avoid doing so, Mama."

"You do not! You are always chafing at him."

"Well, he provokes me."

"He has made you a great heiress. You have no right to object to his wishes."

This was the crux of the matter. Accept the fortune and subject oneself to its conditions. Or return to the penurious scraping of her youth. There was no middle ground. Her grandfather had made that clear. And her mother had begun to view the latter prospect with something like terror. Could she be made to see a third choice?

Harriet squeezed Mama's trembling hands. Perhaps she should have refused the legacy at the very beginning? Her mother had been stronger then. She had, after all, gotten them through years of genteel poverty. Mama might have been outraged, but surely not…broken, as she seemed to be now. But how could Harriet have known? Her grandfather had descended on them with false words of reconciliation. He'd appeared jovial and almost…repentant, at first. He'd lured her mother in, Harriet thought resentfully. And once she was caught, he'd started using Mama's childhood doubts against her.

"We must behave properly." Her mother rose and began to twitter about the room. "Ring the bell. Go and dress. Hurry. Come back when you are ready, and we will go down together." She made shooing motions.

Harriet obeyed with a wisp of relief at leaving her. Both her remaining relatives demanded obedience, in their different ways. It was oppressive. How glad she was that she knew a rogue who did not prize submission. She clung to the thought of getting away to see Jack.

She endured the usual heavy dinner, accompanied by her grandfather's grumbling and constant stream of orders. Harriet tried to keep his attention on her so her mother might be left alone. To do so without arguing was a test of both her ingenuity and her temper. She ended the meal and the day exhausted.

As a result, Harriet slept longer than usual, which spoiled her plan to get out early for a walk. Her mother pounced at the breakfast table with a list of activities that would keep Harriet close by her side all day. She would hear of no deviation, and Harriet struggled with a sharp answer. Mama had never required her to dance attendance in this way before. It could not go on.

Fortunately for her temper, Cecelia came to call at midmorning, bringing a breath of fresh air and a diversion. "How are you today, Mrs. Finch?" she asked.

"How should I be?" replied Harriet's mother. "I am always perfectly well."

Cecelia blinked at her truculent tone, then passed it off with a smile.

They sat down to chat, and Harriet admired her friend's ability to set a group at ease. Cecelia really was a perfect duchess. Mama's fragile mood smoothed so much under her attentions that she did not object when Cecelia asked Harriet to show her the new blooms in the garden. Mama said only, "Be sure to take a parasol, Harriet. The sun is very bright."

Harriet dutifully fetched one, failing to notice a somewhat grubby, folded scrap of paper resting on her writing desk. She rejoined Cecelia, and they walked out together into the fine summer day.

"I have news," Cecelia said when they were well away from the house. "We've found the missing earl. Or James did, I should say."

"So easily?" asked Harriet. "Where was he?"

"In the Travelers camp. Of all places."

"What?" A premonitory shiver ran through Harriet.

"He is living there, calling himself Jack the Rogue." Cecelia looked amused.

"What?" said Harriet again.

"James says he is quite the wag."

"But...that can't be."

"It is odd, isn't it?" replied Cecelia.

"Surely...surely the duke is mistaken?" He had to be. Jack could not be an earl. He was the antithesis of the pretense and spite she'd observed in London society. He represented a different sort of life.

Cecelia shook her head. "He admitted it when James pressed him."

Harriet grappled with an astonished numbness.

"Most reluctantly," continued her friend. "James said he was very annoyed at being exposed."

Events of the past few weeks began to move and shift in Harriet's memory, falling into a new order. She'd ignored the fact that Jack's manner and accent sometimes seemed quite polished. Or not ignored, but simply accepted them because they fit in her world. She hadn't stopped to wonder why an American shipping clerk should sound so familiar. Or why he'd been perfectly at ease peering into Ferrington Hall. Because it was his house! Hadn't her reluctance amused him? He'd mocked the duke with his rustic performance. Without compunction or the least sign of deference. Who but another nobleman would behave so? Harriet felt emotion building in her chest. She'd thought he represented a new sort of life. She wasn't usually so naive.

He had kissed her! She had kissed him. Harriet felt the threat of tears and ruthlessly suppressed them. He'd told her he hadn't written that letter. He'd let her make a fool of herself.

"We're not going to tell anyone where he was," Cecelia added. "It's to be a secret."

"Is it?" Harriet replied through clenched teeth.

"Well, it might be awkward for him if it was widely known."

"Might it?"

"We don't care for such things. But think of Lady Wilton. *Scold* is too mild a word. And other high sticklers might disapprove."

"We wouldn't want *that*."

"Is something wrong, Harriet?"

"What should be wrong?"

"I don't know. But something clearly is. Surely you don't mind that he stayed with the Travelers?"

Harriet let her parasol fall between them briefly and struggled to control her expression. How fortunate she hadn't told Cecelia about Jack, she thought. Her humiliation was quite private. "Of course not," she managed and was glad to hear her voice sounded normal.

"Are you annoyed you didn't discover him yourself?" her friend asked, teasing a little. "You can't have had many opportunities to investigate."

She'd had them, and she'd ignored them, too busy falling in love with a rogue to use her brains. In that moment, Harriet despised herself. She stood straighter and shifted the parasol so she faced Cecelia squarely. There would be no more such failings.

"We're going to slip him into Ferrington Hall as if he's just arrived." Cecelia's smile invited Harriet to share the joke. "Since no one knows him outside the camp."

"Did he say so?" Harriet asked.

Cecelia shrugged. "I don't know. But how could they?"

They might have walked in the forest and encountered a man who claimed to be a rogue, Harriet thought. They might have talked with him and laughed and danced with him and begun to care about a person who did not exist.

"And the Travelers are his friends and will not betray him."

Anger broke its bonds and washed over Harriet. She acknowledged she had never been so furious in her life.

"What is it?" asked Cecelia.

Harriet dug her nails into her palms. Had Jack meant anything he said to her? Why had she been so gullible? No one must know how she'd been duped.

"Harriet?" said her friend.

She forced herself to speak. "Such a surprising development."

Cecelia examined her, clearly puzzled by Harriet's responses.

She tried to find some response to make. "Lady Wilton will be very pleased with you."

"James is writing a letter meant to keep her from coming up here."

Perhaps *she* would contact Lady Wilton and lure her here to torment Jack. Not Jack. He was Lord Ferrington. How would she ever call him that? She wouldn't, because she would never speak to him again. *After* she told him what she thought of his reprehensible conduct.

"I thought you would be amused." Cecelia was quite intelligent. She would discover the truth if Harriet wasn't more careful. Well, given a bit of time, she would be.

"We should go in," Harriet said. "Mama will be looking for me."

"Is she quite well?" Cecelia asked as they turned back toward the house.

"She's finding my grandfather trying."

Her friend nodded sympathetically.

Cecelia departed soon after this, and Harriet nearly went mad as the day progressed at a snail's pace. Each time she tried to get away, her mother made strenuous objections. She reacted to Harriet's mood, which amplified her fears.

At last, in the afternoon, her mother lay down for a rest, and Harriet slipped out at once before anyone could accost her. She didn't even bother with a bonnet and gloves, not wanting to encounter Slade in her bedchamber and have to explain. Feeling rather bare without these garments, Harriet slipped out of the house and through the garden. She took the path that let her evade the watchers her grandfather kept on his borders. All that she wished to say to the perfidious Jack was running through her brain, but she came upon him sooner than expected, right at the near edge of the woodland.

"There you are," he said, looking relieved. "Did you get my note at last? I've been lurking about for hours trying to find a way to see you."

"You!" replied Harriet.

"I wanted to tell you…"

"Are you really an earl? Are you actually Lord Ferrington?"

His face creased with chagrin. "How…"

"Cecelia told me."

His shoulders sagged. "Of course. It would have been too much to expect that dratted duke to keep his mouth shut."

"So it is true?" Harriet realized that, up to this moment, some part of her had thought he would deny the story.

"Well, yes. I meant for you to know first, but we were interrupted when…"

"You lied to me!"

"I omitted some parts of my history."

"Omitted." Harriet put a full measure of contempt in her tone. *Omit* was the word of a weasel. This was the sort of sly evasion common in the upper reaches of society, so those in the know could laugh behind their hands at everyone else. "Jack Mere," she said bitterly.

"I told you that wasn't my real name. You were a stranger then, and I didn't want to be found."

Then. What was she now? "And the letter to Sir Hal? You told me you didn't write it. You swore!"

"I told you I did not *forge* it," he answered. "Which was true, as I am the earl. For my sins."

Had he said that? Yes, perhaps. It was difficult to recall through her hurt and anger. "So it is necessary to test every word you have ever said to me for literal truth?"

"Not anymore. That is…"

"Now that you are Lord Ferrington?"

He winced at the name, or perhaps her tone. "I didn't want Lady Wilton to discover me. Perhaps you can sympathize with that?"

She could, but she wasn't going to admit it.

"I'm sorry, but you have to understand…"

"Don't tell me what I *have* to do!" The dreams she'd woven, out of cobwebs and fantasy apparently, seemed idiotic now. "You've ruined everything!"

"What have I ruined?"

"I thought you were different. Nothing like them. I thought we would…" Harriet bit off the sentence as *Lord Ferrington* gaped at her. Her face burned. She'd imagined they could run away together into a freer sort of life. How silly. How brainless! Humiliation overwhelmed her rage. Choking on it, she turned and ran.

∽

Jack went after her, but Miss Finch rushed directly to one of her grandfather's watchers and requested an escort home. The man looked surprised, glowered at Jack, and of course complied. It took all of Jack's self-control not to leap upon him and pummel the fellow to the ground. But that would only cause more trouble.

He made himself fade back into the forest's edge and watched them go. Harriet was in no mood to listen to him, even if he knew what to say.

He should have told her the truth before she heard it from others. He knew that. He had *tried* several times. Or... Honesty compelled Jack to admit he hadn't tried hard enough. He'd put it off because he hadn't wanted to end their forest idyll. He'd enjoyed being with her in that easy way. He'd behaved badly. He had to make up for that.

He would. Surely, he could. He had to. Had he told Miss Finch how Lady Wilton had hurt him? He must, hard as it would be to admit. He would explain how each small step had led him deeper into his deception. He would tell her he'd only stayed in this country for her. A spike of hope shot through Jack's mire of regrets. She'd thought he was different. And he was. More than that, he'd promise to be as different as she pleased, in any way she pleased if she would just forgive him.

But to do these things, he had to see her again.

Jack wanted to march over to Winstead Hall, find her, and state his case. But he wouldn't be admitted. Jack looked down at his clothes. They hadn't been what Miss Finch's world called fashionable to begin with, and camp living had not improved them. His hands were roughened by work. He ran his fingers through his hair. It had gone shaggy. He was clean, from cold baths in a stream, but compared with a man like that dratted duke, he looked like a wastrel. Jack the Rogue would have to fight his way into Harriet's home, and he would more than likely fail.

Jack turned and walked back toward the camp. He had to find another way, and of course, he had one. From what he'd heard of Harriet's grandfather, the Earl of Ferrington would be welcomed into his house with open arms, whatever he might choose to wear.

Jack wasted a moment resenting this. He would be the same man at heart—rogue or earl. The clutter of externals made no difference. And yet they did. Most people judged their fellows by appearance, the silly, shallow posers. A villain could wear fine garments. A saint might go in rags. Didn't they tend to do so, in fact? Indeed, commented a dry inner voice, right up to the moment when they were speared or burned or otherwise immolated by the self-satisfied pillars of society. And wasn't he being overdramatic, comparing himself to them?

"Yes, all right," muttered Jack.

Back at the camp, he found a note had arrived from the duke, reminding him of his plan and urging him to stage his "arrival" at Ferrington Hall. All was in readiness, the man said, damn his arrogance. Jack gritted his teeth. He did not like being herded.

He threw the note onto his pile of blankets. Was there any alternative? How long did he have before this interfering duke spread the news far and wide?

The only thing that mattered was to see Harriet Finch again, explain, and restore her trust in him, Jack realized. Everything else was secondary. He must take whatever steps were necessary to speak with her, even if they went against the grain.

Retrieving the folded sheet of paper, Jack went to find Mistress Elena.

The old woman was sitting in her usual spot at the back of her caravan. Her dark eyes were wary as she watched Jack approach. He noticed all the Travelers in her vicinity were watching him as well. Some looked hostile. Others merely withdrawn. A few even seemed to appreciate his biographical sleight of hand. It was obvious, however, that the place he'd carved out among them was gone.

"You are leaving," Mistress Elena said when Jack stopped before her.

"Might I stay?" he had to ask.

"I think your time with us is over."

The reality of it hurt, like another punishment for being who he was.

"This is a thing that was always going to happen," she added.

Jack blinked. It was true. He'd never considered settling down among the Travelers. But he'd intended to go in his own time. Not be pushed out.

"You really are a nobleman?" Mistress Elena asked.

"Because I am my father's son," he replied. "And for no other reason. I have no knowledge of these people or connection to them."

"Not even to the girl with red hair?" She looked dryly amused.

Of course she'd noticed. Mistress Elena knew everything that happened in and around the camp. "Except for her," Jack said.

The old woman nodded, her dark eyes flicking to the page he held. "I wish you good luck on your journey."

Jack put a hand to his heart. "I am grateful for your hospitality on the road and after. *Maa'ths.* My thanks."

"*Hu grālt'a.* You are welcome, son of a Traveler woman."

Gesturing at the field around them, Jack added, "This land is mine, it seems. Stay as long as you like. Send for me if you are troubled." That authority was pleasant, at least.

The old woman nodded again.

Jack turned away, filled with a sense of loss. He could come back to visit the camp, but it would never be the same again. Those carefree days were gone.

With the makeshift quill he'd used before, he jotted a two-word acceptance on the back of the duke's note and sent it to Ferrington Hall with one of the boys. Then he went to pack up his few possessions.

Samia sidled up when he was nearly finished and watched him tie the meager bundle. "You're going away," the little girl said.

"Not very far. I'll be living up at the house." He pointed in the direction of Ferrington Hall.

Her solemn gaze said that was quite far. "I don't go there."

It was true that the camp and the manor were two worlds that sometimes clashed but did not meet. Except in him, Jack thought. And no one knew better how uncomfortable that was. Must it be so? "You could visit, if you like."

Samia frowned. This went against everything she'd been taught.

"Come if you wish," Jack added. "And thank you for your company on the road."

She gave him an uncertain smile as he hoisted his bundle onto his shoulder. He walked around the camp to make the rest of his farewells. It didn't take long. Travelers were used to people coming and going. They didn't make a great thing of it.

Soon after this was done, a superior servant arrived and presented himself to Jack. He led him to a pair of horses waiting near the road that led past Ferrington Hall and indicated they were to ride.

Jack thought of questioning him, but he let the idea go. The duke had a plan. This fellow—a valet, he guessed— would be following it and unlikely to take any direction from Jack. Also, he didn't care. For now, he'd let himself be pushed about like a chess piece.

He fastened his bundle behind the saddle, and they rode together some distance to a field that held a tumbledown barn. His guide led him around to the far side of this building, out of sight of the road, where Jack discovered a hired carriage waiting. A young groom held the reins. Another of the duke's people, Jack assumed. This one looked amused.

The two servants nodded to each other. The first took Jack's possessions, placed them in the carriage, and extracted a different bundle from it. "His Grace thought some of his clothing would fit you well enough," he said. The man seemed to deplore the final two words, as if they were some sort of blasphemy.

A sense of unreality descended on Jack. He'd become an actor in a play he hadn't fully read, with no idea of the outcome. Perhaps he shouldn't have taken the role?

"If you would remove your coat, my lord," said the valet.

Jack stared at the man, shocked to be addressed in this way. *My lord* was somebody else. No one had ever called him that, certainly not his great-grandmother. Jack's sense of unreality deepened.

"My lord?" the servant repeated.

With a humorless laugh, Jack began to strip off his familiar garments. He allowed the valet to pull off his boots, but otherwise he undressed himself. Then he donned a set of clothes far finer than any he'd ever owned. There was a shirt of linen so delicate, his roughened hands caught on it, immaculate buckskin breeches, and a neckcloth larger than those he was accustomed to. He tied that himself, not caring to have the valet's hands on his neck. After that, Jack reached for his own boots. The servant had been buffing them with his handkerchief, looking both scandalized and distressed. "They're not covered in dung, man," said Jack. "It's nothing but dust. I didn't have any boot polish."

"Yes, my lord."

Grand English servants could convey disapproval with a

blank face and empty tone. Jack had noticed this in his great-grandmother's staff as well. They went stiff and distant, and censure poured off them, like fog creeping out to choke you. It was an impressive skill. And to hell with them all.

Jack pulled on the boots, snatched up a dark-blue coat with long tails and silver buttons, and shrugged into it. It did indeed fit well enough. He could move his shoulders and swing his arms. He would be able to throw a punch, if he decided to. Or could find some excuse to relieve his frustration in that way.

The valet appeared far from satisfied, however. He brushed and tweaked and muttered. Then he stood back and surveyed Jack as if he was a project that hadn't gone well but could only be abandoned at this point.

"No silk purse here, eh," said Jack.

The man met Jack's eyes for the first time. He looked shocked and perhaps worried. "My lord?"

It occurred to Jack that the fellow's disdain hadn't been personal. Rather, this cobbled together ensemble had offended his professional pride. The valet was a perfection-ist. Perhaps he feared that Jack's ensemble would reflect badly on his reputation.

A sound from the box of the carriage made Jack look up. The groom winked at him.

"Ah," Jack said. He'd never had a mob of servants around him. In Boston, he'd lived in rented rooms—spacious and comfortable, overseen by a landlady who'd been as much friend as servitor. She'd managed those who cleaned and cooked. Jack had never had much to do with them. It seemed things were somehow different for an earl.

The valet was still gazing at him. "Er, well done," Jack said.

"Thank you, my lord." The man produced a hat and gloves from the carriage. Jack put them on, and his transformation was complete.

It almost felt as if he'd donned a new skin with the borrowed clothes and become a stranger. Who was he? This earl? My lord. His great-grandmother had imagined he could become a blank slate for her to write over with her proprieties and affectations. Jack felt a wave of revulsion. That was out of the question. He would not be molded into Lady Wilton's creature. She didn't tell him who he was to be. Nor this interfering duke either. No one did.

The valet mounted up and took the horses away. Jack hesitated.

"Ready, milord?" asked the groom.

He could still run. The Travelers would sell him a horse. He could ride for the coast and find a ship home. He had the funds in his money belt. In these clothes, ships' captains would defer to him. He could easily book passage.

Harriet Finch's lovely face rose before him. Might she come with him to Boston? Should she forgive him, that is. She'd liked Jack the Rogue. Perhaps more than liked. But that fellow was gone, dissolved into the Earl of Ferrington, who had deceived her. And Jack Merrill was really neither of those people. He was still here, beneath this costume.

"Milord?" said the groom again.

Of course, he couldn't leave her. The idea tore at bonds that had formed swiftly but surely in these last weeks. He wanted a life with Harriet Finch. He suspected that, in the end, she would say that life was here. And perhaps he even owed something to his father's legacy. Lords had duties and rights he didn't really understand.

"Is all well, milord?" asked the groom. He looked down from the carriage box with concern on his young face.

"Well enough." Jack stepped into the carriage and shut the door. He would see. He would try. But he was no blank slate. He'd learned a good deal in his time on this earth; he'd achieved some success. Neither Jack the Rogue nor the earl, he was himself. It was time to show England that fact and fill this new role in his own way.

The vehicle started to move, out of his past and into an uncertain future he was determined to shape for himself.

Seven

HARRIET RETURNED TO A HOUSE IN COVERT UPROAR. HER mother had woken, found herself alone, sent a servant to find Harriet, and sunk into muted hysterics when she could not be found. When Harriet came into her bedchamber, Mama rushed over and clung like a drowning man. "Where have you been?" she whispered.

Her eyes were wild. Her mouth and hands trembled. Efforts not to attract any attention from the master of the house had apparently increased the strain.

"I went for a walk, Mama," Harriet said. "As I often do."

"You promised to stay with me!"

This had been more assumption than promise, but that was clearly irrelevant. Harriet patted her hand. There was something clutched in it. Harriet opened her mother's fingers and discovered an empty vial of laudanum. She'd known Mama was taking a sleeping draught at night, but if she was resorting to it in the daytime, that was worrying.

Her mother snatched back the vial as if it was a treasure she could not let go.

Harriet led her to an armchair before the hearth and urged her into it before sinking to the floor to sit at her feet. She dismissed the hovering maid with a nod and leaned against her mother's knee, as she'd so often done as a little girl. "Please tell me what's wrong, Mama," she said.

"I don't know what you mean."

Harriet again took possession of her mother's restless hands. "These last few days, you've been dreadfully upset." She nearly added, *Even more than you've been the whole time since we arrived here.* But she decided against it.

"No, I haven't."

"Mama." Harriet waited until her mother looked down and met her eyes. It took several minutes. "You have. It's obvious."

Her mother flinched as if threatened with a blow.

"Tell me," Harriet urged. "Whatever it is, I will help you."

Her mother gazed down, her face so creased with worry that she looked years older than she had just a few months ago. She swallowed, then sighed. "Papa found out," she muttered. Harriet just barely heard her.

"What?" Harriet squeezed her hands in reassurance. "What did my grandfather find out?"

Her mother's fingers closed in a spasmodic grip and then went lax. "That I spent the last of our money on the season in London. There is nothing left." Her breath caught on a sob.

Harriet struggled to take this in. "But Grandfather was paying all the bills."

"For the house and large purchases. But there were so many small things that were needed as well. The first few times I asked him about something like that, he shouted so—about my foolishness and feckless ways." She grimaced. "If it is not something *he* wishes to buy, then it is a wicked extravagance."

"But…" Harriet knew they had a small capital sum, which

generated a very modest income. Her father had managed to scrape together that much before he died. It had sustained them through her school days and the short time afterward, before her grandfather descended upon them with his oppressive largesse. The thought of this reserve had remained, a comfort, in the back of Harriet's mind when she thought about the future, since no position she could find as a schoolteacher or governess would support them both. Lately, she'd even dared to dream it would sustain her mother should she make…other choices.

Surely her mother would not have used up that sum without telling her. But meeting her despairing eyes, Harriet saw that she had. "Why didn't you come to me? We could have done without…whatever it was you bought."

"Will you also reproach me?" her mother cried. "If he wins you away from me, I don't know what I will…"

"Mama! You know that is impossible. I only wish you had consulted me."

"I didn't want you to worry."

Actions meant as kindness could turn to disaster, Harriet observed.

"I thought you would make a good match—a great success, like your friend Ada. And then it wouldn't matter." Her mother frowned. "Couldn't you have tried harder, Harriet? There were so many suitable gentlemen courting you."

"Because of grandfather's money."

"Well, that is the way of the world. A man can be charming and attractive even so. Isn't it right that he thinks of his family's future?"

"So you wanted me to take the path you refused? A mercenary marriage?"

"Yes!" declared her mother with more spirit than she'd shown in days.

Harriet stared at her, shocked.

"I want you to be happy." She said it like an accusation.

"But you and Papa…"

Harriet's mother pulled her hands free and sat up straighter, her mouth turned down. "Love wears thin when every day is another round of scrimping and falling short," she said. "When each bit of news is bad and no scheme succeeds. After a while, there is nothing to talk about but failures, you see. And the pain of seeing someone you love fretting begins to give way to…irritation."

"It was not Papa's fault that…"

"No, it was mine. I should not have married him."

Harriet's indignation dissolved in stark surprise.

"I should have done as my father wished and refused him," her mother added. "Or avoided him from the beginning. If only I had done that! Never met him at all. How much easier for us both."

"You would have turned your back on love?" Harriet asked.

"It would have been better for everyone if I had. Anthony would have been a great success in business. My father would have made him a partner, you know, instead of wrecking everything he tried to do. He thought him very capable."

"And I would not have been born," Harriet pointed out.

"I would have married someone else," her mother replied.

"An approved suitor. With a title, as Papa wanted. His fortune would have found me one. And you would have been born into a noble family and led a much easier life. You would have had everything you wanted and respect besides. Those girls who snubbed you at school would have fawned over you instead."

"That person would not have been me," Harriet said.

"You would always be my daughter," was the somewhat irrational reply.

"You cannot mean this, Mama. You are distraught."

"Anyone would be!" she cried. "I am squeezed between my father and you. You are always on the edge of dagger drawing. At any moment, our arrangement may fall apart, and there is nothing I can do about it. It is driving me mad."

Harriet almost believed this was literally true. Her mother's eyes were red with weeping. Tufts of her hair stood on end.

"You have endured a trying lifetime because of my wrong choice, Harriet. And don't try to tell me you liked it. The pity and the condescension and the shoddy gowns! You hated all that as much as I did. Except I also had to watch my daughter being slighted." She wrung her hands.

Harriet was not sure she had hated it as much as that. Of course, there had been difficulties, but they had been simply part of her world. She hadn't known anything else until her grandfather turned their lives upside down. Had she felt the sour bitterness she heard in her mother's voice?

"That horrid girl who persecuted you? That wretched dancing master?" Mama bared her teeth. "How I wanted to scratch their eyes out!"

"Mama!"

"I did." Her hands crooked into claws.

"We had happy times," Harriet tried. "I made good friends."

Her mother didn't seem to hear. "All those years. Every minute was a desperate calculation—how to stretch far too little over too many demands. I faced down bailiffs, you know. And that dreadful doctor who refused..." She pressed her lips together and seemed to gather herself. "You *will* have better. I insist!"

It was fortunate Mama knew nothing about Jack the Rogue, Harriet thought. She would break down completely over that adventure. Except—there was no Jack the Rogue, she remembered. He was a fiction, a liar, and she didn't care about him anymore.

Her mother leaned down and grasped her shoulders. "You will have better," she repeated, giving Harriet a little shake. "You're the heiress I ought to have been. You will *not* throw that chance away."

Looking up into her frantic face, Harriet couldn't argue. Not while Mama's unsettling, muted hysterics were so close to the surface. Perhaps when she had calmed down, they could discuss matters more rationally.

"Do you understand me?"

"I have heard you, Mama." Harriet wished she hadn't. Her picture of her parents' perfect love was spoiled.

"So you will do as I say. Promise me!"

She was not going to do that. "I will take care of you, Mama. You must stop worrying."

"I'll stop when you're safely settled. After that, I don't care what happens."

There was a soft knock at the bedroom door, and the dresser looked in. "Did you wish to change for dinner, madam?"

Harriet's mother sprang up. "Is it time? Yes, of course."

Harriet rose as well.

"Wear your jonquil crepe," her mother added. "Your grandfather admired that gown. And be sure to agree with him."

"About what?" Was there some other issue she hadn't been told about?

"Everything, Harriet!"

"Yes, Mama." She would say those words whenever she could to soothe her mother's troubled spirit. But the time would clearly come when she could not utter them. And then what would she do? Harriet's throat tightened with uneasiness.

❦

The carriage pulled up in front of Ferrington Hall, and Jack jumped down before anyone could come out to assist him. "What's your name?" he asked the groom who had driven him.

"Rafe, milord."

Jack nodded. "Thank you, Rafe." He turned to pull his bundle out of the vehicle.

"Bert'll fetch that for you, milord," said the groom.

"Bert?"

"He's the footman. He oughta…there he is."

The door to the hall had opened, and a group of people came out, led by the duke. A dapper young servitor peeled off and approached Jack. "Shall I take your luggage, my lord?"

Would they call him that every time they spoke to him? Jack was sick of it already. He handed over the bundle, which hardly qualified as luggage. "Thank you, Bert."

The young man blinked, startled by this use of his name.

"Hello, Ferrington," said the duke.

"So glad to see you come home, Lord Ferrington," said the woman beside him.

The duchess certainly looked the part—quite lovely, blond with luminous blue eyes, dressed like the society women Jack had glimpsed in London. Her smile seemed sincere, but who could say what lay behind it. Harriet Finch called her friend, and Jack might have trusted that. If he hadn't seen that cordiality depended on one's position in this country.

"These are the Rileys, who have been taking care of the house for you, as you know." She brought forward the old couple he'd spied on from the gardens.

It was odd to meet them after all that covert observation, to receive a bow and curtsy and tremulous greetings. Close up, they looked even older, and worried. Jack realized that they were afraid of being ejected from the house now that he was here. The idea made him angry.

"We've brought some of our people with us," said the duke, indicating the others in the entryway. He reeled off more names.

Jack missed most of them as he considered the way the man said "our people." As if they actually belonged to him. But servants were employees, who were paid. He'd hired and fired workers in Boston. Not like these, he suspected. He nodded in acknowledgment, and the whole circus began to move inside.

"I'm sure you'd like to see your room before dinner." The duchess smiled again. "You are our host, of course, but I've taken the liberty of organizing the household. Naturally, you will be making your own arrangements in future."

Would he? He supposed he must, if he stayed here.

"We won't change," she added.

Startled, Jack wondered if she was actually commenting on the intransigence of the English upper classes? Then he realized that she meant clothing. Lady Wilton had been shocked to find that he possessed no "evening dress," as if this was a sign of his barbarism. Jack couldn't see why one would need a special ensemble to sit down to dinner. Unless it was designed to hide spilled gravy.

He followed the duchess and her entourage upstairs to a bedchamber. "This is the earl's room," she said.

The superior servant who had dressed Jack at the carriage was there. He'd opened Jack's bundle and was sorting through it, which felt like an intrusion.

"You've met Marston," said the duchess. "He is happy to help you until you hire a valet of your own."

As if it was preordained that he would do so. As if strangers had a right to paw though his possessions and turn up their noses at them. Jack grappled with his temper.

"We brought the things you left at…in town," she said.

Was it a good sign she avoided mentioning Lady Wilton? Or a bad one? Did he care?

"If there is anything you need…"

She was indeed acting like his hostess. But the house was his. He was not at their mercy. Perhaps he needed to make that point? Jack surveyed the room. He walked to a window, looked out over the garden. He turned and strolled around the chamber, not hurrying. He opened a wardrobe and found it stuffed with clothing.

"We didn't clear away your great-uncle's clothes," said the duchess. "That seemed…"

"Overreaching?" asked Jack. He observed the flickers of surprise in the ducal couple's eyes with satisfaction. "Perhaps I can use them," he added. "Save a bit of money."

"I fear they are outmoded," replied the duchess.

"I don't care a snap of my fingers for fashion." It wasn't quite a taunt. More of a challenge. They needed to see he wasn't some timid creature ripe for manipulation.

"It can be a bore," said the duke.

"Your Grace!" Marston—the valet—betrayed into the exclamation, looked mortified.

"And yet also a diverting game," said the duchess.

It seemed the Terefords, pictures of modish elegance, might be amused. Jack couldn't really tell. The English nobility seemed to be trained from their earliest years to reveal only what they wished to.

"We'll leave you to settle in," said the duchess. "I've ordered dinner in half an hour. Unless you would prefer another time?"

He was hungry. "That will be fine."

She smiled at him. The duke gave him a nod. And they left, trailed by an escort of "their people."

When the door closed behind them, Jack relaxed for the first time since he'd stepped into Ferrington Hall. There was no one watching him. He was not shadowed by a cloud of mysterious expectations. For a time, at least. Also, he could send all these people away if he wished to. He could live on bread and cheese with the Rileys.

But that would not mend his fences with Harriet Finch.

Jack took a deep breath. She was his reason to be here. He must remember that.

He looked more closely at the grand chamber. The room was spacious but shabby. Windows looked south and west. The blue hangings were frayed and faded in stripes by the sun. Bits of gilt had fallen out of the trim around the fireplace. The furnishings were solid but old. It didn't look like a place to be happy, he thought. And then wondered where that notion had come from.

The atmosphere seemed stifling suddenly, though the ceiling was high. Jack went over and opened one of the casements. Outside air flowed in, carrying the scent of flowers from somewhere in the neglected garden. Neglected. The whole place felt as if no one had cared for it in a long time. He had an odd flash of sympathy.

Jack wondered about the man who'd lived here before him—his great-uncle, the previous earl. Why hadn't he taken better care of his home? Jack's eyes narrowed. Had the Earl of Ferrington been one of those impoverished aristocrats mocked on the stage? Had he stepped into the shoes of such a caricature? Lady Wilton hadn't mentioned money. In fact, he knew next to nothing practical about his new status. That wasn't like him. He was known for sharp analysis and decisive action, not for running from challenges. He'd let Lady Wilton's scolding rattle him. That had to stop.

He breathed in the soft air. He'd taken time to recover from the disappointment his father's remaining family presented. Well and good. More than that, his flight had led him to Harriet Finch and let him make her acquaintance in easy circumstances. Until they became distinctly uneasy. Perhaps it had all been for the best. With a determined nod, Jack turned away from the window.

He joined the duke and duchess at the appointed time and sat down to a meal that was far better than anything Jack had eaten in his life. Each dish he tried was rich with subtle flavors, a revelation on the tongue. "Your cook travels with you?" he asked.

"Not usually," replied the duchess. "We'd heard there was no staff here."

"Syllabub, my lord?" asked Bert, the footman, popping up on Jack's right to offer a dish.

Suppressing a start, Jack said, "What is it?"

"A creamy dessert," replied the duchess.

"I wouldn't recommend it," said her husband. "Sickly sweet."

"It is not."

The duke grinned at her. "One of Cecelia's indulgences," he added.

"Shouldn't you have said 'many indulgences'—to achieve a proper effect?" she replied.

"Not at all. Exaggeration quite spoils commentary."

"Am I some weighty issue then, to warrant commentary?"

"More a work of art," the duke replied.

They laughed at each other. Jack had heard no sting in their exchange. They seemed to enjoy the teasing, and he got the impression of a couple very happy in their marriage. It didn't seem fair they should have a high position, striking good looks, and marital felicity.

The meal concluded, and the servants withdrew. "Are all these *my lord*s and *Your Grace*s necessary?" Jack asked when they were gone. "It becomes oppressive."

The duke looked surprised. "They're customary terms of respect."

"Are they?"

The other man paused. His expression grew wry. "Well, customary at any rate."

"But I am not to use them?" Jack had gathered this much.

"You can say *Tereford*, as I call you *Ferrington*," the duke answered. "Friends use first names."

Jack wondered if they were likely to become friends. It seemed doubtful. "And...my lady?"

"Oh, call her *duchess*."

His wife made a face at him. "That's silly. You two are..." She counted on her fingers. "Second cousins? Something of the sort. Family, at any rate. Why stand on ceremony?" She turned to Jack. "You should call us *Cecelia* and *James*."

He wasn't certain that was more comfortable. Though

these two were friendly, they were also intimidating. Perhaps he could simply avoid using names. "It seems this place hasn't been kept up," Jack said, changing the subject. "I thought that was part of the job."

"Job?" The duke—James—looked blank.

"Of noblemen. Managing their properties."

"Ah, yes. Fecklessness appears to run in our line, however."

"Along with flippancy," said his wife.

"No, no, that is only me. Unless..." He glanced over at Jack. "You are right, my dear. Jack the Rogue had a strong measure of flippancy."

"Had?" asked Jack.

"Do you intend to keep it up? Bravo."

"James," said the duchess.

When their eyes met so warmly, one felt invisible, Jack thought. It was irritating. "The job," he repeated. "What the earl is supposed to do."

"Manage the estate," answered the duke, as if this was self-evident.

"Which includes what, precisely?"

"You should talk to Cecelia. She'd be far better at that sort of thing than I."

Jack was surprised both by that fact and that the duke would admit it.

"I'd be happy to look over the estate records with you and see where things stand," the duchess said.

He nodded his thanks.

"It is a great opportunity to set things to rights," she added. Her tone suggested she was offering him a special treat.

"I suppose." Jack shrugged. "Or one could just sell the place."

Both his companions looked shocked.

"The main estate is probably entailed," said the duchess.

Jack didn't know the term, and he was tired of asking. Well, he would learn and understand before he began giving orders. Should he decide to do so. "I should make the acquaintance of my neighbors," he said.

"Indeed," replied the duke. "A good idea. Unless you want to wait…"

Until he was more like an actual earl, presumably. Jack had no time for that. "The closest house is Winstead Hall, I believe. I shall pay them a visit."

His companions exchanged another glance. "That might be a good place to start," said the duchess.

A little weary of their silent communications, Jack replied with a touch of mockery. "Because they are nearby?"

"We have friends there," she answered.

Who would make allowances for a clumsy earl, presumably. Jack nearly said as much but decided their prejudices didn't matter.

"We can introduce you," the duchess continued. "You will like…the Finches."

And not Mr. Winstead, Jack concluded. He hadn't expected to. But he had to pass the gateway of Harriet Finch's grandfather to reach her. Once in the house, he would find a way to speak to her privately and mend the rift between them.

❧

Harriet looked through the window of her mother's private parlor at the lovely summer day. The morning sun poured rich, golden light over the garden. Dew still sparkled in shaded spots. Birds spread their wings and lifted their voices. Flowers created swaths of color and a symphony of scent. It was wrong to think life had lost its savor. Craven and silly and stupid. She did *not* think that. Her mother's overspending and the reprehensible behavior of one deceitful man could not leach the joy from existence. Perish the thought!

"I believe I will finish this piece today," said Harriet's mother. She sat with her back to the window. A strip of embroidery lay over her knees, its colors echoing the bright outdoors. "You can read to me while I sew," she added with a bright, brittle smile. "I know you don't care for fancywork."

As she was meant to, Harriet heard this as an order not to leave her mother alone for a moment. Mama's spirits had not recovered. She left Harriet only to sleep, and last night she'd come into Harriet's room in the small hours and stood over her, her candle dripping wax on the bed linens, her eyes wide and frightened. Startled and unnerved, Harriet had tried to comfort her, but words didn't seem to reach Mama in the deep night. She'd had to escort her back to bed and sit with her for some time before Mama's eyes closed.

They would walk together in the garden later, Harriet determined. She would insist. Exercise might clear some of the clouds from Mama's brain. She had thought of sending for the doctor, but the suggestion had met with hysterical resistance. There was to be no hint of upset or illness in the household. Horace Winstead despised such weakness.

He was not to know, not to hear…anything. Harriet sighed softly. The doctor would probably just prescribe a stronger dose of laudanum, and that did not seem advisable.

Her grandfather's voice sounded in the corridor. Her mother's head came up like a fox scenting a hunting pack. She crumpled her embroidery in spasmodic hands. The noise seemed to be approaching.

"Is he coming here? Why? He doesn't come here in the morning. What have you done, Harriet?"

"Nothing, Mama. You know I have been with you." But Harriet wondered if her grandfather had discovered her wanderings. She rose to go and intercept him.

Before she could, he entered, saying, "Here they are." His tone was jovial, and Harriet could see the Duke and Duchess of Tereford behind him. Harriet stepped forward. Grandfather shouldn't have brought callers here to this small chamber. He should have summoned Harriet and her mother to the drawing room. Indeed, she couldn't understand why the servants hadn't done so rather than involving the master of the house. But Grandfather went his own way, and he'd ignored this convention, or forgotten it. He was practically rubbing his hands together in glee over the noble visitors. Harriet prepared to greet them as they crowded in.

And then she saw the fourth member of their party, and the smile froze on her lips.

"Our new neighbor has arrived at last," said her grandfather. "May I present my daughter, Mrs. Caroline Finch, and my granddaughter, Miss Harriet Finch. Harriet, Linny, the Earl of Ferrington."

Jack the Rogue offered quite an elegant bow. His dark eyes met hers and held as if he would tell her something. As if she would listen!

His appearance was transformed. His dark hair had been cut in a fashionable style. His clothes were elegant. They must be borrowed. Harriet thought she'd seen the duke in a dark-blue coat with buttons very like that one. Didn't he find this humiliating? Had he no shame whatsoever? No, he did not, she reminded herself.

In his new guise, he looked very like the young men she'd met during the season. Her heart sank. Their time in the Travelers' camp faded. She dropped a small, cold curtsy.

"Papa," twittered her mother. "So unusual...the drawing room."

"Do sit down," interrupted Harriet. If they were to be unconventional, then she would brazen it out. There were enough chairs. Just. She glimpsed the butler hovering in the corridor, looking distressed. She signaled for refreshments.

"A duke and an earl calling on me," muttered her grandfather. His glee was obvious. "So, Lord Ferrington, are you settled in the neighborhood for the summer?" he asked.

"I expect so," said Jack the...no, the *earl*. He was the sneaking, perfidious earl, and he was looking steadily at Harriet. How did he dare? Could he never behave properly? He was going to draw attention. Indeed, Cecelia had already noticed. She was clearly puzzled by Harriet's manner and the fraught atmosphere.

"Good, good," her grandfather said. His beady eyes sharpened. "You're not married, are you?"

Harriet flushed and looked away.

"I am not," he replied.

Grandfather's gaze shifted from the newcomer to Harriet and back again. The idea taking root in his brain was so obvious that he might have been shouting it. Harriet longed to drag him from the room and shut him away until their guests were gone. Or longer.

"Such lovely weather we're having," said Cecelia.

Her husband gave her a sidelong glance. Harriet watched silent communications pass between them, as she'd seen before. "Positively balmy," he replied.

"There is nothing like a fine day in the country."

"To be sure." The duke's deep-blue eyes glinted. "Except perhaps a sunny morning by the sea. In Brighton, say. On the promenade, with all the fashionable world to observe."

"Up to their necks in salt water?" asked Cecelia sweetly.

"They say immersion is good for one's health." Tereford's tone was even, but a smile was tugging at the corner of his mouth.

"*They* being the people who rent out the bathing machines?"

"And, er, experts."

"Oh, *experts*." Cecelia laughed. Her husband clearly appreciated the sight and the musical sound.

Jack the Earl was eying the duke and duchess as if they were some fascinating curiosity he'd never encountered before. Harriet's mother was pleating her handkerchief in nervous fingers.

"Never visited Brighton," declared Harriet's grandfather.

"I don't care for the sea. You never know what's in there, do you? Something could swim up and pull you under. Never be seen again."

"And what would the experts say to that?" murmured the duke.

No one ventured a reply.

Having disposed of that topic, Harriet's grandfather turned to Ferrington. "Our properties share a border," he said.

"Indeed. I noticed you have some men posted there," the earl replied.

There was no limit to his effrontery, Harriet decided. He could sit there and speak of things they had endured together as if he'd only just noticed them.

"To guard against those filthy Travelers," her grandfather replied.

"The ones you wrote the letter about," said Harriet, goaded beyond endurance. "Giving them permission to stay on your land."

Her grandfather glared at her. The duke looked amused, Cecelia curious, Mama distressed. And *Lord* Ferrington held her gaze briefly, before turning back to his host.

"I've always found them to be decent people," he said.

Harriet had to appreciate the way he faced down her grandfather, practically daring him to disagree. A wave of feeling threatened to engulf her. She shoved it away.

It seemed for a moment that Grandfather would choke on the dilemma—his strong need to state his opinions warring with a reluctance to offend his noble neighbor.

"Will you take refreshment?" blurted Harriet's mother.

The butler had arrived with a tray and a means to dissipate the awkwardness. Drinks were poured. A plate of macaroons was passed. Harriet watched Ferrington grow more and more restless. He kept glancing in her direction, as if urging her to come closer. Which was, of course, impossible in this small, crowded room. Should she have wished to. Naturally, she did not. Instead, she indulged in a savage enjoyment of his plight.

The callers stayed a generous half hour. When they rose to go, her grandfather ushered them out.

As soon as they were gone, Harriet missed the reprehensible earl. The energy seemed to go out of the room with his departure.

"Why did Papa bring them here?" wondered Harriet's mother. "You don't think he will do so with other callers? This was to be my private parlor. It was agreed."

Harriet understood her anxiety, but she couldn't assuage it. She had no idea what Grandfather would do. Except that it would be whatever he liked. Moreover, she heard his heavy footsteps returning along the corridor. The chagrin on Mama's face when he walked back in was pitiable.

"This is most convenient," he said, his round face radiating satisfaction. "A fine match plopped down right next door to us, Harriet. And no other young ladies nearby to cut you out."

"Oh, Papa," murmured her mother.

Expecting an annoying thing didn't make it any easier to bear, Harriet observed. "The earl may have his own ideas about his future," she said. And of course, she cared nothing about them. She did *not* wonder why he had come to sit and stare at her like a tongue-tied suitor. He was not a suitor. He was a weasel.

"He'll be on the lookout for a wife. These titled fellows want to secure their succession. And he'll want her to have plenty of money, too."

Harriet had known her grandfather was vulgar. But this was so blatant. "He'll want to look about next season and choose from the debs, I suppose." The idea was surprisingly unpalatable.

"Not if you make a push to attach him, girl." Her grandfather glowered.

"I shall behave with propriety…"

"You'll flutter your eyelashes and bring him to heel. You can't throw away an opportunity like this." His mouth went hard. "Unless you want to be cut off and sent back where you came from."

Harriet's mother made a distressed sound.

"Titled gentlemen don't want to marry vulgar romps," Harriet replied. A memory of dancing around the fire at the Travelers' camp flashed through her mind. But that romp hadn't been vulgar. It had been…joyous. Then. She dismissed an ache from the region of her heart.

Something like a growl escaped her grandfather. He would not be contradicted. He turned on the easier target. "It's up to the mother to push matches forward, is it not? You must be less useless, Linny."

"Mama is not useless!" cried Harriet. Although her mother's cowering posture didn't support her point.

Her grandfather looked at them sourly, like a man who'd

made a bad bargain in the market. "Between the two of you, surely you can find some way to bring this off."

Harriet stood straight and cold and stared him right in the eye. He scowled at her for another long moment, then turned on his heel and left.

"Oh, Harriet."

"Don't begin, Mama!"

"You always make him angry."

"*I* make *him*…"

"You must make a push. You heard what he said."

"So you would have me fling myself at this…stranger to satisfy Grandfather? Like some shameless hussy?"

"You can *try*. You scarcely spoke to the earl today. You might like him very well when you get to know him. He seemed perfectly charming. Not particularly handsome of course, but …"

"He is," popped out of Harriet before she could stop it. She bit off the words.

"But beside the Duke of Tereford, any man would look commonplace," her mother continued. "You need only make an effort, Harriet."

Somehow it was always up to her to make the effort, to adjust and change. "He may have no interest in me at all." She knew this wasn't true. But what *was* his interest, precisely? Why had he stared so?

"Why wouldn't he?" Her mother frowned at her. "You're quite pretty and intelligent and sweet-natured. When you wish to be. I'm sure you can capture his interest if you exert yourself."

She'd dreamed of running away with Jack the Rogue, leaving the constrictions and shameful inequalities of English society behind. Now that man was gone, as if a magician's wand had passed over him and left behind a new-minted earl. And she was expected to marry him simply because he *was* an earl. Her family cared about nothing else. Not his true character. Not her feelings. Or Ferrington's. What did he feel? No one was making any mention of love.

"You will try, won't you, Harriet?" asked her mother.

No, she would not! Her grandfather could rant and rave until he turned blue, she would not be pushed.

"Because if you won't, I don't know what will become of us," her mother added in a quavering voice.

Harriet turned and saw that Mama had begun crying. Her handkerchief was a crushed wad in one hand. Her cherished embroidery had fallen to the floor. She was the picture of misery. And of...defeat. She looked utterly defeated.

Going to comfort her, Harriet tried to think what she should do. There had to be something, some way out. But at the moment, she couldn't see it.

Eight

Jack sat in one of the little-used parlors at Ferrington Hall and thought about the vapid nature of society—capital-S society, which was, as far as he could see, a system for gathering people in a room to chatter about trivialities while they smugly excluded other people, of course. No wonder they called it *exclusive*. They made a great production of leaving people out and then looking down on those scheming and clawing to be invited. Actually convincing them to bother to scheme and claw, somehow. He wondered how many of those who succeeded found their coveted acceptance a dead bore.

He pulled at the fashionable neckcloth, which seemed to grow tighter by the hour, threatening to choke the life out of him. It had been maddening to sit in these borrowed garments a few feet from Harriet Finch and be unable to really speak to her. He'd wanted to pull her to her feet, rush her from the stifling chamber out into the air, and talk as they used to in the Travelers' camp. That really had been an idyll, he saw now. They would not have such freedom again. There, he would have been able to explain everything. He was certain of it. Now, he wasn't sure what to do.

She was still angry with him. The looks she'd shot his

way had shown it. She didn't understand. Jack almost wished Lady Wilton would show up here. If Miss Finch heard how the old lady talked to him, her venom, she would understand what had driven him to hide his identity. And he'd always meant to tell her the truth. Circumstances had conspired against him. And his own foot-dragging, yes, all right. Jack frowned unseeing at a painting on the wall.

The chamber door opened, and the Duchess of Tereford looked in. "There you are," she said. "Why are you sitting in this room?"

"Is this an incorrect place to sit?" Jack heard petulance in his tone. Too bad.

"There are several more comfortable spots."

"But people find me in those places."

She raised her eyebrows, but she didn't go away. "I found you *here*," she pointed out.

"We could pretend you hadn't," Jack answered.

"You will have to do much better than that if you expect to repel *me*," was the surprising reply. "My father practices epic levels of rudeness. And James sniped at me for years when we were...younger."

Jack gazed curiously at her. He'd supposed that no one was ever rude to this elegant noblewoman. She was the sort they all admired, so polished that opposition just slid right off her.

"Good. You've stopped sulking." She entered the room and sat down opposite him. She wasn't going away.

"No, I haven't." He wouldn't give up his grievances that easily.

"I see. How much longer do you intend to continue?" She cocked her head as if asking a perfectly ordinary question.

A thread of amusement ran through Jack. "A while."

"Very well." She folded her hands, assumed a saintly expression, and settled down to wait.

He had to laugh, even though he saw what she was doing. But he wasn't ready to give in. "I never wanted to be an earl, you know. Didn't expect it in the least. Hardly anyone believed my father's talk of noble relations. All sorts of people claim fine lineages in America, and most of them are liars."

The duchess nodded. "And yet here you are."

He'd expected an argument, a lecture on the advantages of his new position. Perhaps a mention of his good luck.

"You might have returned to America. But you did not."

"Yet," he replied, his tone clipped.

"You stayed here in the Travelers' camp, which can't have been entirely comfortable."

"I don't mind rough living. I'm no mincing dandy."

"No, indeed. That would require a great deal of study and effort."

Jack blinked. He'd thought of society women as silly and superficial, with prejudices that distilled into venom when they reached old age. This one was none of those things. He decided to abandon the verbal fencing. "Did you wish to speak to me about something in particular?"

"Yes." She examined him. "I want to know what has passed between you and Harriet Finch."

"I beg your pardon?"

"We'll see."

"What?"

"Whether you require, or deserve, my pardon. I hope you

do not. But now I will have the truth. It was obvious during our call that you and Harriet are...well acquainted."

"It was?" He stared into her luminous blue eyes and decided he'd never met anyone so relentlessly unflappable. Tereford was a brave man to partner her.

"You stared at Harriet like a thirsty man seeing water," the duchess continued. "She glared back as if she wished looks could incinerate. It was blatant, *Cousin Jack*. Why do you think I shifted the conversation into inanities?"

He didn't know what to say.

"Because you think that is the nature of a morning call?" She smiled without humor. "Not mine."

Once, in the North Woods, Jack had glimpsed a lynx pouncing on an unwary rodent. The cat had eaten the little creature in one snapping bite. It was odd he remembered that moment now. Or perhaps it wasn't.

"Harriet is a good friend of mine," said the duchess. "I won't have her trifled with."

"I would never..." Jack's sense of grievance came back. "It was just the opposite."

"The...?" She stared at him. "Do you say Harriet trifled with *you*?"

"She was pleased to be a friend when she thought I was a rootless wanderer. As soon as she discovered I was an earl, she froze me out." He sounded resentful. Well, he was. The fact that the tangle was his own fault merely made things worse.

"Why do I think there is more to it than that?"

The duchess's beauty was a snare and a deception, Jack

decided. It kept a man from noticing the steel underneath until it was too late.

"Ah." Her elegant eyebrows came up.

Jack didn't like the sound of that syllable.

"Did Harriet 'discover' your real identity when I told her? I thought she looked oddly shocked."

"You might have kept it to yourself," Jack muttered. And immediately wished he hadn't.

"*You* might have been honest with Harriet from the beginning."

"Why would I be?" Jack exclaimed. "I'd had my fill and more of society ladies and their opinions. My great-grandmother told me I was a barbarian. I wasn't going to hear any more of *that*."

The duchess sighed. "One could wish Lady Wilton was less…intemperate."

A harsh laugh escaped Jack. He would have used a ruder word.

"But Harriet is not Lady Wilton, of course. And you must have realized that quite soon."

He had to admit it. "Yes."

"And so?"

"I didn't want to spoil a pleasant…friendship." He made a slashing gesture. "And I know saying nothing spoiled it just the same."

"More so," replied the duchess.

"Yes, all right!" His desperation came back. "I meant to tell her the truth. I *tried*, more than once. We kept being interrupted. I should have done more. I need her to understand."

"Why is that important?" she asked.

"What?"

"Why do you care so much what Harriet may think?"

"I…" Jack was not quite ready to tell her everything. There could be no mention of kisses, for example. Who knew what this rather ruthless lady might do with the knowledge? "I wish to regain her good opinion," he replied, knowing it sounded stiff and rather priggish. It was the best he could manage in this moment.

"To what end?" asked his interrogator.

"To…restore our friendship and, er, perhaps more. I hope."

She examined him. Jack tried not to feel like an insect under a magnifying glass. It occurred to him that the Duchess of Tereford might be as terrifying as Lady Wilton in a few decades. Fortunately, she didn't seem to share the old lady's biases. "Harriet's grandfather obviously intends…" She stopped abruptly and went silent.

Jack waited a moment to see if she would continue, then said, "What?"

The duchess frowned. Thoughts were clearly passing through her mind. Jack had no idea what they were.

"All right," she said finally. "I will help you find an opportunity to explain."

"You…will?" He was surprised.

Her answering look was admonitory. "Because I am concerned about my friend," she said. "She seemed…" She paused, then went on, "Whatever comes next, if anything does, will be up to Harriet."

"Yes, of course."

"I won't argue your case. That is up to you."

"Naturally." He wouldn't have wanted her to. The lord knew what she would say. "Why are you helping me?"

"I am helping Harriet, I believe. And that is what society is for—to ease relations between people."

"It is?"

She smiled at his incredulity. "Among other things. So we require an occasion where you can speak to Harriet privately. Perhaps a ride in the countryside. You do ride?"

How did she think he got about? "Yes."

"Good."

"Will Miss Finch be allowed to come?"

"Oh, there will be no problem with that."

Because she would be along, Jack supposed. Harriet's family would not dare refuse a duchess's invitation. But that didn't matter. He'd be with Harriet again and have the chance to redeem himself. Perhaps they could even settle their future together, and he could hold her in his arms in reality rather than dreams.

"We need mounts for that," the duchess continued. "Our carriage horses won't do."

"Leave that to me," said Jack.

❧

Two days later, a party of three riders approached Winstead Hall, reining in by the front door, where Harriet's mount awaited her. Harriet had been ordered to accept this invitation, even though she'd pointed out to her grandfather that she wasn't adept on horseback. She hadn't been able to resist reminding him that the circumstances of her youth had offered few opportunities to learn to ride, since his vengeful spite had created that situation. He'd brushed this aside, of course, as he did any argument that went against his wishes. So all her protest had accomplished was to worry her mother.

Life at Winstead House was becoming insupportable. Her grandfather talked of nothing but marrying her to the earl. Her mother cried a great deal. In truth, Harriet was glad to get away, even though the occasion was certain to be awkward. Tugging at the jacket of the riding habit she'd rarely worn, she wondered why Cecelia had issued this invitation. Had it been her notion? Or Jack the Earl's? What was behind it? She wished she knew. But she trusted Cecelia. Cecelia would stay with her and support her.

She greeted the newcomers as she walked over to the groom holding her horse. "It is very gentle?" Harriet asked him. She'd made this request several times, but Grandfather's servants answered only to him.

"Yes, miss. She's a regular sweetheart."

Was his tone dismissive? Harriet couldn't tell. He helped her mount at the block. She settled in the saddle and took the reins, hoping for the best. In her limited experience, horses were massive, stubborn creatures who stopped at every clump of grass to eat whenever she was astride them. She'd been told she must exert her authority to quell this behavior, that the way she sat and pulled at the traces would master the animal. She had not found this to be true. Or, more likely, she had not learned how to do it. The last time she'd ridden, the horse had spit on her when she dismounted. The laundress had had a terrible time removing the grassy-green stain from her habit.

Why had she agreed to this outing? Would her grandfather have tied her in the saddle if she'd rebelled? Surely not.

They started slowly down the drive. Naturally the duke and duchess rode superbly. They did everything superbly, Harriet concluded with a touch of bitterness. The rogue earl seemed equally at home in the saddle. Harriet tried to line up beside Cecelia and away from the gentlemen, but her mount paid no heed to her wishes. The Terefords moved ahead side by side while Ferrington lingered next to Harriet. When they reached the lane that ran by the house, he pointed left and said, "The Rileys tell me there's a fine prospect down this way."

"Who?" asked Harriet.

"The old couple looking after Ferrington Hall."

"Oh, yes." They'd spied on them together, Harriet remembered, back when everything had been different. She was horrified to find tears threatening. She blinked them away. "Where did you get your horse?"

"I bought all three of them from Meric." He gestured at the Terefords' mounts.

Meric was one of the men at the Travelers camp, and how dared he remind her of them?

"I found a wad of cash in a strongbox locked in a desk, and I was happy to pass some of it along to Meric," he added. "He drove a hard bargain, of course." His smile was admiring.

She wasn't going to chat about Meric, or the camp, or

the dancing and kisses that had occurred there. Perhaps she wouldn't talk at all! Harriet's horse shook its head from side to side and snorted as if it sensed her mood.

"I've been trying out a bunch of keys the Rileys gave me," he went on. "It's like a treasure hunt."

He seemed to think this would amuse her. Did he imagine she intended to *chat*?

"So far, I've found the liquor cabinet and a collection of jeweled snuffboxes."

Harriet kept on saying nothing.

"I never understood the attraction of snuff," Ferrington continued. "Rather unpleasant habit, all the sniffing and brown handkerchiefs."

Did he sound uneasy? She hoped so. Harriet lifted her chin and gazed at the passing countryside. As did her horse, it seemed. She'd spied a juicy tussock at the edge of the lane, and now she ambled over to sample it. Harriet tugged at the reins. The animal kept its head down, chewing and ignoring her.

"What are you doing?" asked the rogue earl.

Harriet turned to glare at him. "*I* am not doing anything." Couldn't he see that? "My *horse* obviously prefers eating to wandering aimlessly about the neighborhood." Where was Cecelia?

~

Unaware of any delay, the duke and duchess had ridden a little distance ahead. "This mount isn't half bad," the duke said to his wife. "Ferrington is a good judge of horseflesh, it seems."

"Spirited but well trained," Cecelia agreed. "The Travelers know their business."

"A truism confirmed." He watched the side of her face appreciatively. "So shouldn't we be moving on?" he asked. "We have found the earl. Our mission here is accomplished."

"I think we should stay at Ferrington Hall a bit longer."

"Ah. How much is a bit?"

Cecelia made an airy gesture. "An indeterminate period. Not too long."

"I see. Why is that? We do have a great deal of other work. I thought you were eager to get the estate in order."

"Friendship comes first," she replied.

"I would scarcely call Ferrington a friend. As yet. He seems a fine enough fellow, but…"

"Not him. Harriet."

The duke raised dark brows, but before he could reply, there was something like a verbal explosion behind them—an exclamation or a shout. The Terefords turned to find Harriet's mount hurtling toward them as if the hounds of hell were at its back. Harriet flailed in the saddle, clearly on the verge of falling off. Ferrington was staring after her, aghast.

Harriet pounded past them, clods of earth flying. In the next instant, Ferrington kicked his mount into action and raced after her.

"What the deuce?" said James as the other man galloped by. "I thought you said Miss Finch wouldn't wish to ride hard."

"She didn't look as if she *wished* to be galloping," replied Cecelia. The other two riders disappeared around a curve ahead. Cecelia put her heels to her horse and went after them. James followed suit.

༺ঌ༻

Bent over his horse's neck, pounding along the lane terrified for Miss Finch's safety, Jack tried to work out what the hell had just happened. He'd gone over to her recalcitrant mount. He'd advised Miss Finch to yank the reins with some authority, which had earned him a scorching look. He'd then administered a slap on the rump to admonish and encourage the beast. It had been a perfectly normal slap—really, no more than a tap—a mere touch that any rational horse would have understood as familiar marching orders. But this animal had taken offense, jumped off its hocks like a rabbit, and shot off down the lane as if a race had been declared.

Jack had lost a moment to sheer disbelief. This behavior made no sense. But then he'd noted Miss Finch's imbalance in the saddle. She wasn't a good enough rider to control this kind of bolting. Heart in his mouth, he went after her. He didn't even notice the Terefords as he galloped past.

"Pull her back," he shouted when he drew nearer. He didn't think Miss Finch heard. She looked frightened and was fully occupied with clinging on.

They came to a low place in the high hedges that lined the lane; Miss Finch jerked at one of her reins for no reason Jack could see. Her horse tossed its head, half reared, twisted, and jumped over the line of bushes. The pair disappeared in a way that made Jack fear the ground was much lower on the other side. Picturing Miss Finch and her mount lying in a broken heap in the ditch, he urged his mount a bit farther along, then put him at the hedge. The Traveler horse accepted the challenge and jumped.

The tips of branches brushed the horse's hooves and stomach. But they cleared the obstacle and landed in a meadow that slanted swiftly downward toward a line of trees that probably ran along a stream. Jack looked left and right. There was no sign of Miss Finch in the flower-strewn meadow grass. He headed for the trees.

They concealed a small, placid river. And Miss Finch sat right in the middle of it, a few yards downstream. Her horse had stopped a little farther along, cropping grass on the bank as if it had never misbehaved in the whole of its equine life.

Miss Finch looked dazed. The water came up to her shoulders. As Jack moved closer, she flailed at it and managed to stand, but the heavy skirts of her riding habit dragged her down. The current caught the mass of soaked fabric, threatened to topple her off her feet, and pulled her along. She lurched and stumbled, hands grasping but finding no hold in the water.

Jack jumped from the saddle and lunged into the water, half diving to reach her. He caught her around the waist and steadied her.

"I am *not* crying!" she declared.

"It's just river water splashed on your face," he replied.

"I…" Her breath caught on a sob. "Yes."

Holding her tight against his side, Jack turned toward the shore and found he couldn't move. His riding boots had sunk into a layer of sucking mud. He heaved at his right foot, finally got it free, took a step, and sank in again. The stuff was pernicious. He pulled up his left foot, managed another step. It took much of his strength. At the next try, he nearly lost a boot to the muck and almost dumped Miss Finch into the increasingly murky water.

Between the resistance of the mud and the tugging weight of her skirts, the trek to the bank was strenuous. But at last Jack stepped up onto the mossy bank, pulling Miss Finch along with him. "Are you hurt?" He ran his hands over her arms and ribs. Nothing seemed broken. She was standing without effort.

Miss Finch pushed at his chest. "You hit my horse!"

"I just tapped her rump, the sort of thing anyone does to urge a mount along."

"Urge? She lost what little mind she possesses. It was like being carried off by a whirlwind."

This seemed an exaggeration, but Jack made allowances. "There's something off about that animal." He eyed the still-browsing mount.

"Everything at my grandfather's house hates me," Miss Finch declared, clenching folds of his coat in sudden fists.

She was all right. She hadn't broken a leg or suffered a knock on the head. Her spirits were clearly not broken. "Thank God," said Jack.

"What?" The word crackled with indignation.

"That you are all right. Not that your grandfather's... I was frightened out of my wits."

"You were?"

"Of course I was. If you'd been hurt…" He ran his hands up her arms again to reassure himself she had not.

Miss Finch gazed up at him. She was breathing hard from the trek through the mud. Water dripped from their sodden clothing. Her green eyes were wide and still a bit wild. Jack found himself getting lost in them, and their surroundings seemed to drop away until nothing but the two of them existed. He bent his head. She raised her chin. Their lips met in a kiss of unutterable sweetness.

❧

Harriet was ambushed by a sense of rightness. This felt like…home—his arms around her, his mouth tempting hers. Despite her sodden clothes, heat shot through her. Her hands slid up to his shoulders and gripped. Her body melted into his. She was aware of nothing but her dear, dizzying rogue.

❧

Neither noticed when the duke and duchess rode through the fringe of trees a little way upstream. The Terefords sat on their mounts, observing their soaked, passionate companions.

"Ah," said the duke. "So that's the way the land lies."

"Apparently," replied his wife. "I hadn't expected such… abandon."

He glanced at her. "But you had expected something? What?"

"A frank exchange of views?" she answered with a half smile.

"Cecelia! How dreary. I don't believe you can mean that."

"Well, the situation is not as simple as it might look," she replied.

The duke eyed the embracing couple. "I wouldn't call that simple. More suggestive." He raised one teasing eyebrow.

She laughed. "I suppose we had better stop them."

"That seems rather mean."

"We are the chaperones. It is our duty."

"What a lowering reflection."

The duchess sighed. "It is, a little. But Harriet will catch a cold if we don't get her home and into dry clothing." She raised a hand. "Hello?" she called.

❧

Harriet stiffened at the sound and at once became aware of her scandalous position. What had she been thinking? Or rather *not* thinking? What had come over her? She pulled away. The rogue earl resisted briefly, then let her go. She was glad, of course. Not the least bit sorry.

She turned and watched the duke and duchess ride closer. "My horse tossed me in the river," she said when they stopped a few feet away.

The Terefords looked down from the height of their saddles. It was like being observed by slightly amused gods.

"F-Ferrington helped me to the bank," Harriet added.

"The mud is knee-deep on that river bottom," he said. He

exhibited a boot caked with mud, which clearly had oozed over the tops onto his feet, as if he had to verify his statement. Did he imagine it excused the way they'd been discovered? Did he dare to look smug?

Harriet was wet and cold. Her riding habit clung to her like the gowns of wantons who dampened their petticoats. No, worse than that. She could tell by the way the duke was carefully not looking at her.

"We must get you home at once," said Cecelia.

"Right." The rogue earl squelched over to catch the reins of her wretched horse, still nose-deep in the rich grass of the riverbank.

"I will *not* get back on that beast," Harriet declared. She scowled at the creature. The mare looked back with bland innocence. A tuft of grass dangled from her jaws.

"I will lead her," said Ferrington. "She won't run away with you again."

Harriet wondered if one could explode with rage. And why her sodden garments weren't steaming from the heat of her anger. "She wouldn't have done so this time if you hadn't struck her!"

"I didn't…" Ferrington looked up at the Terefords. "It was the merest tap. Just to get her moving."

"You certainly managed *that*," replied the duke.

"You could ride behind one of us, I suppose," said Cecelia. She looked dubious.

Harriet considered her dripping skirts. The cloth was streaked with odoriferous mud. She couldn't plaster Cecelia with that. And she refused to ride behind either of the others.

"Oh, very well," she said. "But if she spits on me, *I* shall strike her."

"Spits?" Ferrington said. "Why would your horse…"

"Someone will have to help me up," Harriet interrupted. She stomped over to the earl. It would have to be him, of course. She couldn't ask the immaculate Tereford. Resolutely, she paid no attention when Ferrington put his hands on her waist and boosted her into the saddle.

They made their way back up to the meadow, Harriet's mount being led by the earl. Finding a sparse place in the hedge, they pushed through, to Harriet's vast relief. She could not have faced another jump.

There was little conversation on the short ride back to Winstead Hall. Harriet was in no mood for chatter, and the others seemed to realize this. Once home, she sent them on their way and rode straight to the stables. She hoped to evade her mother and grandfather in her bedraggled state, though some servant would probably report it.

She managed this, reaching her room without seeing them. She was stripping off her muddy riding habit when Slade entered. "I've ordered a bath," the abigail said.

Harriet could only be grateful, though this meant word of her soaking had spread through the household. Well, she would face the questions when she was clean and dressed.

And the rogue earl could just keep his…delicious, delirious kisses to himself.

Nine

SITTING WITH HER MOTHER IN HER PARLOR THE FOLLOW-ing morning, Harriet wondered a little at the servants' silence about her mishap. Though most of them surely knew in what state she'd returned, none seemed to have told Grandfather or Mama. Her grandfather had questioned her closely about the outing, yes. But his inquiries had focused on the earl's level of interest in her, the chance of an early proposal, and ways she could encourage him to make an offer. Mama had followed this dinner conversation like a gambler who'd wagered more than she could afford on a hand of cards, her head moving anx-iously back and forth between them. Otherwise, she'd barely mentioned the ride. Harriet appreciated the staff's restraint. It made her feel a bit more at home in Winstead Hall.

The butler entered to announce, "The Duchess of Tereford." Cecelia followed him into the room, serenely ele-gant as always in a chip-straw bonnet and sprig muslin gown.

They exchanged greetings, and Cecelia was offered a chair. "I had thought we might walk in the garden, Harriet," she replied.

Taking in their caller's determined expression, Harriet saw she intended to talk about the ride, all of it. "It is rather windy," Harriet replied. "Won't you be more comfortable inside?"

"I find the weather invigorating," Cecelia answered.

"It looks as if it may rain," Harriet tried.

"I don't think so."

"There are clouds blowing…"

"I wish to speak to you privately," interrupted the duchess. "About a matter of some importance."

It was unsporting of her to be so forthright, Harriet thought. Because, of course, this stirred up her mother, who immediately looked worried. She watched them go with an anxious frown. Harriet wasn't even able to dally in fetching her hat. Cecelia followed right along to her bedchamber.

"So," the duchess said when they had left the house well behind. "Ferrington."

Harriet pretended to admire a spray of delphinium. It *was* windy. The blossoms dipped and swayed.

"The man you were so enthusiastically kissing by the stream," Cecelia added.

"That was *not* enthusiasm," Harriet blurted. "I was, er, overset by relief after my fall."

"Ah, relief."

Harriet could practically feel her friend's gaze on the side of her face. She certainly heard the skepticism in her tone.

"I can't say relief has ever moved me in precisely that way," said Cecelia.

Shifting ground, Harriet said, "He took me by surprise."

"Did he? A swooping descent? And yet it didn't look as if you wished to push him away. In fact, it seemed to me that you might have kissed him before."

She had no way of knowing that. Harriet was not going to admit it.

"Did he manage to plead his case with you?" Cecelia asked.

"What case?"

"He told me he was very eager to regain your good opinion."

"You talked about me?"

"Only a little. I noticed the constraint between you when we called here, and I asked him about it. He seemed...distressed by whatever has passed between you, Harriet. And eager for a chance to explain."

"He is a complete rogue," replied Harriet.

"He seemed to think that is what you liked about him. At one time. That's what I gathered, at any rate."

It was true, but it sounded foolish when spoken aloud. "He lied to me."

Cecelia nodded. "About his identity. He tried to conceal it from James as well."

"Who was too clever to be fooled," responded Harriet bitterly.

"The situations were rather different."

"Lies are lies." She'd meant to sound stern, but her treacherous voice trembled.

There was a short silence. Harriet gazed at the gravel path at their feet.

Cecelia took Harriet's arm and guided her into the shrubbery. The thick bushes cut off some of the wind. Cecelia led her to a sheltered bench, sat beside her, and then said nothing for a bit longer. "It is important to know your own mind," she said finally.

Harriet glanced at her, then away.

"Which is not always easy," the duchess continued. "Or simple."

Platitudes were not less annoying when they were true, Harriet noted.

"But once you do." The duchess paused. She pressed her lips together, then gave a small nod. "A woman can take her fate into her own hands, you know. My mother taught me that."

"I thought she died when you were quite young," said Harriet, startled by this change of topic.

"She did. My aunt told me the story. Of how my mother settled her own destiny."

"Destiny?" Harriet wasn't certain what she had expected. A warning to be more careful perhaps? Reminders about propriety and appearances? Not this, at any rate.

"My mama arranged her own marriage," Cecelia continued. "She went to my father and presented a list of the advantages of marriage. When he heard them, Papa conceded."

"Conceded," said Harriet.

"I know. It doesn't sound romantic. You would have to be better acquainted with my father to understand the significance. He is a…tiger for argument. He hardly ever gives in. To have convinced him was a true achievement. I think he must have wanted very much to marry her. But would he ever have bestirred himself to ask?" Cecelia shrugged.

An interesting tale, but Harriet didn't see that it applied to her.

"I've been telling her story to other young ladies. Those who don't think they can do anything about their situations. Why should they not?"

"Family, society, training, fear," suggested Harriet.

"Yes, it is hard to surmount those things, but not impossible. I did something rather like my mother."

"You?" She'd imagined the duchess's life as serene and perfect, including her marriage to the handsome duke.

"Our cases were not quite the same," replied Cecelia with a secret smile. "But the point is, I decided to act, and I did. I would like to spread that idea throughout the female half of society."

"A kind of amative philanthropy?"

Cecelia considered this. "More like fomenting a petticoat rebellion."

Harriet had to smile at the picture this presented. "Ladies to the barricades? But with no better cause than marriage. As ever."

"Do you not wish to be married?" the duchess asked. "It certainly looked as if you and Ferrington…"

"I thought he was a…a free spirit," burst out of Harriet. "Someone living a different sort of life. Far away. And then he turned out to be an *earl*."

"Which many would see as a great advantage and a wonderful surprise," replied Cecelia.

"Many." Harriet nearly spat the word. "The many who comprise society, which is…no more than a glittering scum disguising wretched behavior."

"Scum wouldn't really be much of a disguise…"

"You know what I meant, Cecelia."

The duchess paused, then nodded. "There are problems, of course. And those of us who care work to improve things."

"I don't know what you think…" Harriet began. And stopped. She saw Cecelia's line of reasoning laid out before her—Ferrington an earl, marriage to him, a position that could influence others, favorable change. Somehow, the cool logic was vastly dispiriting. "My grandfather sees marriage as another kind of business deal. I thought better of you, Cecelia."

Her friend seemed unaffected by the reproach. "You did not appear to be kissing a business partner beside the stream," she replied dryly.

"I was…" Harriet was a muddle of conflicting feelings.

"I merely offer observations," added Cecelia airily. "And perhaps…possibilities. Who knows?" She stood. "I must go."

Harriet rose as well.

"There is a lovely little path through the woodland," the duchess said, turning in that direction. "It goes past the Travelers' camp and right over to Ferrington Hall. Perhaps you know it?"

Meeting her eyes, Harriet said, "Yes, Cecelia. I do."

"I thought you might."

Harriet walked with her to the garden gate and then turned back toward the house. The wind, which had been at her back, pushed into her face now and threatened to pull her hat from her head. Skirts billowing, she hurried along the path and slipped through the nearest door, which happened to be the one nearest to her grandfather's study.

She paused and considered going back out into the gale. She would have to pass his lair to reach other parts of the house, and the door was open. She listened. He was hardly ever so silent. He must not be there. She hurried along the hallway, passed the study safely, turned a corner, and nearly ran into the old man in the hallway.

Her grandfather effectively blocked the corridor. His dark eyes drilled into her. "There you are. What did the duchess have to say?"

"It was just a friendly visit," Harriet replied.

"Linny said it was a matter of importance. She thought the duchess came to speak to you about the earl."

She did wish her mother would be less forthcoming. She hadn't *had* to tell him that. She hadn't known it was true.

"Well, what was it?" He frowned at her. "What's wrong with you, girl?"

"Nothing." She had to think of some sop to offer him. Harriet said the first thing that came into her head. "He enjoyed the ride."

"Did he?" Her grandfather rubbed his hands together. "Would the duchess be willing to act as matchmaker, do you think? I could pay her."

"No!" It was a horridly vulgar suggestion. Cecelia might laugh, but Harriet would be mortified.

"I don't suppose she needs the money," he conceded.

"Indeed not!"

"You needn't look so sour. Plenty of noblewomen hire themselves out as go-betweens and would be very happy to take my money."

She couldn't deny it. "The duchess is not one."

"Ah, well." He waved the idea aside. "Perhaps she may be helpful without prodding. She said he enjoyed the ride, eh? Came over to tell you that. Nothing else?"

Harriet shook her head. She edged along the wall, hoping to slip past him and escape.

He moved to block her. "You should arrange another then."

She would not be getting on a horse any time soon. Perhaps ever. "I'm a poor rider," she said.

"You think you don't show well on horseback?" He considered this while Harriet absorbed the sensation of being spoken of like livestock. "You should walk out toward Ferrington Hall and hang about until you run into him."

The fact that she'd done precisely that not so long ago, when the earl was Jack the Rogue, somehow made her even angrier. "So you're no longer worried about the Travelers?"

"Oh, them." He looked disgusted. "Why won't they move along? I wish I *had* chased them off. The whole neighborhood would be grateful once the thing was done."

She shouldn't have reminded him of that. "I won't lurk on the earl's property hoping to ambush him," she declared to distract him. Though it was also quite true.

Her grandfather came a step closer and glowered down at her. "A fine match has dropped into your lap like a ripe plum, Harriet. If you don't make a push to snag it, I will understand you have no intention of heeding my wishes."

"I cannot guarantee…"

"In which case, our deal will be at an end."

"Deal?" She hated the sound of the word.

"I will look elsewhere for an heir," he said. "One who is a better investment and not a weak failure like her mother."

"Don't speak of Mama that way!"

He shrugged. "It is no more than the truth. I can't help that."

"It isn't. She retreats because you are cruel to her."

He rejected this with a brusque gesture. "Get on with it, girl. My patience is not endless. And so I've just told Linny."

At last, he stepped aside. The spiteful gleam in his eyes told Harriet he knew very well what effect his threats had on her mother. He enjoyed it. She would find Mama in frantic tears, ready to echo Grandfather's demands in a far more affecting mode.

But her mother was not in her parlor, which was rather a relief. Harriet went to take off her hat, tidy her windblown hair, and gather her resolution before searching further.

She found her mother lying in her bed, deeply asleep, with a fresh laudanum bottle clutched in her hand.

"Mama," she said, shaking her shoulder.

There was no response. Her mother's breathing remained steady. Harriet pried the bottle from her limp fingers. It was about half full. Harriet went to the bell pull and jerked it sharply.

When her mother's maid responded, Harriet held up the bottle. "Do you know anything about this?" Like Slade, she was new to them, hired when they arrived in London for the season to make sure Mama was turned out properly.

"It was full the last time I saw it, miss," said the maid. Her face showed no opinion.

"Full!" Harriet was appalled.

"She's taken as much before," the woman added. "At night, mostly."

"How do you know? Did you provide it?" If she had, Harriet would see that she was dismissed, no matter what her grandfather thought.

"No, miss. Your mother said her doctor recommended a soother." The woman's mouth turned down. "I don't hold with it myself."

"No." Harriet's fingers closed more tightly around the vial. "I will take this away with me."

"There are others. She hides them."

The final three words made Harriet's heart sink. She met the woman's inexpressive eyes. It was impossible to tell whether she was a real ally. "Do you know where?" she asked her.

The maid directed her to six of the small bottles, tucked away in various spots around the room. She could not guarantee this was all, however. Harriet searched until she could think of nowhere else to try and found no more.

Her mother slept heavily through all of this. After getting the abigail's assurance that Mama had slept this soundly before without lasting harm, Harriet took the vials away to her own bedchamber. She put them on a small table, sat down, and gazed at the little glass containers.

Harriet knew laudanum was widely used—for pains, anxiety, even to soothe fretful babies. But she could not think it was a good idea. The drug dulled and deadened the senses. What else might it do? She wondered whether the recent change in her mother's temperament was partly due to taking it. No, this should not go on. She would talk to Mama and convince her to stop. Her grandfather could not find out; that was out of the question. He would treat Mama even more cruelly.

But would Mama listen to her? Would she give it up while Grandfather continued to bully her?

Harriet rose and began to pace, trying to think what to do. She knew how to survive on the small income they'd had previously. But the capital was gone. Her mother had spent it without consulting her. It was no longer possible for Mama to return to their old life while Harriet went out to find some employment. And in her mother's current state—pushed there by her grandfather's spite—even less was possible. Anger at the old man flamed through Harriet. He would not destroy her only remaining parent!

She clenched her fists and paced on. So much in her life had been done without her consent. When she'd been a child, there was no help for it. But she wasn't a child any longer. She had to do something.

Her school friends would be sympathetic. She and Mama could go and stay with one of them—Ada would be the best choice as she was married now and had her own household. But this was not a permanent haven. They couldn't live as penniless dependents.

Returning to the chair by the hearth, Harriet gazed into the distance. An idea rose in her mind, sparked by Cecelia's visit.

Out of the question!

And yet it would resolve many problems.

Nonsense!

It even had certain attractions.

Never!

No other possibility presented itself.

She could pull it back later, an insinuating inner voice suggested, after she'd had time to think of another plan. With a bit of peace and quiet, for Mama as well, surely she would be able to do so.

Harriet remembered her mother, sleeping so sonorously. Dead to the world, people called it. The phrase made her shudder. Would it be a fact, if Mama went on as she was?

She rose, went to the writing desk, jotted down a few lines, sealed the note, and took it downstairs to be sent off.

~∕∽

Jack read the note from Miss Finch with surprise and a surge of hope, particularly because she'd asked him to meet her in the garden as they used to do in better days. He sent her messenger back with an enthusiastic acceptance and set off not long after the lad in his best borrowed garb. The path through the woodland seemed a familiar friend, though he had to keep one hand on his hat to prevent the wind from snatching it.

He found her, as promised, in the shrubbery of the Winstead Hall garden, on a bench they had used before. The thick, evergreen hedges cut off most of the blustery gusts and made the spot feel quite private. Jack bowed over her hand. "I was so glad to receive your summons." She gestured an invitation, and he sat down beside her.

There was a short silence, broken only by the rustle of the branches above their heads. Jack wondered if he should remark on the weather or some other bland topic. He hoped she didn't expect it, because sitting so close to her, within reach of the sort of embraces they'd more than once shared, had tied his tongue. She looked so very lovely. He longed for her. "I do apologize once again for deceiving you." He hadn't meant to emphasize *once again*. That happened on its own. But he *had* apologized several times already.

Miss Finch's lips tightened. Her green eyes flashed over him and then fell.

She'd noticed the emphasis. Of course. She noticed everything. Her ardent intelligence was one of the things he admired about her. Along with her beauty and her quicksilver emotions and her adventurous spirit. He thought of her whirling in the dance around the Travelers' fire and ached for that happier time. "Did you ever think that it was for the best we met as we did?"

"What?"

"If I'd been introduced to you as the Earl of Ferrington and you to me as the distinguished Miss Harriet Finch, in some stuffy London house or even here, we would never have become…friends."

"Friends," she repeated as if the word surprised her.

"But we met as…only ourselves. With no stifling conventions coming between us. No families hanging about to cause difficulties."

Did she turn a little pale? She seemed so subdued today.

Jack went on, hoping to rouse her, even in argument. Also, he was more and more pleased with his theory. "The idea of an earl seemed to repel you, but I'm not really an earl. Nothing in my life made me so."

"You *are* the Earl of Ferrington," she replied.

"In name, perhaps. But actually, I am Jack, the man you called a rogue." He tried a smile.

"You are not a rogue either."

"I can't help but think that fortunate," he teased. "You would not wish to meet a true rogue, I promise you."

Once, she might have laughed at this or disagreed. Now she just sat with folded hands.

"Is something wrong? You summoned me." Why had she done so?

"I wished to speak to you about a…delicate matter," she said.

She sounded prim and stiff, not like the forthright girl Jack had gotten to know. He could endure reproaches over his conduct, even anger. This stuffiness was worrisome.

"I must suppose you know what it is," she went on.

Must she? Jack wished she wouldn't, since he had no idea.

"I am referring to the incident at the stream."

"Ah." Did she wish to thank him for hauling her out of the water? There was no need, though he wouldn't mind a bit of gratitude. Or any sort of emotion, really.

"Its scandalous nature," she added.

She was a wretched rider. They'd been wet. The mud had stunk. She'd melted into his… "Oh."

Harriet raised her eyebrows.

"Do you mean…?"

She appeared to lose patience with him. "The Terefords saw us kissing," she said. Slowly, as if to a poor student.

They certainly had, although Jack hadn't been aware of them at the time, or of anything really, except scorching desire.

"So, do you have something to say to me?" Now she sounded annoyed.

That he'd enjoyed it immensely? That he would like to do it again, right now? He didn't think that was what she meant. "I don't think they will say anything," he tried.

"I beg your pardon?"

"They don't seem the type to spread gossip."

"What?"

"Quite down-to-earth people, for a duke and duchess."

"You…" She seemed to grope for words. "Do girls in America kiss whomever they please?"

"No." Well, some did, of course. But not those Miss Finch was likely to meet.

"I have been compromised."

She said these words slowly, in such a strange tone that Jack couldn't puzzle it out. Was she angry or bewildered or regretful?

"My reputation is damaged."

Still the same odd voice, as if she repeated phrases from a lesson she'd disliked learning in the first place. "I hardly think…" Jack began.

"Unless you do the right thing."

In one dazzling moment, he understood. It was like being handed a prize you'd been desperately longing for as a free gift. He couldn't quite believe it. "Marry you, you mean?"

Miss Finch put a hand to her throat as if something was stuck there. She started to speak, stopped, then, jaw clenched, finally said, "Yes, Lord Ferrington."

Why was she angry? Oh. He'd been obtuse, inept. He'd made her say it starkly aloud. He was a dolt. Nearly the barbarian his great-grandmother had named him. He had to make up for that. Jack slipped off the bench and sank to one knee on the gravel path. He took her hand. "Miss Finch, would you do me the great honor of becoming my wife?"

She stared at him. Her green eyes swam with emotion. It didn't look like happiness. For a bewildered instant, Jack thought she was going to refuse. But she said, "Yes."

Elation raced through Jack. He could hardly believe his luck. He surged to his feet, pulling her up to face him, and then into his arms. "You have made me the happiest of men," he declared and kissed her.

At first, she was like a statue in his arms, stiff and wooden, nothing like she'd been on the riverbank. He held back and coaxed until her mouth softened under his. Jack pulled her closer, and at last she melted into his embrace, her body pliable under his hands, her fingers tangled in his hair. He was swept away on a flood of passion.

But all too soon, she pulled away. "We must go and tell my grandfather the news."

He could think of so many more pleasant things to do. "Can't we wait just a...?"

"No."

The word couldn't have sounded bleak. He must have imagined it. Or the thought of her grandfather disheartened her. He could sympathize with that.

She led him inside and along a corridor to a room with a large desk. Mr. Winstead sat there, surrounded by documents. He looked up when they entered, like an ill-tempered spider at the center of a vast web.

"Grandfather, we have come to tell you that we are engaged to be married," said Miss Finch.

The old man's habitual glower faded slowly into a grin, like a rarely used piece of machinery grinding into motion. "Ha." He stood. "Good for you, girl."

He spoke to her as if she was a servant who'd done well at her assigned task. Jack didn't like it.

Winstead rubbed his hands together. "Countess of Ferrington," he muttered. "And my great-grandson will be an earl. By God, he will."

He had no thought of wishing anyone happiness, Jack observed. Actually, he doubted the old man understood the meaning of the word.

"I'll tell the vicar to post the banns," Winstead added.

Not caring to be chivvied about, Jack said, "You're quick off the mark."

"You have some objection?" The grin was gone, replaced by the glower of suspicion that was Mr. Winstead's natural expression.

Jack had a few. At some point, he would have to show this old curmudgeon that he was not in charge. But this was not the moment. Jack was ready to marry Miss Finch tomorrow, had that been possible. "No," he said.

There was a tug on Jack's sleeve. Looking down, he gathered that Miss Finch—Harriet—wished to go. He certainly had no objection to *that*. Leaving Winstead to his gloating, he followed her into the corridor and along it to the front entry of the house. They could go back to the garden now and resume their vastly more pleasant activities.

She stopped beside the door, however. "Thank you for coming," she said, opening it and waiting.

As if he'd paid a morning call, and not a particularly welcome one. "Miss...Harriet, is all well?"

"Why wouldn't it be?"

This sounded like a challenge or a riddle he should be able to solve. Which was ridiculous. He was imagining things.

"I must go and inform Mama," she said.

That made sense. "Shall I come with you?" And then they could return to the garden.

"No."

Jack had never proposed marriage before, so he couldn't be certain. But this didn't feel like the aftermath of a joyous agreement. "I'm glad you've forgiven me for...withholding a bit of the truth."

"Are you?"

"Of course I am." What was the matter with her? "And gladder still that there is no need for secrets anymore."

"Until the next time you decide there's something I mustn't know?" she asked.

"That will never happen again," Jack assured her.

"I count on that," Harriet replied. She gestured at the open door, and before he quite knew what was happening, Jack found himself outside with the panels closing on his heels.

Ten

Harriet had left orders that she should be told as soon as her mother awoke, and so she was summoned to her bedchamber later that afternoon. Mama was still lying down, dazed from the dose she'd taken, but she brightened when given the news of Harriet's engagement.

"You're not joking?" she asked, sitting up against her pillows.

"No." Nothing could be further from a joke, Harriet thought.

Her mother clasped her hands together. "Papa will be so happy. Have you told him?"

"Yes."

"Was he pleased? Of course, he must have been."

"He was." *Triumphant* might be a better word.

Her mother smiled. "This is splendid. Oh, I am so happy, Harriet." She reached out and squeezed Harriet's hand.

Taking in the dark circles under her mother's eyes, the new lines around her mouth, the sagging skin that showed lost weight, Harriet could not be sorry for what she'd done. Mama *required* a respite, and given the circumstances, she'd seen no other way to manage one. Now, her mother looked so relieved.

"You will move to Ferrington Hall after the wedding," her mother went on. "Quite a fine house, I thought. Though in need of some attention. You will be comfortable there. Papa will hand over your portion to your husband, so there can be no doubts about the money any longer."

More of a pernicious system than an advantage, Harriet thought, but she said nothing.

"He won't be able to dangle it before us while threatening to snatch it away," Mama said. "You will be all right. Settled. And I..." She blinked and looked uncertain, as if she'd lost her train of thought. Or, more likely, she had no idea how to finish that sentence.

Harriet nearly said that of course they would both move to her new home, where neither of them would have to care what her grandfather thought or wanted ever again. Except...her engagement was a ruse. She was going to think of another plan for the future and then break it off. Wasn't she? Yes, of course she was. She'd made the rogue earl propose. He hadn't been intending to. He hadn't said he loved her. She couldn't actually marry him. And that fact was not the least bit melancholy. But her mother looked so forlorn. "You will come with me when I marry," she declared. That was perfectly true. *If* she ever married.

"Oh, Harriet," said her mother.

"I won't abandon you. You cannot live here with Grandfather."

Tears welled up in her mother's eyes. She blinked them away like a prisoner who did not dare hope for release. "You must see what your future husband thinks."

In other words, she was to exchange one tyranny for another. Harriet was assailed by a muddle of emotions, with rebellion at the head of the stampede.

Mama squeezed her hand. "You are such a good girl."

She wasn't. She was a selfish schemer. But she would set things right, as soon as she came up with another way forward.

Her mother rose from her bed and went to the dressing table to tidy her hair. "Ferrington seems quite charming. I expect you'll be happy with him."

There was nothing to say to this.

"And you like him. Well, of course you do. You accepted his offer, and I know you too well to think you would have done so if you did not. Like him, I mean." Mama's fingers picked at the folds of her gown, smoothing creases left from her nap. "And why shouldn't you? He has a lovely smile. I think he must be kind." Her eyes in the mirror found Harriet's and held them. "Is he kind?"

"Yes, Mama." Harriet would have confirmed this in any case, to reassure her mother. But she realized it was quite true. The rogue earl was kind; she'd noticed it with Samia and in other ways. Her thoughts stumbled as she wondered if he'd offered for her out of kindness. Or even pity? The possibility scalded along her veins.

"His smile quite makes up for his commonplace looks," her mother added.

Harriet didn't think his looks were commonplace. On the contrary, he was very attractive, as well as quick-witted and capable and amusing. His kisses were deliriously… She cut off this dangerous line of thought. "We should dress for dinner."

The necessity distracted her mother, as Harriet had known it would, and she was able to escape to her room.

Harriet's grandfather was uncommonly affable at dinner that evening. Every so often, he paused, fork suspended, and stared into space as if contemplating some pleasant prospect. "We will hold an engagement party," he said at one point. "Perhaps a ball. Yes, why not? The workmen are nearly finished with the new ballroom. Or, if they are not, they can bestir themselves." He frowned in a way that boded ill for the carpenters. "Our high-nosed neighbors will have to come, since you're marrying the earl. And when they hear that your friends the duke and duchess will attend, well, they'll abandon their snobbish ways soon enough."

Harriet wanted to object. But what was to be her reason?

"You don't look pleased, Harriet," the old man added. "I thought all girls loved balls."

"Of course she is pleased," said Harriet's mother. "Aren't you, my love?"

"Yes. Er…"

"Those friends of yours are arriving for a visit next week, aren't they?" asked her grandfather. "I daresay they'll be delighted to hear there's to be a ball."

Harriet *hadn't* forgotten that Charlotte and Sarah were coming. She'd simply been busy thinking of other things. A flush warmed her cheeks when she imagined their arrival. What would they think of her engagement? They'd be astonished is what. They would expect to have heard a great deal about Ferrington beforehand, but she'd never mentioned him in her letters. Until very recently, he had been Jack the

Rogue, and she hadn't known how to speak of *him*. Her friends would ferret out the true story. They were experts at doing exactly that. It was all too easy to imagine Charlotte's acerbic opinion of her conduct.

"How shall we manage the arrangements?" her grandfather wondered. "I don't suppose you can plan a ball, Linny?"

This roused a flash of her mother's old spirit, which Harriet was glad to see. "Naturally, I can, Papa."

He took a large bite of potato and surveyed her, chewing. When he'd swallowed, he said, "You will come to me with the details for approval at each stage."

Harriet's mother nodded, accepting this humiliating prospect without argument. Was she perhaps a fraction less cowed? A tiny bit irritated at his contempt? Harriet dared to hope so. If she was, that made her scheme worth it.

❦

Jack announced the change in his status at the Ferrington Hall dinner table. The Terefords took in the news of his engagement with a slight pause.

"Congratulations," said the duke then.

"This is rather sudden," remarked his wife, focusing her gimlet gaze on Jack. "How did it come about?"

He wasn't sure what to say. If he agreed it was sudden, which he actually did, that implied some irregularity. That wouldn't do. Clearly, he couldn't mention kisses and damaged reputations. In any case, the duchess knew about those. She'd seen their embrace on the riverbank, and

Harriet had implied her disapproval. Why then was she asking? "Ah," he said.

His two polished houseguests gazed at him. *Not* like cats trying to decide if they were observing a mouse. The duke's eyes showed some sympathy, didn't they?

There were, in fact, no details of his proposal that Jack cared to share, he realized. There'd been no talk of love or even esteem, as one would expect on such occasions. He'd blurted out some hackneyed phrases. Harriet must think him a bit of a clod. He ought to have prepared pretty speeches. He *would* have if he'd known what was afoot. Of course, Harriet had thought he *ought* to have known. Jack supposed that was true. A gentleman didn't go about kissing young ladies unless his intentions were honorable. But she'd been so angry with him so recently. He'd thought things had to be smoothed over before an offer would be acceptable. And so, he'd stumbled through his first, and only, he trusted, proposal. By the time he'd gathered his thoughts, Harriet was ushering him out the door. He'd made a mull of the thing from start to finish. But she'd said yes. He clung to that happiness.

The silence had stretched too long. "When is the wedding to be?" asked the duke politely.

"Quite soon," Jack replied. "Harriet's grandfather talked of posting banns at once."

"I suppose we are staying for the ceremony then?" the other man asked his wife.

He might have consulted Jack, as their host and the prospective groom, but Jack didn't blame him for turning to the true authority.

"One doesn't wish to miss a wedding," said the duchess.

Something had perplexed her. Jack had no idea what.

"Lady Wilton will be so pleased," she added with a tiny brush of wickedness.

"Will she?" Jack frowned and muttered, "That would almost make a fellow draw back, just to spite her."

"But of course, that would be ridiculous," said the duchess.

Jack had no objection to providing entertainment, but he liked to do it on purpose. With the Duchess of Tereford, he was seldom granted that opportunity. "I don't see why Lady Wilton should keep sticking her nose in," he said.

"An inborn conviction that she knows best strengthened by decades of habit and the cowardice of her offspring," replied the duke.

His tone was dry, but his blue eyes glinted. Jack laughed. Until another thought occurred. "Do I have to invite her to the wedding?"

"It would be customary," said the duchess.

Jack groaned.

"You needn't worry," said the duke. "Grandmama will be pleased with the match."

"So she likes Miss Finch?" Jack wasn't surprised. Who could dislike Harriet, after all?

"Miss Finch is an heiress," the duke replied. "Grandmama encourages all her family members to marry money."

"I was not an heiress," said his wife.

"I'm sure she saw your lack of fortune was outweighed by your many sterling qualities."

"And your lengthy resistance to any marriage at all."

"And that," he agreed, smiling at her.

Jack had decided it was no use trying to understand all the nuances of the Terefords' conversation. They practically had a language of their own. "Will people say I married Miss Finch for her money?" he asked. He didn't like that idea.

"Oh, I shouldn't think so." The duke shrugged. "It's not as if you were a penniless fortune hunter."

He'd forgotten. He was an earl. With a great estate. His acceptance of that fact had changed everything, particularly regarding Harriet's grandfather.

"I can recommend someone if you like," said the duke.

"What?" Jack hadn't been listening.

"To help with the settlements, the marriage contract."

"Contract?" Jack knew about legal agreements. He ran a business, after all. But he'd never thought of marriage in those terms.

"Families with large estates must make a variety of arrangements," explained the other man.

"Did you do so?" Jack looked from one to the other. The Terefords were obviously in love. The story of their engagement was probably crammed with romance. Yet the duke spoke of contracts without constraint.

"Oh yes," was the reply.

"I suppose I'd better consult with your fellow then."

The duke nodded.

"I expect Harriet's mother will be moving with her," said the duchess.

"Moving?"

"Here to Ferrington Hall. It would be cruel to leave her behind. Mrs. Finch finds living with her father quite trying."

Jack could see that. Winstead was no charmer. But he hadn't counted on a resident mother-in-law.

"You don't mind?" asked the duchess.

Mrs. Finch seemed all right, if a bit limp and weepy. "Whatever Harriet wants," said Jack.

"Umm," she replied.

How could one word—not even a word, really, more of a hum—convey skepticism and concern and sympathy? And what was the need for these things? Jack gazed at the gravy congealing on his dinner plate and thought how much he needed to see Harriet again. Some…things needed to be clearer. And he should make those pretty speeches he hadn't yet composed. He considered asking the duke for advice about that. And decided against it. Tereford wouldn't laugh out loud, but his amusement would be all too apparent, nonetheless. As for the duchess… Jack suppressed a shudder.

⁓

One advantage of being an engaged man was he could call at Winstead Hall whenever he pleased, Jack decided. And so he set off the next morning to walk through the woods, determined to sit down with Harriet and thrash everything out.

Before he was halfway there, however, a mob of children swept out of the trees, shouting and laughing, leaping over sprigs of bracken, and waving sticks as if they were swords. Jack paused to enjoy their sheer, exuberant joy. But as soon as they spotted him, the gang stopped short, lowering their mock weapons to stare. The tiny, dark-haired, and bright-eyed ringleader put her hands on her hips.

"Hello, Samia," said Jack.

"Hullo, uh...Mr. Earl."

"I'm still just Jack."

"No. Mistress Elena said I was to call you..." The little girl frowned in concentration. "My lord, it was."

"I wish you wouldn't."

"Mistress Elena *said*."

There were murmurings among the other children. The Travelers did not question Mistress Elena's decrees. Jack felt again his separation from these people, a sad loss. "What are you playing?" he asked.

"Pirates," replied Samia.

"Don't pirates need a sailing ship?"

"Up in the trees sways just like a ship," she informed him.

"Got a real crow's nest," said one of the smallest boys. "With crows."

"Ah." It was a clever idea. No doubt Samia had come up with it. She had a vivid imagination.

"You going to the camp?" the little girl asked him.

"No, I am on my way to Winstead Hall. That's the house..."

"Over yonder." She pointed in the right direction.

"Yes. I'm calling on Miss Finch. We're going to be married." He wasn't certain why he added that bit of information. Perhaps he just liked saying it aloud.

"Today?" asked Samia.

"No. Soon." Jack resumed his walk. The children tagged along at his heels.

"Can I come to the wedding?" Samia bounced at his side, occasionally beheading a weed with her wooden scimitar.

"Yes," said Jack. Harriet's grandfather wouldn't approve, but it was his wedding, and he would invite whomever he liked.

The unruly group came out of the woods into a meadow. A burly man rose from a stone where he'd been sitting and waved a quarterstaff. "You rabble keep away from here!" he shouted.

The children slid to a stop, then melted back into the trees. Annoyed that he'd forgotten Winstead's border guards, Jack walked on.

"No comin' through here," the man declared.

Jack was wearing clothes tailored for a duke. He was on land he owned. He summoned his father's haughtiest accent and kept moving. "I am Lord Ferrington," he said. "I'm on my way to call at Winstead Hall."

The guard squinted at him. "Ain't I seen you about here before? Dressed different?"

"I arrived at Ferrington Hall only recently." Neither an answer nor a lie, Jack thought as he approached the man's station. His father had been expert at that sort of response, providing no information in a supercilious tone. Jack tried to mimic one of his expressions as well—serene confidence that no one would think of questioning his wishes.

The man lowered his staff and stepped back.

A spot between Jack's shoulder blades itched as he passed

by and walked on. But no blow came. He'd cowed the fellow. He supposed that was a triumph, but he didn't much care for the feeling.

The servant who opened the front door at Winstead Hall was far more welcoming. He ushered Jack in with a bow and held out a hand.

Did he want a tip just for admitting him?

"May I take your hat, my lord?" the footman said.

"No. Miss Finch and I are going to walk in the garden. If she is free, I mean."

It seemed his new status was known to the household, because there was no nonsense about inquiring whether the ladies were at home. The servant took him directly to a small parlor at the back of the house where Harriet and her mother sat. The latter seemed delighted to see him. His fiancée less so.

"I thought we might walk in the garden," he said to Harriet when he had made his bow.

"Perhaps you would care to talk to my mother?" She looked severe. He seemed to have a special knack for making her do so.

"That's all right, Harriet," said Mrs. Finch. "You go and get your things." She beamed up at Jack.

"I think, Mama, that we might..."

"We will have a chat while you do that," interrupted the older woman.

Jack was careful to show no reaction as Harriet frowned, then turned and went out.

"Do sit down, Lord Ferrington."

He did so.

"I'm so happy you will be joining our family."

She sounded sincere and kind, which made a nice change. Jack looked at her closely for the first time, this small, brown-haired woman who didn't much resemble her daughter. She was more like her father, Winstead, he realized, though without the man's glower and choleric temper. He had thought of her as plump, but she wasn't. In fact, she looked wan and quite weary. Jack wondered if she'd been ill. "Thank you, Mrs. Finch," he said.

"Oh, you must call me…" She cocked her head like a sparrow. "Now, what shall you call me?"

He caught a glint of humor in her tired eyes.

"Mama-in-law perhaps," she went on. "Nothing that would offend your own mother."

Jack remembered Lady Wilton's searing disapproval of his lineage. And then he thought of his feisty, red-haired mother. She would have been offended by many things he'd encountered since coming to England but not by Mrs. Finch.

"Will she be coming over for the wedding?" that lady asked.

Fleetingly he thought she meant Lady Wilton. But of course, she was referring to Mam. "She died several years ago."

"Oh, I am so sorry." She leaned over to press his hand briefly.

The warmth in her voice and the touch of a sympathetic hand moved Jack. For a moment, he couldn't speak. He thought he heard a sound in the corridor, but no one appeared. "I could call you Milady Mother," he suggested. "Or what about Materfamilias?"

⤜

Standing outside the open parlor door, Harriet listened to her mother laugh. It was a sound she hadn't heard for some time.

"Is that Latin?" Mama asked the rogue earl.

"Yes, it means the female head of the family."

The fact that he knew Latin struck Harriet as another deception. She remembered the ridiculous accent he'd put on for the duke. Had Ferrington been laughing at them the whole time?

"Oh, that name would not be proper for me then," replied her mother.

"No? You must educate me in English proprieties."

"I didn't mean… It is just that I am not… Our family does not…"

"I'm sure you can tell me just how to go on," said their visitor, interrupting Mama's fumbles. He sounded warm and encouraging. Harriet was struck by his gentle tone.

"Oh, no. I have been living quite out of the fashionable world for many years."

"Not as out of it as I was."

"Over in America."

"Yes. Where my father was sent."

From the corridor, Harriet heard a sound rather like a snort. It took her an instant to realize her mother had made it. "I've heard Lady Wilton tell that tale," Mama said. "I found her actions absolutely unforgivable!"

She hadn't sounded so spirited in months.

"Did you?" asked Ferrington.

"I certainly did. And I am not the only one. Lady Wilton must be a hard, cruel woman to have done such a thing."

Harriet heard the pain of her mother's own rejection in her tone, along with true sympathy for Ferrington's case.

"I must admit I found her so," said the rogue earl.

"There is *no* excuse to…to *throw away* a child."

As Mama had been discarded, Harriet thought. As she still was, by Grandfather's dismissive attitude. She'd known there was hurt in that, but perhaps she hadn't understood the full depth of it.

"I agree," he answered.

A similar sort of pain, Harriet noted. Not as deep as her mother's, but the relationship was more distant. Still, they had this wound in common. She hadn't really considered that. What must it be like to be…expunged from a family after nearly twenty years of domestic life?

"She has you back now, however," said her mother. "Which may be more than she deserves."

"It is certainly less than she likes," said Ferrington. "Lady Wilton discovered nothing to approve in me. Thoroughly undistinguished, she said. With the manners of a barbarian."

"Well, that is *obviously* not true," said Mama.

She was hotly defensive. Harriet enjoyed her fire. She'd missed that so much.

"Thank you, ma'am. I've been trying to…"

"There is no need for you to *try* to do anything. You are perfectly charming as you are."

There was a short silence. Though she couldn't see them, Harriet felt it was fraught with emotion.

"Much obliged," said their visitor.

His voice trembled just a bit. She could hear the appreciation and gratitude in it. Harriet realized this man could not have been more different from her grandfather, with his coldness and constant criticism. Ferrington had a quick sensitivity beneath his insouciance. He listened. Her mother would be comfortable in his household. Content, even joyful. Except... That wasn't going to happen, was it? Feeling uneasy, Harriet stepped into the room. "I'm ready," she said.

They both started, like people caught in a private moment, deep in rapport. They seemed to have briefly forgotten her existence. It was so very unexpected.

Her mother recovered immediately. "Have a lovely walk," she said and positively twinkled at Harriet. She couldn't have approved of this match any more if the rogue earl had been a fairy-tale prince.

Ferrington rose. He looked shaken out of his usual lightness. The emotion in his dark eyes was...endearing?

No, it was not. Harriet turned away, reminding herself of all the times he'd been irritating and deceitful. One mustn't forget the lies! But they seemed harder to condemn this morning after hearing him talk with Mama. She'd caught a glimpse of a younger, more tender person, and he had evoked a wave of sympathy. Her anger was slipping away, moment by moment. What would be left if it was gone? She strode out of the parlor, tapping the tip of her parasol sharply on the floor with each step.

All doors were opened to them now. Servants radiated goodwill. Clearly everyone had heard of the engagement and approved. Or, more likely, they appreciated the softening of her grandfather's mood. *That* must make working here easier.

"Your mother is a lovely lady," said Ferrington from behind her.

Without warning, Harriet's throat grew tight with tears. Mama *was* lovely. Her meekness and anxiety might sometimes be irritating, but no one could fault her heart. Harriet had to do whatever was required to protect her.

Stepping through the outer door, Harriet snapped her parasol open and positioned it like a shield. She struggled with emotion as she moved rapidly down one path and up another.

"Is this a race?" asked the rogue earl.

"You wished to walk. I am walking." If she stayed ahead of him, she didn't have to see his expression. And possibly be undone by it. That would not do.

"More of a trot, if we're speaking of gaits."

"Ha, ha."

He came up beside her, brushing aside sprays of flowering shrubs on the narrow path. Their pungent scent filled the air. "Why are you angry?" he asked.

"I am not angry."

"You are giving a good imitation of it then. I seem to have a positive genius for making you angry. And yet I never mean to do so."

If he weren't so irritating... No, that wasn't fair. She was angry at the situation and at herself for creating it. Recalling the animation in her mother's voice when she spoke to Ferrington, Harriet wondered what she was going to do.

She kept the parasol bobbing between them, hiding her confusion. "Was there something in particular you wished to speak to me about?"

"Yes. Any number of things. None of which I can recall just now." He touched her elbow. "Here, will you sit? This bench is in the shade, so you can close that dashed parasol."

"I…." His hand had shifted to the small of her back, warm and insistent. She couldn't think of a reason to refuse.

They sat. He took the parasol gently from her hands and shut it. "That's better. Now I can see you." He smiled.

Why must he smile? From the beginning, that smile had been her downfall. It was open and warm. So terribly alluring.

"I thought we should talk about our future," he went on. "And I also wished to tell you, as I didn't have the wit to do yesterday, that I sincerely, ah, admire you." He cleared his throat.

Admire was such a paltry word, Harriet thought. She'd never noticed that before. He was straining for compliments, the man who'd been so fluent when they were together in the forest. She'd forced him into an uncomfortable position. Harriet couldn't bear that idea. It worried her so much that she leaned forward and kissed him.

And discovered a remarkably effective means of silencing a man.

Indeed, it was useful for driving every thought from one's own head as well. The touch of his lips required all her attention. He was, it seemed, something of an expert in gently fiery, tantalizing kisses. The strength of his arms as he pulled her nearer on the stone bench demanded even more concentration. Really there was no room for anything else in her consciousness. She could only respond, shifting with him, pressing closer, twining her fingers in his dark hair. It felt a bit like a dance, and yet not like that at all.

When his hands began to wander, Harriet discovered spikes of sensation and waves of desire that swept all else before them. Her parasol fell over with a clatter. It was made of satin and lace and would be spoiled by dust. Harriet could not have cared less.

She nearly whimpered when he drew away. Her pulse was racing, and her breath was near a pant. He was breathing hard, too, she noticed. "I see this engagement business has both advantages and drawbacks," he said in a thick voice.

Harriet groped for the scraps of her reason. She had no idea what he was talking about.

"One is allowed more privacy," the rogue earl continued. "But only enough to make one want…a great deal more."

More, thought Harriet dreamily. Yes, she wanted that.

"I'm more thankful than ever that your grandfather wants a quick marriage. They tell me this reading of the banns in church takes three weeks?"

"Three Sundays," Harriet managed.

"Ah, too bad Sunday is just past and we missed our opportunity."

Harriet came back to earth with a jolt. If the vicar read the banns, all would become public and official. As things stood now, people might hear of the engagement, but mistakes could still be claimed.

"Well, the details don't matter, do they?" Ferrington said, taking her hand and kissing it.

She tried to ignore the wave of heat ignited by his touch. Of course they mattered. There was the detail, for example, that no one had spoken of love. She pulled her hand away and stood. "I should go in."

"Perhaps so," he said with obvious regret. "It's all I can do to keep my hands off you." The words sent a thrill through Harriet as he bent to pick up her parasol and began brushing off the dust. "I don't care for this thing, but I didn't wish it ill," he added with a wry look.

A tender and teasing smile this time, joined by an irresistible glint in his dark eyes. Harriet found herself transfixed by his lips and leaning toward him.

In the next instant, the parasol fell back into the dirt, and they came together as if their lives depended on it. The rogue earl's muscular body pressed against hers, kindling all her senses. How had she never known that physical passion was easier than thought? And so much more compelling? The world dissolved in a whirl of desire.

"Oh dear," said a feminine voice behind her. "I've done it again. So maladroit."

Harriet pulled back. The Duchess of Tereford stood a few feet away. Clearly, she had just come around a corner in the path.

"I do beg your pardon," she said, taking a step backward.

Naturally, they separated. That was the correct thing to do, the only thing to do. Ferrington again retrieved the parasol, though this time, he seemed to wish to hold it in front of him like a shield. Harriet squared her shoulders, wondering how disheveled she looked. Rather tellingly so, she assumed.

"Hello, Cecelia." She liked the duchess very much, but she did wish that her friend hadn't arrived at this particular moment. Or…perhaps, on the other hand, it was providential that she had. Harriet's senses were still swimming.

"Harriet, Ferrington," Cecelia replied. She might be hiding a smile, but she was very good at being unreadable. She waited. Harriet thought she was interested in what might be said next. So was she. What was there to say about blatant kisses?

"We were discussing the wedding," said the rogue earl, taking the bait Cecelia had dangled.

"Were you? It seems it will prove an interesting ceremony." She was certainly laughing inside, Harriet concluded.

"Before…" Ferrington seemed to realize he had nowhere to go with that sentence. "Fine day for a walk in the garden, eh?"

Cecelia looked up. Clouds were gathering. "Do you think so?"

He shrugged and offered one of his beguiling smiles. "You told me once, when in conversational doubt, fall back on the weather."

"Conversational doubt?" The duchess's smile escaped this time. "I can't remember using any such phrase."

"That was the gist," he answered. He held out the parasol, like an actor covering flubbed lines with a bit of business.

Harriet took it in the same spirit and snapped it open. "Have you come to see me?" she asked Cecelia.

"Yes. Though if you are occupied…"

"Lord Ferrington was just going."

"Oh, is that what he was doing?"

"A...uh...fond farewell," said the rogue earl. He grinned at them, bowed, and took himself off.

Cecelia laughed.

Harriet turned to walk in the opposite direction, half hiding behind her parasol.

"I keep coming upon you kissing Ferrington," said Cecelia, falling into step beside her.

She might have said Cecelia seemed to appear whenever it happened, but she chose not to.

"And giving every appearance of enjoying it?" The duchess made this a question, and she gazed at Harriet like a lady who *would* have an answer.

The silence stretched. Finally, Harriet murmured, "Yes."

"Well, that's good." Cecelia nodded and smiled. "Passion is an important part of a marriage."

Cecelia would know, Harriet thought. She'd seen the way the duke looked at her. And vice versa. She could imagine...all sorts of things she mustn't think about. Because in her case, there wasn't going to be a marriage. She had to set things right very soon. Even though she had no alternate plan. And the thought of relinquishing her rogue earl was becoming more and more distressing.

Eleven

"I SHOULD LIKE TO LEARN MORE ABOUT MY RESPONSIBILI-ties as earl," Jack said to the duke and duchess at dinner that evening. This was part of preparing to be married to Harriet, and anything to do with that happy event cheered him. "People speak of 'managing the estate.' What does that entail precisely?"

The duke gestured at his wife. "Cecelia is the expert in that regard. You could do no better than consult her."

He'd said such things before, and Jack was always surprised at the ease with which he admitted it. Few men of his acquaintance would have done so.

"There are times when I think she loves dusty old records and documents more than she loves me," Tereford added.

"And *I* wonder if you married me in order to have your work done for you," replied the duchess.

They laughed at each other. Clearly this was an old joke between them. Jack realized living beside the Terefords had given him hope for his future. Though they were of the highest rank, they had never been stuffy or disapproving. He'd watched for signs. Time had passed, and he'd seen none. They'd convinced him his great-grandmother was wrong. He could be accepted by English society as he was. Lady

Wilton's harsh tutoring was not required. "I'm ready for a new job," he declared. "I can't bear idleness."

The duchess nodded as if she approved.

Jack was glad of that. He'd been the target of several speculative glances from the duchess since she'd caught him kissing Harriet. Again. He might have preferred receiving more easygoing instruction from the duke. And yet he wanted to really learn and pitch in.

"Why don't we meet in the estate office in the morning?" she said.

"Is there one?" Jack asked.

"Yes. Haven't you looked over all the rooms of your new home?"

He had not. In fact, he hadn't really thought of Ferrington Hall as home. But now he must, because it would be Harriet's. He wanted to make it fine for her. And her mother also. Having talked a bit with Mrs. Finch, he was glad to offer her a refuge. "I should do that, I expect," he replied.

"Mrs. Riley would be happy to show you," said the duchess. "She's worked here since she was fourteen, you know."

Once again, he hadn't. "So long?"

"She came as a kitchen maid and worked her way up."

"And has she been happy here?" Jack asked. He still didn't entirely understand such long-standing relationships.

"I would say so. She is proud of her accomplishments."

"That's good." For some reason, Jack was reminded of the laborer he'd questioned in the field near Winstead Hall. That fellow had said the earl looked after people, lent a helping hand. And what else? Settled disputes, that was it. How was that done? He was no judge. Jack had a sudden sense of a great many people spread out over the lands around him ready to rely on his perspicacity. He didn't mind responsibility, but that seemed a bit daunting.

After breakfast the next day, the duchess led him down a corridor near the kitchen. She opened the door and gestured him in. Jack entered a small room furnished with a desk and some chairs. Two walls of shelves held ledgers and document boxes. The place reminded him of the headquarters of his shipping business. This had a grander ceiling and fancier carving on the shelves, but the room gave him a sense of industry and purpose he appreciated. He felt comfortable suddenly, more so than anywhere else he'd been in Ferrington Hall.

The duchess started to sit at the desk. Then she stopped and gestured for him to take that seat. Jack did so. There were several stacks of papers set before it.

"I've looked over a few things," she said with a smile and a shrug as she sat down across from him. "I couldn't resist."

As if documents were special treats created for her entertainment, Jack thought. It was amusing, really.

"Some of your tenants have pressing questions or requests," she went on. She pointed to one of the piles. "And some farms lie vacant and should be let."

"The estate is all rented out?"

"Nearly all. There is a home farm, which you can use for your own purposes."

"Such as?"

"Agricultural experiments, specialized livestock breeding."

Jack had no idea what these experiments would be. He decided to save that question. "And these rents are how an estate makes money?"

She nodded.

"So there's really nothing for me to do?" He wanted a task that required his opinions and energies.

"Not at all. The landowner is responsible for upkeep and improvements. You must decide how much of the income is to be turned back into buildings and tools. A threshing machine, for example, that can be shared by all the tenants in turn."

Her face glowed with enthusiasm. Jack couldn't quite visualize a threshing machine. "And the remainder is the profit," he observed.

"Yes. Your income. But it is well worth investing some part of the rents in the land. Over the long run."

Jack nodded. "It seems I must learn a whole new business."

"Some landowners leave oversight to stewards and agents," the duchess replied. "That can work well if you find good men." She made a wry face. "Always men, of course."

"I suspect you are a rare creature."

She smiled. "There are other women who are just as knowledgeable, though they get little chance to show it. A good landowner is a caretaker, and women are often good at service."

"Service?" repeated Jack.

"Well, that is how I see it. Tending the land and the people it supports, as well as the future."

He raised his eyebrows, inviting her to go on. He was finding her perspective on this subject fascinating.

"You are, I believe, the ninth Earl of Ferrington."

"Seemingly," he replied.

"So your people have been here for centuries." The duchess gestured at the ceiling. "The beams in a house like this last that long. But eventually, some will need to be replaced. And so you plant oak trees to be ready when that time comes."

Jack was speechless at the thought of such a span.

"And there's something else. What do you do with the money you make with your shipping business?"

"I live on it," he replied.

"And the surplus? Perhaps you make charitable donations?"

"Not as many as I might have," he admitted.

The duchess nodded as if she understood. "It is another thing to think of. I know Harriet is interested in several charitable causes."

"Is she?" That was interesting information.

"She will be bringing a goodly sum to the estate. I'm sure she'd like to have some say in how it is used."

"Of course. Why wouldn't she?"

This earned Jack his first look of total approval from the formidable Duchess of Tereford.

❧

"Did your instructional session go well?" the duke asked his wife later that day as they strolled arm in arm through the unkempt gardens of Ferrington Hall.

"Yes," was the absent reply.

"Ferrington was willing to listen to you?"

"Quite. He is an apt pupil."

"Then why aren't you smug with success?" he inquired.

"I beg your pardon?"

He smiled down at her. "Now I have your full attention."

"And you are smug with success."

"Completely."

The duchess shook her head but returned the smile.

"Something is nagging at you," observed her husband. "I don't think I can be the cause, because I have been excessively accommodating."

"Excessively?"

"I have given a near stranger my clothes, along with the services of my valet. Which Ferrington does not value as he should, by the by. I have not complained…"

She raised her eyebrows.

"Well, not nearly as much as I might have. It is rather dull here, Cecelia. Aside from your company, of course. But you do go off on mysterious errands."

"Poor James." She pressed his arm. "I'm puzzled about Harriet Finch. There's something odd about her lately."

"So you have said before. She is a bit unusual compared with other debs, but surely…"

"She is behaving oddly, I mean. Haven't you noticed?" When the duke made no reply, she looked up at him. "You would if you tried. You are an acute observer."

He put his free hand to his heart. "My dear, I am overwhelmed."

"Tease all you like, James."

"Thank you, I will."

The duchess laughed. "As long as you help me discover what's going on."

"Is this one of those unspoken requirements of marriage? To become a coconspirator?"

"Yes," answered the duchess with a bland expression. Her eyes danced, however.

"Then I must rally 'round, of course."

"I will be very grateful."

Their eyes held, and a familiar, delicious heat rose between them. They smiled wickedly.

"No, my lord!" cried an urgent voice behind them.

The Terefords turned to see the earl and the old caretaker Mr. Riley on the other side of the garden, beside a decrepit trellis. Ferrington had put a hand to the structure, and as they watched, it trembled and fell over, burying Riley in grapevines. The earl sprang forward and pulled him out, brushing bits of leaf from his smaller companion's clothing.

"I need a way to bring them together," said the duchess.

"I don't see how they could be more so," replied her husband, watching the earl and Riley contemplate the unsupported mound of vines.

"Ferrington and Harriet, I mean."

"Oh. Not another ride, I think."

"Harriet wouldn't come. I know! That's perfect."

⌘

Thus it was that Harriet found herself carried off to Ferrington Hall the following day to look over the house and note any changes she would like to make as countess. She'd tried to resist the invitation, but Cecelia was not a duchess for nothing. She'd been unstoppable, countering all the objections Harriet could muster and enlisting her mother and grandfather in the scheme. Mama had thought it a lovely idea. She'd positively beamed. Grandfather seemed to view it as planting their flag on a rival's bastion. He'd had to be discouraged from coming along and making suggestions of his own. Harriet feared he was even now reviewing the clutter of objects that crammed Winstead Hall and choosing the gaudiest, most ostentatious to send with her when she married the earl.

Harriet had been driven back and back until she ran out of excuses. And so now, she was walking through the rooms with the rogue earl at her side and Cecelia lurking behind them, more instigator than chaperone. There was to be a luncheon in the garden afterward, for which the duke would join them. Harriet had prayed, unsuccessfully, for rain.

"The Rileys say there have been no changes to the furnishings in forty years," Ferrington told her as they passed through the drawing room, dining room, and two parlors on the lower floor. "Only in the wine cellar. My predecessor was…"

"A connoisseur?" suggested Harriet.

"I would have said a drunkard. But I am a blunt colonial."

"Is that your new designation?"

"I prefer it to barbarian. Or rogue." His smile brought back a rush of memories. They'd tossed that last word back and forth in so many different tones. At this point, it seemed like an endearment.

Conscious of Cecelia's sharp ears, Harriet walked on.

"Apparently he stocked the cellar with hundreds of bottles," Ferrington continued as they walked. "We shan't drink it up until we're old."

"A great deal of drink is required for large house parties," said Cecelia at their backs.

"Ah." The earl looked at Harriet. "We'll have as many of those as you like."

"I've never been to any," she replied. Her youth had not included such invitations.

"Neither have I."

He was more like her than her close school friends, Harriet realized. Even with them, she'd sometimes felt like an outsider when they chattered about their connections in society. And the gentlemen she'd met during the season often had no other topic of conversation. Their talk was filled with unfamiliar names and shared occasions, along with the expectation she would know of them and be impressed. Ferrington was the only nobleman she'd encountered who never did this. Because, like her, he could not.

In the antiquated kitchen, Cecelia's cook had many suggestions for improvement, all of them sensible. They agreed she would note them down for future reference and moved on to the upper floors.

"I'm told this room is known as the countess's retreat," Ferrington said, opening a door and gesturing for her to enter.

Harriet stepped into a beautifully proportioned chamber with long windows on two sides letting the light flood in. There was a tiled fireplace on the right with a design of curling vines. The hangings and furniture were faded and worn, as was the striped wallpaper. But a rug covering the center of the floor glowed with jewel colors. With a little freshening, this could be a charming place to sit.

She went to look outside. The windows overlooked the garden, which cried out for attention. Her grandfather's gardener would be a good person to consult. He and his helpers had created a riot of flowers at Winstead Hall. It would be a pleasure to restore these grounds. A series of patterned beds would provide a lovely view from this vantage point. For someone. She turned away.

They looked into the bedchambers used by the earl and countess with their adjoining dressing rooms on the opposite sides. Neither looked occupied at present. They had the same faded quality as the countess's parlor. Harriet wondered which room Ferrington was occupying now.

"I set up in a smaller chamber," he said as if reading her thoughts. "I wasn't ready for this sort of state when I arrived."

It must have been odd to move from the Travelers' camp to the hall, Harriet acknowledged.

"But I am now," he added. He seemed to think she needed this reassurance. "Mrs. Riley tells me the linen is a disgrace," he went on. "I don't know exactly what that means. Does it go out cavorting with the tapestries in the drawing room during the hours of darkness?"

Harriet laughed. "It's probably just threadbare." The problem was not unfamiliar.

"How disappointing."

"They can be mended." She'd darned many torn bed linens.

"You should just replace them," said Cecelia from the doorway.

Harriet nearly jumped. She'd almost forgotten her friend's presence.

"Worn-out sheets are good for polishing furniture," the duchess added.

She could do that, Harriet realized. She could replace outworn linens and hangings, even furniture. There would be no need for scrimping. She could create her own sort of household, about which she discovered she had definite ideas. She wanted an informal, comfortable, bountiful home such as she never had before. Later on, perhaps it would bustle with children. Her mother would be so happy in such a place. Tears thickened Harriet's throat at the picture.

They examined the guest bedrooms, and Ferrington expressed some enthusiasm about installing newfangled bathing facilities. They saw the servants' quarters required extensive refurbishing before returning to the ground floor. Cecelia slipped away to "see about luncheon," blatantly leaving them alone in the drawing room.

"We shall do whatever you want with the house," the rogue earl said then. "I'm sure you know exactly how things should be. You should buy anything you like."

"As long as I cleared the expenditure with you, I suppose," Harriet replied.

"No need for that."

"But I would have to come to you for the money," she pointed out. He must know her grandfather's money—his payment for a title, in his mind—would go to her husband.

"That doesn't seem right," Ferrington answered. "We'll put you in charge of the funds."

He said it as if it was only sensible and not a revolution. Was this some American attitude? No, things weren't so very different there. It was his unique outlook.

She could simply stay silent and marry him, Harriet thought. Would that be so very bad? Everything about this visit, about *him*, urged her in that direction. But she'd forced him to propose. He hadn't even thought of it himself, seemingly. He'd stepped forward out of obligation. He'd never said he loved her. If she married him, wasn't she being as greedy and pragmatic as her grandfather? Hadn't she made a deal, just as the old man had ordered?

There were those searing kisses. But men kissed easily, she'd been told. Passion flamed and died, or so she'd heard. Chaperones and novels were full of warnings about that. As the latter were rife with stories of gentlemen manipulated into marriage and the disastrous consequences thereof. She'd railed at him about withholding his identity, called him a liar more than once. Wasn't she as bad or worse? She must speak to him clearly and honestly. And if he then drew back… Tears threatened again, and she shied away from the thought.

❧

Later that day, when luncheon was finished and Harriet gone, the duke and duchess took another stroll through the Ferrington Hall gardens. "What do you think?" she asked him.

"Ferrington is smitten," the duke replied. "I have no doubt about that."

She nodded.

"About your friend, I'm not so sure."

"You don't think she likes him? I thought she did, but…" The duchess bit her lower lip. "There is some constraint there."

He nodded this time.

"I don't understand it. I would have said they were perfectly suited."

"You know her far better than I do," he said. "But to me, she seemed just slightly…furtive. Perhaps guilty?"

"About what?"

"I have no idea. And as I said, you know her better."

His wife frowned. "Could it be because I caught them kissing? Twice?"

"Is Miss Finch so straitlaced?"

"I wouldn't have thought so. Besides, they are engaged. A kiss is not a scandal now." She shook her head, perplexed.

"Is this really your affair?" the duke asked gently.

She had to admit it might not be any of her business. "But I want Harriet to be happy," she replied. "As happy as I am."

"Is that possible?" he teased.

He got the smile he'd hoped for. "Do you imagine we are unique?" she asked.

"My imagination is fertile," he suggested. He met her eyes and held them. "Shall we go in?"

A bit breathlessly, she agreed.

Twelve

No magical solution occurred to Harriet as the first banns loomed closer. When she tried to think about how to approach Ferrington, her brain veered off into memories of those melting kisses. A sly inner voice repeated the temptation—she should simply marry the man. Why not? Parts of her thought it a fine idea. They were not parts she knew well or fully trusted, however.

One sad irony was she'd established a new harmony in her home. The relief was considerable and the idea of losing it hard to contemplate. Her mother was bubbling with good humor and had not asked for the laudanum since the engagement was announced, a heartening sign that she was not too dependent. Harriet's grandfather remained jovial at the dinner table. He hardly barked out any contemptuous criticisms these days. This was partly because he directed his ire at the workmen constructing Winstead Hall's new wing. His increasingly grandiose plans for a celebratory ball were held back by the lack of a ballroom, and he was driving the carpenters to complete it. This outlet for his impatience was a boon for Harriet and her mother, if not for the workers.

And so, in this increasing muddle, they somehow came to the day set for Charlotte and Sarah to arrive for their visit. For weeks, Harriet had looked forward to seeing her old friends. Now she was worried they would think ill of her. No, that was silly. They never had and never would. But they would certainly be surprised at the state of things. Which they would ferret out down to the least detail. She had no doubt about that.

The post chaise came in good time, and the visitors stepped down in a flutter of ruffled skirts and merry greetings. Harriet felt something ease deep inside when she saw their smiling faces. These two—along with Ada Grandison—had been drawn to Harriet by common interests and lively curiosity in their first year at school, at age thirteen. Unlike many of the other girls there, they had not disdained her poverty. They didn't care that Harriet paid for her schooling with household chores and teaching younger, slower students. Their steady friendship had helped Harriet endure the many little slights and disparaging remarks thrown her way, and even the school's dancing master's disgusting little compliments, whispered in *her* ear because she was poor and powerless. They had become her extended family when Harriet had no one but her mother. Together, the four of them had discovered a love of solving mysteries and had a number of successes. Indeed, they had helped uncover an ancient lost treasure and made Ada's happy marriage to her indigent duke possible. It was a delight to have them with her.

Here was Sarah, a smiling, round little person with sandy hair, pale brows and eyelashes, and a sprinkling of freckles. Sarah's light-blue eyes sparkled with intelligence, and her head was full of esoteric bits of knowledge gleaned from constant reading. She was a scholar and a peacemaker, and her even temperament was always a comfort.

Beside her, Charlotte was much taller, her stature made more pronounced by a slender frame. She had black hair, pale skin, a sharp, dark gaze, and was the most methodical person Harriet had ever known. Charlotte could draw charts that reduced the knottiest problem to precise order. She also cut roast beef into precise bits, all the same size, before eating them. There was a constant edge of dispassionate analysis in those eyes.

"It's been such an age since we saw you," exclaimed Sarah.

These summer weeks had been both like and unlike the school holidays. They'd come back together after being separated. But the reunion was not really the same. The absences would only increase as they established themselves. Ada was already gone. The others would soon follow into whatever fate life brought them. But they were here now, and Harriet was very glad. "Come in and say hello to Mama," she said. "Grandfather is occupied, but you will see him at dinner."

They exchanged looks that perfectly conveyed their mixed attitude toward Mr. Winstead. Harriet loved how much they could say without words and the similarity of their opinions.

"Here are Sarah and Charlotte," Harriet said when they reached her mother's sitting room.

"Oh!" Mama dropped her sewing and stood. "You've come. Harriet has missed you so."

"And we, her," replied Charlotte.

"Of course, now that she is engaged, she has other things to think about as well."

Naturally Mama would mention this immediately. It was foremost in her thoughts. Harriet had foreseen this.

"Engaged?" cried Sarah. "What, when...?" She glanced at Charlotte to see if she had known. Charlotte shook her head. "How could you not write us about that?"

"It's quite recent," said Harriet.

"Well, who is he? My goodness, Harriet."

"The Earl of Ferrington," answered her mother, her face glowing with pride.

"Lady Wilton's missing heir?" Sarah's blue eyes went round. "You found him?"

"More than found apparently," said Charlotte with raised brows. "Found, beguiled, and bagged, all in a few weeks."

Harriet frowned at her. The word *bagged* was an obvious provocation, but she wasn't going to be baited.

"And you solved the mystery without us," said Sarah.

"The Terefords did most of it."

"Are they here?" asked Charlotte.

"Staying at Ferrington Hall. Lady Wilton sent them up."

"I wouldn't think the duke would submit to being sent," said Sarah.

Harriet shrugged. "You know Lady Wilton."

They'd all seen this lady's dictatorial ways during the past season. Harriet didn't intend to mention the letter about the Travelers that had brought the duke and duchess here. Not yet at any rate. She was used to telling her friends everything. But the story of the rogue earl was...complicated.

Charlotte gazed at her as if she could see her ambivalence. "It seems there's been a great deal going on. How did the Terefords recover the missing earl? Where was he?"

"And how did you fall in love with him?" asked Sarah. "I want to hear everything."

"Everything," echoed Charlotte.

"The duke is very clever," said Harriet's mother.

"And Cecelia is even more so," said Harriet.

"Indeed. And so they..." Charlotte raised her eyebrows and waited.

"Found him," said Harriet. She glanced at her mother and then back at her friends.

They got the point and fell silent. There was a short silence, indicating that Sarah and particularly Charlotte would require more than this. Eventually.

"You must invite your earl to call immediately," said Sarah then. "We have to make certain he's worthy of you." She smiled to show she was joking.

Harriet's mother was not amused. In fact, she looked worried. "He's very kind, a true gentleman," she declared.

"You like him?" asked Charlotte.

"Anyone would. You mustn't...play any of your tricks."

"I was only funning, Mrs. Finch," said Sarah. "Any man Harriet has chosen must be wonderful. Her standards are so high." She smiled at Harriet.

Her friends had teased her about this during the season. They hadn't understood what it was like to be a newfound heiress, tossed into the marriage mart like a fox among the hounds. *Sarah* had never been courted with blatant calculation or totted up like a column of numbers. During her time in London, Harriet had seen so many varieties of greed—desperate, arrogant, pathetic, relentless. Smiles and flowery compliments might hide mercenary motives for a while, but something had always revealed the grubby truth in her town suitors. Her rogue earl had shown no trace of that, another mark in his favor and reason for her heart to ache.

"Your grandfather must be pleased," Charlotte said to her. "An earl."

"Yes." Harriet had never been on the opposite side of one of Charlotte's probes. Her friend's tenacity, which she'd always admired, was less pleasing now that Harriet was a mystery herself. "Shall we have some tea?" she asked.

Her mother frowned at her. "You should show them to their rooms, Harriet. They will want to settle in. They haven't even taken off their bonnets."

At any other visit, she would have been eager to get her friends alone for a good talk. This time, it would be more like an interrogation.

"I should like to see my room," replied Charlotte, confirming her conclusions.

Harriet gave in. The questions had to come. And she *wanted* to tell her friends what had happened. She just didn't want them to think ill of her.

"All right, what's going on?" asked Charlotte as soon as they were alone in her bedchamber. "Did your grandfather force you into this engagement?"

Sarah gaped at her, then turned to Harriet.

"How could he?" Harriet asked.

"By threatening to change his will again," replied Charlotte impatiently. "That's the sort of thing tyrannical old people do. And he is among the most tyrannical."

They knew her too well. She hadn't fooled Charlotte in a long time. "Let us sit down at least."

Bonnets, gloves, and shawls were shed. Sarah and Charlotte took armchairs, and Harriet sat on the bed. It might have been any cozy afternoon in the past six years. But it wasn't.

"It all began with a rogue," said Harriet.

Charlotte frowned.

"Soon after we arrived here, I walked over to Ferrington Hall, which I supposed to be empty. I wanted to see the place because Lady Wilton had made such a mystery of her missing relative."

Her friends nodded, perfectly in harmony with this mission.

"I found a…fellow lurking about there. I thought he was from the Travelers' camp nearby. Perhaps planning to rob the place. But he didn't seem just like them, and…"

"He turned out to be the missing earl," said Charlotte with the air of one cutting to the chase.

Harriet nodded.

"How did you know that?" asked Sarah.

"It is a simple logical progression," Charlotte said. "An unidentified gentleman surveying the hall. An heir gone missing. Harriet centering her tale on this person. Who is he likely to be?"

"Easy to see in retrospect," Harriet commented acidly. "As many things are."

"I expect it was not so clear at the time," said Sarah.

"Precisely."

"Because Harriet was falling in love with him," Charlotte replied. "I've noticed love clouds one's perceptions to a marked degree. It is sad to see."

"I wasn't." But she had been, Harriet acknowledged. When he was the rogue. Her plans for a free-wheeling future flitted through her mind.

"All very obvious," finished Charlotte in her most superior tone.

"Charlotte the all-knowing," said Sarah.

"I can follow a clear train of logic."

"Like the time you were convinced that workman was a spy for Napoleon," said Sarah.

Charlotte glared at her. "He was skulking beneath the school building."

"He was checking the drains," said Harriet.

"I was fourteen. You are not."

That was inarguable, Harriet acknowledged. She was nearly twenty, and she'd been taken in by her own rosy imaginings.

"If you were not falling in love with him, why did you end up engaged to him?" asked Charlotte. She was clearly not to be diverted.

"And how did he propose?" asked Sarah. "You must have been so downcast, since your grandfather insists on a great match. And then, like a miracle, the lurker turned out to be an earl."

"Ugh," said Charlotte. "You are so romantical, Sarah.

Next you will be comparing Ferrington to a knight of the grail or some such thing."

"No, I won't. Those days are long gone." She sighed. "So, when he told you, Harriet…"

"He didn't. Cecelia let it drop. And I found out he'd lied to me. He told me he was plain Jack Mere."

"Mere?" repeated Charlotte. "What sort of name is that?"

"Exactly!"

"You might have noticed it sounded odd. *I* would have."

"He told me it wasn't his real name," Harriet admitted.

"Was that when you first met?" Sarah put in, smoothing the waters. "Before you had become well acquainted?"

Harriet nodded. She *had* noticed, of course. She'd just brushed it aside in her headlong plunge into fantasy. "I understand he was wary at first. Lady Wilton was quite unkind to him, and he was…" Wounded, melancholy? "But he had ample time to tell me the truth later."

"What sort of time?" asked Charlotte. "How did you become acquainted with this lurker?"

"I called him a rogue," Harriet said. She thought of the walks, the conversations, the dancing. The kisses.

"Perhaps he didn't tell you because he could see you wanted him to be a rogue," said Sarah. "Not a real one, of course." She shook her head. "A real rogue would have… taken advantage. But a dashing, chivalrous adventurer. And he didn't wish to disappoint you."

The other two stared at her. "That's rather…deep," said Charlotte.

"And you are surprised because?"

"I *wanted* him to be honest," said Harriet. But Sarah's reasoning had struck a chord. She still sometimes wished Ferrington was less earl and more rogue.

Charlotte let out an impatient breath. "I see that, and he should certainly apologize." Examining Harriet's face, she said, "Has he done so?"

"Well, yes."

"And you forgave him," said Sarah happily.

Harriet realized she had, somewhere along the way.

Charlotte eyed her. "So, he turned out to be an earl, and now you are going to marry him. Why aren't you blessing your luck?"

"How did he propose?" asked Sarah again.

Harriet's two best friends focused their keenest gazes on her. There was no deceiving them. Harriet didn't even want to. "It was Mama," she said.

They looked skeptical, well aware of her mother's gentleness.

And with that, the story of her mother's trials and her grandfather's meanness came pouring out. Every bit of it—the lost income, the threats, the laudanum, her rising anxiety, and her making the earl offer for her. "And so, I engaged myself to Lord Ferrington, and now everyone is happy," she ended.

"Everyone," said Sarah uncertainly.

"I don't understand," said Charlotte when she had finished. "Why should the earl give in to your urging?"

"We'd been alone so much," Harriet murmured. "At the camp. Compromising."

Her two friends gazed at her. It was very likely they saw more than Harriet wished.

"I've made a muddle of it. He had no thought of marriage. He is doing the honorable thing. I have to break it off before the first banns are called on Sunday. But then my grandfather will probably throw us out. And I fear Mama will break down completely." Harriet bit her lip. She would also lose Jack the Rogue, which might be worse than all the rest.

Charlotte turned to Sarah. "Clearly we must get to work," she said to her.

Sarah nodded. "The first thing is to meet this rogue person."

"Lord Ferrington," murmured Harriet. They ignored her.

"Undoubtedly," said Charlotte. "We must examine him thoroughly, and then we will see."

"Indeed," replied Sarah.

"I don't think—" began Harriet.

"There is no need for you to do so," interrupted Charlotte. "We are here now."

"You know we will take care of you," said Sarah.

Harriet did, but this wasn't some schoolgirl mishap, and she didn't see what they could do.

⁂

Jack was glad to be invited to call at Winstead Hall. He'd begun to fear Harriet was avoiding him. The fact that he was to meet her visiting friends was a good sign. But also a challenge. The opinions of one's friends could make a difference.

"What if they take against me?" he asked the Duchess of Tereford as she approved the borrowed clothes he'd donned for the call.

"Why would they?"

"Lady Wilton said my manners were not fit for polite society. And presumably these young ladies are part of…"

"*I* am an established member of the *haut ton*," interrupted the duchess. "And James—well, he is a nonpareil."

Jack gazed at her. She looked back, as always the picture of blond perfection with the piercing eyes of a hunting hawk. The *haut ton* was what the English called high society. They'd fought the French for years and yet, for some reason, they used their enemy's language to describe elegance.

"And *we* find your manners perfectly acceptable," added the duchess.

Indeed, he'd seen no sign of the contempt Lady Wilton had predicted. The Terefords hadn't mocked him for his dress or his variable accent or a brief confusion over items of cutlery. And yet Lady Wilton's rejection still rang louder in his consciousness than their cordial welcome. "You are unusual?" he suggested.

She smiled. "We are discerning and intelligent, with exquisite taste. You can rely on our judgment."

"So Lady Wilton…"

"Is an antiquated relic." There was a touch of impatience in her tone, as if she thought he should put this issue behind him.

Jack enjoyed hearing his great-grandmother criticized. He couldn't help it after the way she'd treated him. But he wasn't quite convinced. "Some probably agree with her, and these young ladies might be among them."

"They are not. I am well acquainted with both of them, and they are clever and kind and curious." She smiled again. "They like solving mysteries."

"What? Finding lost thimbles or straying lapdogs?"

"If you wish to turn them against you, say something like that," replied the duchess.

"Like what?" asked her husband, strolling into the drawing room with his usual languid elegance. "And turn whom?"

His wife explained.

"Oh, by no means mention thimbles, Ferrington. Do you remember, Cecelia, when Mrs. Moran asked them to use their skills to find hers? You'd have thought she offered them a mortal insult."

"She was a bit patronizing, James. Also, the thimble was right there, perfectly visible. She'd simply put it on the wrong finger." She turned back to Jack. "These young ladies helped recover a treasure trove that had been lost for centuries."

If she thought this sort of information would ease his nerves, she was mistaken.

"Watch out for Miss Charlotte Deeping," added the duke. "She has a sharp tongue. Practically makes an art of the satirical."

"Oh, James."

"She told young Pelot he was less intelligent than his horse."

The duchess bit her lower lip. "I believe he was about to walk into a lily pond in the park at the time. And his mount was pulling on the leading rein, trying to turn him away."

The duke shrugged. "It's true that a thing doesn't exist for Pelot if he can't hunt it, shoot it, or, er, mount it."

"James!" She shook her head. "That was *not* an example of polished manners," she told Jack.

"Indeed." Both the Terefords' eyes were gleaming with humor, and Jack had to wonder if they really understood how their exalted positions gave them license that a "foreigner" might not be granted. He reminded himself he was an earl.

He set out for his neighbor's house on foot, knowing the walk would ease his nerves. At Winstead Hall, he was admitted like an old friend and conducted to the parlor where Mrs. Finch customarily sat.

The small room was remarkably full today. Beside Harriet and her mother stood the two visitors—a small, sandy-haired girl and a taller, dark one.

Introductions were made. Jack bowed to their curtsies. Everyone sat. Now he would have to produce polite conversation.

Jack longed to see Harriet alone. He wanted to talk more of their future. The idea of creating a family of his own had been growing in his mind. He knew it might not be easy. His parents' match had been tempestuous—loud disputes, fiery reconciliations, and bitterness when his father fell into the abyss of drink for days at a time. But nevertheless, he had hopes. He would never behave so.

And, of course, he wanted to hold Harriet close again. Memories of her lingered in his hands, on his lips. He thought of her constantly, and his dreams were full of her. To be so close and not be able to touch was frustrating.

"So you are the missing earl," said Miss Deeping.

Maybe it was to be not-so-polite conversation. The duke's warning came back to Jack. He wasn't afraid of this slender, sharp-eyed young lady. He was only…wary. "Missing no longer," he answered.

"No, you turned up out of the blue."

The gleam in Miss Deeping's dark eyes told Jack she knew quite well where he'd come from. It seemed Harriet had confided in her friends. But how much? Her mother looked mildly bewildered. "I'd been taking a look around England," he replied. "Seeing my father's country."

"Yes? Which parts precisely?"

"The ones between London and here."

Miss Sarah Moran giggled. "Did you find it very different from America?" she asked. "I would be interested in your views on the comparison."

She spoke like a schoolmaster. Which Jack found odd from a small, delicate-looking girl.

Harriet rose as if there were springs in her legs. "I'll see about refreshments," she said and left the room.

"The servants will bring them," said Mrs. Finch, looking even more bemused.

Miss Deeping leaned forward. Jack found himself drawing back just a little.

Harriet stopped in the corridor outside and leaned against the wall. Of course, the servants had refreshments well in hand. There was no need to ask. She'd just found it too unsettling, sitting there with her rogue earl and her mother and her old friends. She had different ways of speaking to each of them, and she didn't know how to match these up. Time was running out. She had to break off this forced engagement. But she couldn't make herself do it. So she stood there and eavesdropped, well aware she should not.

"The two countries have many things in common and others that are different," said Ferrington.

He sounded uncharacteristically stiff.

"Can you be more specific?" asked Sarah.

"Harriet said the Terefords are staying with you," Charlotte put in.

"Yes."

"It was the duke who found you, I understand." Charlotte was in full interrogation mode.

"He did, er, track me down." Before she could go on, he added, "He lent me this coat as well. They are determined to make me fashionable."

"Are you interested in fashion?" asked Charlotte.

"No, are you?"

"Is that a comment on my attire, Lord Ferrington?"

"It is simply the same question you asked me."

Leaning against the corridor wall, Harriet admired his spirit. People could be offended or intimidated by Charlotte. He was obviously neither.

"Well then, I find fashion tedious and shallow," Charlotte answered.

"There we can agree, Miss Deeping."

"You see," said Harriet's mother. She sounded both relieved and uncertain.

"One large difference between here and Boston is my friends," said Ferrington. "I miss them."

"Oh, you do have friends?"

"Of course he does, Charlotte," said Mama. "Don't be silly."

"A good number, though only a few really close ones."

"That's the way, isn't it?" said Sarah.

"My business partner and some other mates."

"Are you in business?" asked Charlotte.

"What is the matter with you?" said Harriet's mother.

"I am a partner in a shipping concern. And *that* is one of the differences between England and America, it seems. There, one is not despised for such activities."

"You think you are here?"

"Lady Wilton assured me I would be. She warned me never to mention it."

"Oh, Lady Wilton," replied Charlotte dismissively.

"If she didn't want you to make your own way, she shouldn't have thrown your father out," said Harriet's mother, with the fire this topic always inspired in her.

"What were you supposed to do?" asked Sarah. "Starve?"

"That is rather what I thought." He sounded surprised.

Harriet felt a surge of warmth for her friends as well as Mama. They were sensible, sympathetic people.

"Lady Wilton is a goose," added Charlotte. "One of those ill-tempered ones who dashes at people, flapping and squawking."

Sarah giggled.

"I was told she is one of the chief arbiters of polite society," said Ferrington.

"By whom?" asked Charlotte.

"Well…"

"Lady Wilton herself?"

"Ah. Yes."

"There you are then."

Harriet could visualize the gesture Charlotte always made when she'd scored a point in an argument.

"You are not what I expected," said Ferrington.

"How so?" asked Sarah.

"I was told society people would disapprove of…everything about me."

"By?" asked Charlotte acidly.

"Ah. Lady Wilton."

"I must say that woman has far too many opinions," declared Harriet's mother. "Nearly all of them wrongheaded."

The laughter that followed both pleased and concerned Harriet. It was pleasant to hear him finding common ground with her friends and family. Except… What was that going to accomplish? Beyond making things harder when she broke the engagement.

"The high sticklers in society don't think much of me," said Charlotte. "And the feeling is mutual."

"You don't care?" Ferrington asked.

"About them? No."

"You have to pick and choose among the people you meet," said Sarah.

"But can you? I was told…"

He stopped. Harriet could imagine Charlotte and Sarah cocking their heads at him. She had exchanged knowing looks with her friends so many times that she could see them in her mind's eye.

"Right," said Ferrington. "Lady Wilton."

"Where in the world can Harriet be?" wondered her mother.

She could be at a loss, Harriet thought. She had to go back. A muted rattle made her turn, and there was one of the housemaids a few feet away, holding a tray. She looked puzzled. Harriet nodded as if lurking in the corridor when she had visitors was not at all strange, beckoned, and stepped back into the parlor. "Here we are," she said.

The maid came in behind her, providing a diversion, placed the tray on a low table, and departed.

"Macaroons?" said Harriet.

Charlotte looked at her as if she knew she'd been eavesdropping. Her mother simply stared.

"You didn't tell us Lord Ferrington had a shipping business," said Sarah to Harriet.

She'd half forgotten. Because she'd thought he was a rootless rogue and then a deceptive earl. Instead of seeing an individual, she'd been far too ready with assumptions. She'd called him a shipping clerk, she remembered. Harriet wondered what else she didn't know. Well, scads of things, apparently.

Ferrington kindly refrained from saying so.

"What sort of things do you ship?" Sarah asked him.

"A good deal of machinery. My partner, Nathan, is

fascinated by power looms and that sort of thing. We trade American timber and ore for innovations, as he puts it."

"Harriet's grandfather might be interested… Or, er…" Sarah's face changed. No doubt she'd remembered Harriet would not be uniting two enterprises with a wedding. Not to mention Harriet's disinclination to help her grandfather in any way. Sarah reached for a macaroon and bit into it. "Oh, these are delicious," she added.

❧

Jack lost track of the conversation briefly when Harriet sat across from him. Once she was in a room, it was hard to look elsewhere. She offered him only her profile, however, seeming uncomfortable. Where had she gone for the greater part of his visit so far? For that matter, why had she put off his last two attempts to see her? That was worrisome.

He thought he'd done all right with her friends. He had at least not alienated them. At most, they liked him. But now that they were here, it would be next to impossible to catch Harriet on her own.

A servant came to fetch Mrs. Finch about some household problem. The proper amount of time for a morning call had elapsed. When Jack said perhaps he should be going, no one objected. In fact, he was afraid Harriet looked relieved. He rose to go, hoping she might see him out. She made no move. Feeling thoroughly dissatisfied, he made his farewells and walked out.

He was well down the corridor when he realized he'd

forgotten to deliver the duchess's invitation to dinner in a few days' time. He turned back and was a step away from reentering the parlor when Miss Moran's voice floated out to him. "I really don't see why you want to break it off with him, Harriet," she said.

Jack felt as if someone had thrown a bucket of icy water in his face. He couldn't move.

"I've told you," Harriet replied.

"He seems…acceptable," said Miss Deeping.

"Well, but it seemed to me that you both…"

"Sarah! The engagement is a lie."

Jack surged through the doorway into the parlor. The three young ladies looked startled, none more so than Harriet. "A lie?" he repeated. "What the deuce?"

Harriet stared at him. Her lips parted, but she didn't speak.

"What do you mean by that?" he demanded. Jack caught movement in the corner of his eye. Miss Moran was plucking at Miss Deeping's sleeve and pointing to the door. Miss Deeping shook her head. He wished they would go. "Well?"

"I pushed you to offer…" Harriet began.

"Because you'd been compromised." Jack's world was falling down around his ears. "But now that your society friends are here, you find I'm not good enough after all. Not polished like your London beaus."

"No! It's nothing like that."

Jack made a slashing gesture. Yet he still couldn't quite believe it. There had been more than this between them. He was sure of it.

"Grandfather was nagging at Mama," Harriet began. "He insists…"

"That you marry a nobleman," said Jack. He'd gathered as much. "And I am a thrice-damned earl. So I fulfill his conditions. Quite nearby, too." Jack had never been so insulted in his life or so hurt. "He forced you into it." He waited for her to contradict this.

"No, I…my mother."

"She wanted it, too," Jack said. That had been evident. "When I think how you railed at me for being deceptive…"

Still, she just sat there, offering him nothing.

"Well, you need not worry. I declare the engagement ended."

"A gentleman cannot end an engagement," said Miss Moran. "That is ruinous to a lady's reputation."

"Be quiet, Sarah!" said Harriet.

Jack set his jaw. Even now, he could not do that to her. "I suppose you must do it then."

"I had planned to…"

"So all is going as you wished. My felicitations." He gathered the rags of his dignity and marched out.

෴

Silence fell over the parlor. No one spoke for quite a time, in case he returned again. Finally, Sarah rose and shut the door. Charlotte said, "That didn't go very well."

Harriet was clenching her jaw so hard, it hurt. She'd been witless, idiotic. Why hadn't she explained? The hurt in his eyes had cut her to the quick and rendered her silent. "I must go after him," she said, rising.

The parlor door opened again, and they all jumped. But Harriet's grandfather, not Ferrington, stood there. "The ballroom is ready at last," he said. "Come and see. Where is Linny?"

"There was some question in the kitchen," replied Sarah. She and Charlotte were watching Harriet with concern.

Harriet's grandfather made an impatient gesture. "Typical, she is never around when wanted. But never mind. You will do. Come along and let us talk about the decorations for the ball. Linny's ideas are too plain."

"P-perhaps a bit later, Grandfather," Harriet tried. "I must go and…"

"Nonsense!" he snapped. "There's nothing more important than this. Come along!" He chivied them out with an unanswerable scowl.

Thirteen

JACK NOTICED NOTHING OF THE SULTRY SUMMER DAY ON his march back to Ferrington Hall. He entered through a side door and went up to his bedchamber, staying only long enough to throw off his borrowed garments and put on his own plainer clothes. It felt like resuming his own skin, or emerging from a failed disguise. He slipped out again without seeing the Terefords, though he passed one of the new housemaids in the hall.

He was glad not to see his noble guests. He wasn't ready to tell them what had occurred. In fact, he thought as he strode through the garden, there was no need to inform them at all. The false nature of his engagement was none of their business. The thing would limp on for a bit. Harriet would break it off, and if they wanted reasons, they could ask *her*. No one need know about the plans falling about his ears or the bitter unhappiness in his breast. Indeed, wasn't it time for the duke and duchess to depart? All this talk of acceptance and friendship seemed to be a sham when it came down to it.

That idea brought a picture of an emptier home and himself rattling around within it. His vision of a new family filling the place with happiness shriveled and died, and his mood darkened further.

He'd had no particular goal in mind, but he found his feet taking him to the Travelers' camp.

The scatter of caravans and tents remained just the same. The horses had been moved to fresh pasture. A man coming from the meadow with a brace of rabbits raised his hand in greeting. Another, chopping wood, nodded as Jack passed. A woman tending a pot hung over a fire greeted him with a smile. Once, he had been part of these daily rhythms. Yet he hadn't really been one of them. Here, too, he'd lived on the margins. Tolerated? Was that to be his eternal fate? He noticed some Travelers were packing items away in wooden crates and bundles.

Samia came running up to him. The tiny girl wore a pink dress today, which made her cheeks looks rosier against the sweep of her dark hair. "Good day to you...my lord," she said.

"Please don't call me that."

"Mistress Elena said..."

"She is correct, as always. But I still don't like it." He noticed two youths folding up a small tent. "Are you leaving?" he asked.

Samia shrugged. "In a few days. Mistress Elena will know when it feels right to go." She spoke as if this was commonplace.

Jack walked faster. Samia danced along beside him. He found the wizened old woman in her customary place, at the back of her painted caravan. She sat in the open doorway under the carved overhang, her feet on the lowest step. The kerchief that hid her hair was embroidered with poppies. "Are you going?" he repeated. "I thought you would spend the summer here."

"The countryside in its beauty calls to us," she answered. "You know we like to move."

"But you're welcome on my land. More than you might be elsewhere."

Mistress Elena gazed up at him. "We have used much of the downed wood and the rabbits. We do not care to take too much from a place."

Jack had no answer for that.

"We are tired of those men and their muttering, too." She gestured toward the border with Winstead Hall land with one gnarled hand.

"Perhaps I could convince Mr. Winstead to remove them." He was, after all, a favorite of the old man. For now.

Mistress Elena shrugged. "But we like the road, my lord Earl. It calls us. We make a round, meeting our kin here and there each year."

"I will visit all my cousins in the north," said Samia.

Jack saw they wouldn't be convinced, and that made him feel more alone than ever. Soon this field would be as empty as his life in England seemed destined to be.

"You are sad," said Samia. She turned bright eyes to the old woman. "Shall I read his palm?"

Mistress Elena gave Jack a long, penetrating look. "No, get the cards."

Samia's eyes widened, and her lips made an O. She wriggled around the old woman and into the caravan, returning with a small, silk-wrapped bundle.

The old woman took it and held it in her lap. "These are precious," she said. "They came to me from my grandmother. I don't show them often, lest people be tempted to steal."

Jack watched, curious, as she folded back the silk to reveal a stack of cards. They were a bit larger than a normal deck, and the backs—all he could see—were heavily decorated.

"Samia, bring me that," the old woman said, pointing.

The little girl darted over to a small table, hardly bigger than a chessboard, and brought it to sit before them. She hovered over it with bright anticipation.

"You know that you do not tell what you see," Mistress Elena said to her.

Samia nodded, though she nearly danced in place.

The old woman turned to Jack and indicated a round of tree trunk that functioned as a chair. "Fetch that and sit," she said.

Puzzled and intrigued, he did so and waited to see what came next.

Mistress Elena held the deck with both hands and murmured some words he couldn't hear. He suspected he wouldn't understand them even if he did. Then she spread the cards in a wide fan on the small table. "You will choose three without turning them over," she said. "Be slow. Think well."

Not sure what he was to think about, Jack let his hand hover over the cards. They all looked alike. Finally, he pulled one card each from the left, right, and center of the fan, lining them up in a row before him.

Mistress Elena reached out and turned over the one on Jack's left. What she revealed was not a normal playing card with pips and numbers or kings and queens. Instead, the card showed an odd figure of a man dressed in medieval motley, somewhat awkwardly drawn, with his back to the viewer. He gripped a stick in one hand and what might be a sword over the other shoulder. His profile showed a pointed beard, and a cat pawed at his leg. At the bottom of the card was written *Le Fol*.

"Le Fol," said Mistress Elena in a passable French accent. "The Fool. This card represents your past."

"Well, that's certainly apt. I've been a fool." The words slipped out with more bitterness than Jack meant to reveal.

"It is not so simple as that," replied the old woman. "Or so unfortunate. The Fool is a free spirit. He acts in the moment. He may make mistakes, but he also opens up many possibilities in life."

That might sound good, Jack thought, but a fool was a fool. And he certainly felt like one today.

Mistress Elena turned over the middle card. This one showed a similarly garbed man flanked by two ladies, each with a hand on him while he kept his to himself. Overhead, a strange, half-naked figure surrounded by sunrays aimed an arrow straight at the fellow's head. The label was upside down. He couldn't quite…

"L'Amoureux," said Mistress Elena. "The Lovers. This card stands for the present. But it is reversed and so suggests disharmony, some imbalance come upon you now."

Jack said nothing. This was a bit too apt. Mistress Elena had in no way guided his choices, but still.

"The third card stands for the future," she continued and turned it over.

On this one, a skeletal figure seemed to be digging in tumbled earth. There was no label.

"Ah, La Mort," said Mistress Elena.

"Death?" Jack sat back. Of course, this was all silly superstition. It didn't really mean anything. But the image was unsettling.

"It means endings, change, transformation," said Mistress Elena. "Not dying, necessarily."

"Necessarily?"

"Most often not," she replied.

"Well, that's reassuring." He sounded flip and sarcastic and feared he might have offended her.

But the old woman merely surveyed the three upturned cards. "Draw one more," she commanded.

Partly to humor her and partly to expunge the last picture, he did so, turning it over himself as he chose. On this one, two people stood close together under a large, many-rayed sun disk.

"Le Soleil," said Mistress Elena. Samia forgot herself and clapped her hands. "The Sun indicates warmth and success," continued the old woman. "All will be well for you in the end."

Jack didn't see how. And fortune-tellers always predicted happiness and riches and justice, didn't they? How else would they stay in business? And what was "the end" anyhow? Old age? That didn't help much right now. But he didn't say these things to her.

"You don't believe," said Mistress Elena.

"Not really. I'm sorry."

She merely smiled, myriad wrinkles shifting across her

face. She restacked the cards and wrapped them away again. Then she pointed over Jack's shoulder. "A visitor for you."

His heart leaped, thinking of the times Harriet had sought him here. But when he turned, he saw her mother standing uncertainly at the edge of the camp. Mrs. Finch looked small and pinched and nervous about her surroundings.

Jack rose and went to greet her.

"One of your gardeners saw you come this way," she said. She looked around as if wondering why.

"Is something wrong?" Jack saw she was wringing her hands.

"Sarah said… She *wouldn't* say really. You and Harriet haven't quarreled?"

Mrs. Finch seemed terrified by the prospect, which seemed excessive. Jack was not inclined to tell her what had happened. Let her daughter explain her conduct.

"All is well between you?" the woman added. "I had to come and see. Even though…" She looked around the camp as if she might be accosted at any moment. "Harriet is behaving so strangely lately."

"Is she?" Jack didn't know whether he was glad or sorry to hear it. "How so?"

"First she's sharp-tongued. Then she mopes. She was rude to my father about the ball. I *wish* she would not provoke him."

Jack suspected it was difficult not to, from what he'd seen of Mr. Winstead.

The hand-wringing had returned. "Papa is so very happy about this match. Things have been so much easier."

That would soon end, Jack noted. He was sorry for her, but it was not his fault.

"I thought all was well, with Harriet's affections engaged in a match he approves." She frowned at him. "Nothing must go wrong!"

But Jack had been transfixed by one word. "Affections?"

"What?" Harriet's mother looked confused.

"You said her affections were engaged."

"Of course."

"You seem certain."

Mrs. Finch peered up at him, her face creased with worry. "Is this the trouble? I know my daughter, my lord. I can assure you they are."

Jack felt a tendril of—not hope, but speculation.

His visitor put a hand on his arm. "If you thought otherwise, you are wrong." All trace of timidity had disappeared from her voice and stance.

"Umm," said Jack. He would have to learn more about this.

"Nothing is wrong between you? Nothing about the banns?" The small woman looked ready to shake an answer out of him.

"What?"

"They will be calling the banns in church on Sunday. Sarah seemed to think... I didn't understand why she should care about that. It is all settled."

"Banns. Ah, that is an official announcement of the engagement. To the whole neighborhood."

Mrs. Finch nodded, frowning at him.

"No denying things after that," Jack noted.

Her fingers tightened on his arm, an iron grip. "Why would you wish to do so? Tell me you do not!"

He needed time, Jack concluded. There were matters to explore. He shook his head, allowing her to take it as a denial. "Allow me to introduce you to Mistress Elena," he said as a distraction.

"Who?"

"The leader of the Travelers." He gestured toward her caravan.

"That's an old woman," said Mrs. Finch.

"Yes."

"She can't be the leader."

"They look to her to make decisions," Jack replied.

Mrs. Finch stared. She seemed both fascinated and scandalized by the idea. "My father says Travelers are filthy thieves," she said.

"He is wrong."

She glanced up at him, startled and perhaps pleased, and then back at Mistress Elena. "I shouldn't."

"It would be courteous to say hello as you have come to their camp."

The threat of rudeness swayed her. She followed Jack to the caravan, and he performed the introductions.

"Are you really the leader?" Mrs. Finch looked around, her gaze pausing at various large, muscular men as if expecting one of them to come up and contradict the claim.

"They look to me for counsel," said Mistress Elena. "Wisdom comes with years."

"Not for me," said Mrs. Finch.

"Maybe you aren't old enough," said Samia.

The visitor looked down at her in astonishment, whether because a small child had expressed this opinion or at the notion itself, Jack could not tell. "I feel old," said Mrs. Finch.

"Wait until you are four score and see," replied Mistress Elena.

"Four score! I can't imagine it."

"You will find much happiness at that age," said the old Traveler.

"How can you...?"

"I see it."

Mrs. Finch blinked at her. She took in Samia's emphatic nod and Jack's shrug, then shook her head. "I don't think that's likely."

"Unlikely things happen every day."

"Not to me." Mrs. Finch shook her head again. "I must go. It was...interesting to meet you."

Mistress Elena bowed her head in acknowledgment.

"I will escort you home," said Jack to Harriet's mother.

She seemed glad to take his arm and move out of the camp. They walked in silence for a bit, Mrs. Finch thoughtful. Finally, she said, "How could she think I would be happy? Those times are gone."

"What times?"

She waved his question aside. "Never mind."

"Please. I would like to hear about when you were most happy." Jack had actually found this a telling question as he was making new friends. People's replies revealed a great deal.

"I shouldn't say," she answered.

"Why not? Is the answer scandalous?"

"No!" She tapped his arm with her free hand. "Of course not."

"Well then?"

"It is just… I was happiest when I lived alone."

"Indeed?" This surprised him. If he'd had to guess, he would have mentioned a time when her husband was alive.

"You think that very selfish."

"No, I don't."

"Harriet was at school," Mrs. Finch added hurriedly. "I knew she was all right, even though she had…difficulties there. She had good friends as well. She wrote to me about them. Sarah and Charlotte are two of the closest."

Jack nodded encouragingly.

"I remained at our cottage in Tunbridge Wells. It is…was small but very cozy."

"You weren't lonely?"

She looked surprised he should ask. "I have… I had a wide acquaintance among ladies in the town who enjoyed fine needlework. There are a great many of those living there. People call the town stodgy, but I never found it so. I taught fancywork to a group of girls as well. We would gather every Wednesday." She sounded wistful. "And I had a small room at the front of the house where I exhibited my embroidery. There's no sense keeping it all in chests and wardrobes, you know."

Jack wondered how much of the stuff there was.

"Especially when someone might need a lovely collar or wristbands. Even a fine tablecloth."

"It was like a shop?" said Jack.

Mrs. Finch flushed bright red as if he'd accused her of obscenity. "Nothing like that!" she exclaimed. "It was simply a place where friends and acquaintances might find beautiful things."

"They didn't pay you for your work?" Jack was too surprised to be tactful.

"Of course not! They sometimes, if they cared to, offered the cost of the silks. Which can be quite dear. But they never… I never asked… There was no question of…"

"Of course," interrupted Jack. "I understand perfectly now."

They walked a while in silence as she calmed down. Her hand actually trembled on his arm.

"You long for that life," Jack suggested when she had recovered.

"Oh yes, so much."

"Why not go back to Tunbridge Wells then?"

"Oh, I can't afford that anymore."

Jack thought if she actually opened a shop and charged a fair price for her needlework, she might be able to afford it. But that was clearly out of the question for Mrs. Finch. And perhaps those friends and acquaintances wouldn't patronize a shop as they did her home. "Your father wouldn't give…"

Mrs. Finch stopped short and dug her fingers into his forearm. "You won't tell him what I said."

She was really frightened of old Winstead. The man must be even more unpleasant than he'd thought. "No. Not a word."

Her grip eased. As they started walking again, she threw

him uneasy glances. Jack wondered what was going through her mind.

"I shall like living at Ferrington Hall," she said after a while. "If that is what you really... I mean, Harriet suggested... Of course, I would never expect... Only Harriet thought..." She became tangled up in words and subsided.

She'd thought of her dependence on him, Jack realized. It was either him or her tyrannical father. She had no other choices. The idea was distasteful. He didn't want to be one of the many things this small woman apparently feared. Yet he wasn't certain how to reassure her without rousing more anxiety. He settled for, "You are very welcome."

Mrs. Finch's face relaxed. They had come to the edge of the Winstead Hall gardens. "I will leave you here," said Jack.

"You won't come in?"

"Not just now." He wasn't ready to face Harriet yet. He had a good deal to think about. But more than that, he wanted to move, to act. Since he'd come to England, he'd spent far too much time reacting to other people's wishes and opinions, Jack decided. He'd imagined that, in a foreign country, they knew best. But they—in particular his great-grandmother Lady Wilton—did not. Not for him. A restlessness that had been building in him burst out. He was accustomed to making decisions and seeing them carried out. He was good at it. More often than not, he'd been right. It was time to see what he could do here and now. Ideas began to surface as he strode home.

Back at Ferrington Hall, Jack searched out the duke. He found him in the drawing room behind an open newspaper.

Tereford closed the pages when Jack came in, saying, "There's a certain futility in day-old news. It is over. There's nothing to be done. Should one even read it?"

This probably qualified as a witticism. It was at least an invitation to exchange the kind of banter Jack found pointless. He shrugged. "You mentioned a man of business who could manage all sorts of matters."

The duke put the newspaper aside. "Dalton, yes. Cecelia thinks very highly of his firm."

She would have made certain they were competent, Jack thought. "I should like to write to him."

"Cecelia can give you his direction. She will have it neatly listed."

Jack was sure she would. "Do you know of a place called Tunbridge Wells?" he went on.

"Tunbridge Wells?" The duke looked surprised at the change of topic.

"It's a town, I understand. Do you know where it is?"

"About twenty miles east of here. But, my dear Ferrington, you don't want anything to do with Tunbridge Wells. It's full of terrifying dowagers and fubsy-faced widows. Dreadfully unfashionable."

"Is it?" Jack saw this as a point in its favor.

"It is. Whence comes this odd request?" Tereford's blue eyes had grown curious.

Jack saw no need to explain himself. "Call it a whim," he replied. He had heard the duke say this to his wife.

Perhaps the man remembered because he smiled. "I see."

Jack turned to go, the letter he would send this Dalton

fellow already forming in his mind. Then he remembered another point. "This calling of banns in the church," he said, turning back. "I'm not familiar with the process as I have never set out to marry before. They are quite a public announcement, it seems."

"Yes, but they aren't necessary," replied the duke.

"Oh? Mr. Winstead seemed to think they were important."

"He might not know, because banns are customary for… country people."

"And grubby tradesmen?" Jack suggested, unable to resist.

"You make too much of this label, Ferrington."

Having just seen Mrs. Finch's reaction to the idea she'd run a shop, Jack doubted this. "Banns," he repeated.

The duke nodded. "Having just gotten married myself, I am familiar with the process. You need not post banns. You can procure a common license and marry in a parish where one of the couple has lived for at least four weeks, as Miss Finch has here, of course."

"I see." This simplified matters. He could gain a bit of time to discover if Harriet's mother was right about her affections. As long as he convinced her grandfather to use this method rather than public banns. Jack had a few thoughts about how that could be accomplished, and he expected to enjoy besting the old man.

"You apply at the registry for the jurisdiction," the duke continued. "I don't know where that is in this case, but someone will. You give your oath there are no impediments to the marriage, and the thing is done."

No impediments except the bride's determination to break

it off. Despite the fact that her affections were engaged. Jack clung to this phrase. "That is helpful," he said. "Thank you."

"Of course. No waiting for three weeks, eh? Marry whenever you like."

He hadn't thought of that.

"Three weeks for what?" asked the duchess, coming through the half-open door.

"The wedding," answered her husband. "I was telling Ferrington how to procure a license. So they needn't wait for banns."

"Oh."

It was one simple, short word, but Jack heard an odd uncertainty in it. The duchess was Harriet's friend. She might know more than he wished to discuss just now. "I should inquire about this registry," he replied before she could say anything else. And with a brief bow, he left them.

❧

"And once they are married, we can be on our way," the duke said to his wife.

Cecelia looked at him. "You are eager to go."

"Cornwall is lovely at this time of year," he answered. He came to put an arm around her. "And this… What is the place called?"

"Tresigan House."

"Right. It's said to be picturesque."

"I told you that. And you know it is probably falling to pieces."

"Prime for your talents then," he replied.

Cecelia hid a smile. "And why would you be less bored there than here?"

"That place belongs to me. I can order people about more."

She had to laugh. "Ferrington Hall is good practice for your neglected estates. Putting a house in order is more than just repairs and dusting, you know."

"What do you mean?"

"A house is people as well as buildings. And since you don't intend to live in all the ones you own, they will need inhabitants."

"Good caretakers, of course."

"Or more than that," she said. "Look at this place. It felt so neglected when we arrived, even though the Rileys were conscientious. Then Ferrington came, and soon…"

"Your friend Miss Finch will add her homely touches," James finished.

Cecelia hesitated. The future looked far from certain just now. She settled for, "A home should be loved."

James looked down at her with a mixture of fondness and exasperation. "Are you proposing we install people in all the Tereford properties who will…love them?"

"I like the idea."

"It's mad, Cecelia. Also, they belong to me. If anyone is going to love them…"

"You will?" She gazed up at him, savoring the feel of his arm around her.

"I love you," he replied. And kissed her.

This was unanswerably sweet. Cecelia leaned into his arms.

"You can love them, and I will love you," he murmured against her lips.

The next kiss was searing.

They might have different philosophies on estate restoration, Cecelia thought before she was swept away by desire, but on this they always agreed.

Fourteen

HAVING DECIDED TO TAKE CONTROL OF HIS DESTINY, Jack wasted no time in laying plans. Convinced that advance preparations were never wasted, he made a variety of arrangements and then caught up with the duke again as Tereford returned from his daily ride. Jack caught him as he came in from the stables. "Had a good gallop?"

"Capital. I've become rather fond of Blaze."

This was one of the horses Jack had bought from the Travelers. Jack thought the duke was surprised by its quality as well as rather bored at Ferrington Hall. Tereford usually went to Brighton in the summer, he understood, and then on to large house parties. Certainly, his houseguest was accustomed to far more society than he found in this neighborhood.

"Would you consider selling him to me?" Tereford went on.

"Of course, if you like. There are some other promising horses at the camp as well."

"Perhaps I'll have a look," said the duke.

"You should go soon if you wish it. They will be moving on in the next few days." The idea still saddened Jack.

Tereford nodded and started to move on toward the house.

Jack fell in beside him. "I am going to see Mr. Winstead," he said.

"Oh, yes?"

"I wondered if I might ask your advice?"

"Of course." They walked into the study and sat down.

"What do know about Winstead's business?" Jack asked then.

"Nothing whatsoever."

"And you make a point of not learning."

"Well, he's in trade."

"Which is some sort of stigma? Similar to a plague? So a noble Englishman must avoid any contact lest he be sullied?"

The duke laughed. "I wouldn't go so far as that. It is simply thought to be..."

"Distasteful? Grubby? Vulgar?" Lady Wilton had certainly said as much.

Tereford shrugged. "I suppose there's a good deal of envy involved. Fortunes are being made in trade these days, while some of the ancient families teeter on the edge of ruin."

"We may be in rags, but we have our lineage?" Jack suggested.

The duke examined him. "You are going to be a breath of fresh air in the House of Lords."

Would he be? Jack wasn't certain whether he'd bother. On the other hand, he could imagine speeches that would make these lords sit up and take notice.

"But all I know is Winstead does some sort of trading," Tereford added. "You should ask him. I daresay he would be happy to tell you about his business."

Jack nodded. Perhaps he would. It might even be interesting.

"You're going to speak to him about the marriage settlements?"

Jack allowed him to think so.

He was received at Winstead Hall with a gratifying show of welcome and only a trace of surprise when he asked for its master rather than his fiancée. After a brief wait, he was ushered into Mr. Winstead's study. A cowed young man, being hustled out as he entered the room, threw him a covert, curious glance. "The Earl of Ferrington," Winstead said as he shooed the fellow away. "Going to marry my granddaughter."

The young man murmured something that might have been a congratulation.

"You get that letter to Grankle today," Winstead added.

"Yes, sir." The weedy lad put a hand on his coat pocket as if to assure himself of its contents and went out.

"Sit down, my lord. You'll take something, I hope? A glass of wine."

Jack accepted the offer and the chair. Winstead, small and round but not the least jolly, sat down behind his large desk. He reminded Jack of a drawing he'd once seen in a book of fairy tales—a crafty gnome preparing to cheat the hero out of a hidden treasure. And then cut off his head, if Jack remembered correctly.

"I expect you're here to discuss the marriage settlements, eh?" the older man continued.

There was to be no pretense of polite conversation then. Jack was relieved, as he had none to offer.

"Best to get things clear." Winstead probably thought he was smiling. The effect was something else entirely.

Predatory, Jack decided. "You needn't worry that I'll try to cozen you. We'll have the documents drawn up all right and tight. The money to be settled on her at marriage. No loopholes for backing out." He laughed as if this was a joke.

Jack tried to imagine having a granddaughter he would bargain over in this way. Without even mentioning her name. He couldn't. He'd run a business. He'd negotiated bargains and made the best terms he could. But not about people he loved. Obviously, Winstead loved no one. Jack's idea of asking about the man's trade and possibly exploring some joint efforts died a definitive death. "There's the matter of banns," he said.

"Yes?" Winstead instantly looked suspicious. Clearly, it was his natural state.

"There's no need…"

"Has that granddaughter of mine done something to put you off?" Winstead interrupted. "I'll soon teach her better if she has. Don't you worry about *that*!"

"No," Jack began.

"You can't shab off now. Try it and I'll ruin you." His scowl was ferocious.

He was one of those men who must have every detail go his way or he threw a fit of temper. Jack had seen them before, and he didn't think much of them. For them, power was oppression. It came to him that he could not leave Harriet and her mother in the clutches of this man, whatever happened. "There's no question of that," he said.

"There had better not be. I'll make you pay."

Jack didn't think his influence would extend into the ranks

of the English nobility. But there was his partner in Boston to consider. They did business in England. Jack summoned his father's most refined accent. "It is simply that I've discovered banns are a bit…common," he drawled. "Tereford told me so." Let Winstead chew on that—the pronouncement of a duke.

"Eh?" The old man was brought up short. "Common?"

"And unnecessary," Jack added. "The duke himself simply procured a license from the proper registry." Parroting what Tereford had told him, he sounded supremely confident, which was the idea.

"We always did the banns," Winstead replied.

Jack let the remark sit. He tried to look like an aristocrat pretending not to notice a social lapse.

Seemingly he succeeded, because Winstead flushed.

"I thought I would take the duke as my model," Jack said, heaping coals on his head.

"What's this registry?" the older man growled.

"I intend to look into that."

"I'll find out." Winstead glowered. He had a broad repertoire of threatening expressions. "I'll brook no delays. And if you think you'll see a cent of my money before the knot is tied…"

"This is actually faster than banns, I believe."

Winstead glared. He didn't like being opposed, even when he was being given something he wanted. He would almost…almost prefer to throw it away. But not quite. How had Harriet and her kindly mother resulted from such a forebear? The man was a monster of selfishness, and the sooner they got away from him, the better. However that separation was accomplished.

Could it not be marriage? The pang that followed this thought laid Jack's soul bare—he loved Harriet. With all his heart. This had made her denial of the engagement a greater blow than any rejection from society. He adored her. If she did not love him, then…a sudden pain twisted in his chest. But her mother had been sure about her affections. Jack sat straighter. Whatever the truth, the first step was to wrest control of the situation from this tyrant. He was quite able to do *that*. "So we are agreed. There will be no banns. I will procure a license…"

"I'm to trust you to do it then?"

Had Winstead bullied his way to commercial success? Jack supposed he had. Such things happened, unfortunately. "Tereford said the bridegroom generally does." He was wielding the duke's name like a duelist's sword.

Winstead growled what might have been an assent. "I'll tell the vicar there's to be no banns," he said, reasserting his primacy. "Useless fellow might have let me know about the license," he muttered. He glared at Jack. "You'd best have it in hand before the ball."

"The…oh yes." He'd heard there was to be a ball. Winstead had been lashing his builders along to finish his new ballroom.

"I'll have the whole neighborhood here, and I want everything in order." Winstead leaned forward, bracing for an argument.

Jack refused the gambit. "Indeed." He rose to go.

"What about the settlements?"

Right, he was expected to care about those. "Perhaps you could have something drawn up?"

"You would allow that?" Winstead seemed incredulous.

"I can look the documents over, and we can discuss any points of contention." Actually he would ask the duchess to read the things. She would ferret out anything that needed negotiating. If he was getting married. He so hoped he was.

Smirking like a man who's put something over on a rival, Winstead stood. "Very well, my lord. I shall have the papers for you in a few days."

Jack nodded and, gratefully, took his leave. Once they were married—should they be married—he and Harriet would spend as little time as possible with her grandfather, he decided.

"I shall expect to hear you have the license," Winstead called after him.

Of course, he had to have the last word. With a wave of his hand, Jack gave it to him and made his escape.

❧

"You have just missed him," the Duchess of Tereford told Harriet not long after Ferrington had gone out that day. "I believe he went to see your grandfather."

"He what?"

"James said he intended to discuss the marriage settlements."

That couldn't be right. Not after their last encounter

when everything had gone so wrong and she'd been too tongue-tied to explain. Harriet had come to Ferrington Hall today to do so and set things right.

"Is that surprising?" Cecelia asked. "Why shouldn't he? It must be done."

Only if they were to wed. Harriet wasn't certain of that after she had so wounded the man she…loved. During a dark, tearful night, Harriet had faced it. She loved Jack the rogue earl, and she had hurt him. The look in his dark eyes when he'd come back into the room after overhearing their careless talk had cut her to the quick. Her throat had been tight with remorse, her mind frozen.

"Will you tell me what's wrong?" asked Cecelia.

Harriet looked at her beautiful, concerned friend—the perfect duchess, with a perfect life.

"I want you to be happy," Cecelia added. "I would like to help."

As did Sarah and Charlotte and her mother as well, should Mama learn there was a threat to their settled future. Which must not happen! Harriet did not need another helper. She had a surfeit of those and a dearth of solutions. "I merely wanted to speak to Ferrington," she said. "Will you tell him so?"

"Of course. I'm sure he'll call on you as soon as he learns you wish it."

But he did not.

Harriet returned to Winstead Hall. She chatted and strolled in the garden with her friends. She changed her dress and went down to dinner without having heard from the rogue earl. It seemed he was refusing to see her. Silently. So she didn't know if he was angry or despondent or vengeful. Was he longing to be free of the engagement now? The uncertainty was driving her to distraction. Her friends were giving her concerned looks. Finally, although she tried to avoid conversation with her grandfather whenever possible, she had to ask him, "Did Ferrington call today?"

"Yes, he came to see me."

"What did he...did you talk about?" Harriet asked, avoiding her mother's worried glance.

Her grandfather dabbed gravy from his lips. "Settlements. Nothing that need concern you."

Of course not. It was only her life, her future. Why should she be concerned about *that*? Or why a man who did not answer her summons was talking to her grandfather about them? A familiar anger rose in Harriet.

"The fellow is clever," added her grandfather. "He knows his own mind. Not that he'll get the better of me." His laugh grated.

Harriet couldn't keep quiet, even though her mother obviously wished she would. "Clever about what?" she asked.

"There are to be no banns," was the astonishing response. "It's more fashionable to get a license from the registry. The duke said so."

"The duke?" Grandfather didn't chat with the duke. They'd barely exchanged three words when they'd last been in a room together.

"Well, he told Ferrington as much. The earl will procure the license, and then we can set the ceremony whenever we like, you see. No need to wait three weeks. The vicar is a fool. I've always said so."

"No banns," murmured Harriet. That meant she had no public announcement looming over her. But did it also signify the earl didn't want to be pushed into marriage? She had to speak to him!

As soon as they rose from the table, Harriet sent a note over to Ferrington Hall, with orders for the messenger to await a reply. It came from Cecelia. The earl had gone away for a few days. She wasn't certain where. James did not know either. Ferrington had left before Cecelia had an opportunity to pass along Harriet's summons, as she had not been aware of his plan to go.

Harriet sat in the drawing room with the open page in her lap. Gone? Where had he gone?

Sarah and Charlotte came and dragged her over to the pianoforte, where they pretended to look over music they might play. "What has happened?" asked Charlotte "You look dreadful."

"Thank you, Charlotte," replied Harriet.

"You did seem shocked when you read that note," said Sarah.

Harriet had always valued her observant friends. But in the past, they had not been observing *her*. "Ferrington has gone away."

"Where?" wondered Sarah.

"Cecelia does not know. Nor the duke."

"Perhaps he went to get the license your grandfather spoke of," Sarah suggested.

"Cecelia said he had gone for a few days."

"The license shouldn't take that long," said Charlotte.

"And why would he be procuring one when we are not... not to be wed?" Harriet stumbled over the phrase.

"That's easy," answered Charlotte. "To remove the threat of the banns."

"Threat?"

"Well, the last time I saw Lord Ferrington, he was extremely angry and wanted to end the engagement himself. So he wouldn't want to be pushed by the posting of banns."

The words were like a blow. "Is that how he seemed to you?"

"Of course. How else would he be?"

Charlotte's famous bluntness could be unwelcome, Harriet observed.

"I thought he was surprised," said Sarah.

"*He* was?" said Charlotte. "He popped back into the room like a jack-in-the-box. Ha, he calls himself Jack, does he not?"

"And hurt," Sarah added, ignoring the jest. "Which he had some right to be, perhaps."

Harriet winced.

"*He* did?" said Charlotte.

"Stop saying *he* as if it referred to some bizarre, alien creature," said Harriet.

"Perhaps it does."

"I wish you would stop quizzing me, Charlotte."

"I won't."

"Because you are determined to be annoying."

"No, because you are one of my dearest friends, Harriet,

and I care about you. Also, I know you rather well, and I can see you are not telling us everything."

"I don't have to tell you everything," Harriet retorted.

"Very true. You have a right to your secrets. I want to help, however."

Sarah nodded in agreement.

"And we can't do that if we don't know what it is you really want," Charlotte finished.

And wouldn't it be nice if she had the least idea? As she shook her head, Harriet realized she was very glad she was still engaged. She shouldn't be, perhaps. But she was. She decided to keep that inconvenient fact to herself.

Fifteen

COMPLETION OF THE BALLROOM SENT HARRIET'S GRAND-father into a frenzy of planning for his grand ball. He wanted everything done at once and made no allowances for timing in invitations. He seemed to think he could summon the entire neighborhood for one week hence and have them all fall into line. Irritatingly, he appeared to be right. Acceptances flowed in, lured perhaps by the promise of a duke and duchess in attendance. Her grandfather reveled in what he deemed his social success and harried the servants at Winstead Hall from task to task, contributing more to disorganization than to accomplishments, in Harriet's opinion. He didn't seem to know Ferrington was away, and no one mentioned it to him. It was not as if he cared to hear anyone's voice but his own.

Whenever she could get away, Harriet took to walking in the woods alone. It was a relief to be away from her grand-father's manic gloating and her friends' constant concern. There was peace among the trees, though each turn of the path reminded her of happier days here with Jack the Rogue. Where had he gone?

As she returned to Winstead Hall on the third day of Ferrington's absence, Charlotte and Sarah pounced on Harriet in the garden. "There you are!" said Charlotte.

"We've been looking everywhere," said Sarah. "Where were you?"

"Walking. Is something wrong?" She had thought her friends were sitting with her mother, who had sensed Harriet's turmoil and reacted to it. "What is Mama doing?"

"Sorting her embroidery silks," replied Sarah. "She told us to go and enjoy ourselves."

Mama had found solace in her workbasket many times over the years. So this was welcome news. But her mother's restored equilibrium had come at the price of so many new problems that Harriet had not foreseen. Was life to be like this? Did the actions one took to mend matters inevitably cause more trouble?

"How are you feeling?" asked Sarah.

Tired of being asked this question, Harriet thought but did not say. Her friends were wonderful. She was grateful for their support. But she really wanted to take all her roiling, untidy emotions, package them up, tie the container with a stout rope, and chuck it down a well.

"You went walking alone again?" asked Charlotte.

"Yes. I like walking alone."

"Really? I didn't know you had hermitish tendencies. How could I have missed that in all these years?"

"Very funny," said Harriet.

"Walking in a forest alone can be quite restorative," said Sarah.

"Are you restored?" Charlotte asked Harriet. "You don't look it."

"I am…invigorated. I saw a fox near the Travelers camp." Sarah could often be diverted by mentions of wildlife.

Not this time, however. "I thought you said your grandfather had posted men to keep us away from there," Sarah replied. She had wanted to visit the group.

"Yes, but…"

"You know how to slip past them," said Charlotte.

Harriet had to admit it.

"So we can go and see them," said Sarah.

"Yes. All right. We will."

"When?"

A muted roar came through the window of Harriet's grandfather's study, followed by the rise and fall of one of his temper tantrums. They couldn't hear the details, but the outrage was familiar.

"What about now?" suggested Charlotte.

"Good idea," said Sarah.

Harriet's mother emerged from a side door like a cork popping from a champagne bottle. Seeing them, she rushed over. "Fresh air," she said breathlessly. "Join you for a turn about the garden." Grasping Harriet's arm, she urged her toward the shelter of the shrubbery.

"We're going to visit the Travelers' camp," said Sarah with the air of one offering a treat.

This was a problem, after all her grandfather's railing. Harriet waited for a flurry of fears and objections. But her mother merely nodded and walked faster. "I will come with you," she said.

"You will?" Where were the warnings, the anxieties? Harriet wondered.

"They seemed…interesting," was the surprising reply. "Lord Ferrington likes them."

Harriet stared at her as they passed into the shrubbery and out of sight of the house. "How do you know that?"

"Oh, well. I met him there the other day."

"You did?" Her mother had said nothing of this.

"We had a lovely chat. He is such a kind gentleman, isn't he?"

"What did you chat about?" asked Charlotte, relieving Harriet of the necessity.

"This and that." Harriet's mother made an airy gesture. "My embroidery."

"Your…" Harriet tried to picture it.

"What does Lord Ferrington know about fancywork?" asked Charlotte.

"He appreciates skill," answered Harriet's mother with quiet dignity.

One of the gardeners ran past the entry of the shrubbery carrying a palm tree in a pot. Its fronds were brown and curling at the ends.

"We should go," said Harriet's mother. "Papa has discovered the plants sent from London for the ball are not suitable. He's…disappointed."

"And his disappointment is so very loud," said Charlotte.

This earned her an anxious glance. As one, they headed for the far edge of the garden.

Harriet led them along the path that avoided her grandfather's lax sentries, who were thoroughly weary of their useless jobs by this time. They entered the camp from the woodland, and she noticed some things had been packed up in preparation for moving on. Harriet greeted those they passed, heading toward Mistress Elena's caravan. It was proper to present visitors to her first.

Samia came running up as they approached, her face bright with curiosity. "You haven't been here for ages," she said to Harriet.

"It has been a while." Harriet introduced her friends to the little girl. "We were going to say hello to Mistress Elena," she added.

"She's busy with Meric," was the reply. "Making plans. Do you want to come and see the horses?" Samia asked the others.

She proceeded to lead them around the camp, offering a running commentary on its activities. "We are going north soon," she said at one point. "I will see my cousins, and there will be a festival."

"When do you go?" asked Harriet.

"Soon, I think. That is what they're planning."

"I will miss you."

Samia's smile was brilliant. "Me, too. But we may see each other again. We might come here next year. We like this place."

Harriet tried to picture herself in a year's time. Where would she be?

"I'll read your palm and see," added Samia as if answering her inner query.

"You did that already," Harriet pointed out.

"But I didn't *finish*. Come." Samia led them to a space off to the side of the camp. There was a bench made of twining branches and several log rounds turned up to serve as seats.

"You sit here with me," Samia told Harriet. The little girl hopped onto the bench and patted the seat beside her with a presence beyond her years.

Charlotte and Sarah each took a log and gazed at Harriet as if she'd become the day's entertainment. After a moment, Harriet's mother sat as well. Predictably, she looked uneasy.

"Come," said Samia again.

Harriet sank down beside her and let the girl take her hand.

"So, I told you before, this is your Life line." She traced the crease that ran diagonally down Harriet's hand. "And this is your Heart line." She indicated the more horizontal mark and put a small fingertip on one spot. "And there is the big change we saw."

It hadn't been exactly *we*. But it was true about the change with her father's death. Did Samia remember these things? Or were experiences actually recorded in her hand?

"Your Heart line is very strong," said Samia. "And here, farther along, is another crossing. With the line of your head, your mind. It is a choice to be made. Soon, I think."

"What sort of choice?" Harriet couldn't help but ask.

"I cannot tell. Only that it will be very important for you."

This was nonsense, Harriet knew. But Samia sounded so authoritative. "If you can't tell me anything about this choice, what's the use?"

"You can know it is coming and be ready."

Harriet had to shrug.

"You will have a long life."

"Do you always say that?"

"If I see a long life," Samia responded seriously. "If I do not, I am silent."

"I suppose people won't pay to hear they'll die young," Harriet quipped.

"I did not ask you for payment," answered Samia, letting go of her hand.

"I'm sorry, Samia. I didn't mean to offend you."

The little girl looked away, more like a disgruntled adult than a child.

"Please forgive me," Harriet continued. "It was a silly thing to say."

"Very well." Samia looked back at her. "Not all is for money."

Harriet nodded solemnly to show she understood. Samia had offered a gift, and she had not valued it sufficiently.

"Do me," said Sarah, leaning forward on her log.

"Perhaps it is enough," the little girl replied. She was not completely mollified.

"Oh, please," said Sarah. "I so want to hear what you see."

After a pause, Samia bowed her head in agreement.

Harriet and Sarah switched places.

"We will find a story together, engraved in the hand," said Samia. It was the same thing Mistress Elena had said, Harriet remembered. The little girl had learned her elder's confident tone as well.

"That's a wonderful description," said Sarah. She held out her hand.

Samia took it and bent over the palm. "The line of your mind is very strong," she said after a while.

"All those books you've read," said Charlotte in a satirical tone.

"Or vice versa," Sarah replied.

"What?"

"Perhaps I read because I was always destined to."

"Trust you to concoct a fantastical explanation." Charlotte and Sarah made faces at each other.

"Hmm," said Samia.

"What?" Sarah looked down at her hand in the child's fingers.

"There is something." She traced a line. "Health and success and fate cross together here. That is not common. It means some great thing coming to you, I think. You must take care."

"An adventure?" asked Sarah, thrilled.

"There might be danger," Samia replied, frowning earnestly over her task. "You should be watchful."

"We'll never hear the end of this," Charlotte said to Harriet. "Sarah will be waiting for her adventure when she is a querulous old lady."

"It will be sooner than that," said Samia. Harriet couldn't tell whether she understood Charlotte's ironic tone.

Sarah's eyes gleamed. "Your turn next, Charlotte," she said.

"No, thank you."

"I will try it," said Harriet's mother, surprising her.

They shifted seats again and waited while Samia examined the older woman's palm. "You have had many trials," she said after a bit.

That might be true of any older person, Harriet thought. And yet she was being drawn into this process. Samia sounded so certain.

"But things grow better now," the little girl continued. "See the lines smoothing out down here? A happier time is coming for you and going right on to the end."

Mama looked pleased. Harriet imagined she was thinking of her marriage to the earl and their new home at Ferrington Hall. Which could hardly be inscribed in the stars or whatever the proper phrase was in palm reading.

Samia released her mother's hand. "Charlotte, you must give it a try," said Sarah.

Charlotte shook her head.

"But we all did."

"Some people are scared to look into the future," commented Samia. Harriet glanced at the girl in surprise. Had her tone held a brush of mockery? And how could she have known Charlotte hated to be accused of cowardice?

"I am not frightened," declared Charlotte. "I simply think it's a pack of nonsense."

"Then what harm can it do?" asked Sarah.

"Oh, very well." Charlotte came over to sit on the bench. "I don't believe a word of any of this," she said to Samia.

The little girl nodded, undaunted. She took up Charlotte's right hand. Then she frowned and traded it for the left. "Ah, you use this one," she said.

Charlotte looked startled.

"Our teachers at school tried to make her change, but she wouldn't," said Sarah.

"Don't give her hints!" said Charlotte. "That is how they fool people. They tease out information and watch for reactions."

Much as Mistress Elena had said, Harriet acknowledged. Perhaps Samia had seen Charlotte using her left hand? But she didn't think so. There'd been no opportunity.

Samia bent over Charlotte's hand. As she gazed, her expression slowly shifted to a frown. She looked some more, then straightened. "It is enough for today, I think."

"But you haven't told Charlotte anything," said Sarah.

"I am tired."

Charlotte's dark eyes narrowed. "You're trying to coax me. Make me beg you."

"No."

"Then you've run out of guff to peddle. Can't think of anything new."

Harriet raised a hand. Samia was just a little girl.

Samia's dark eyes flashed. "I don't lie."

"Right." Charlotte pulled her hand away. "This is ridiculous. Enough of children's silly games."

"It is not a game."

Charlotte gave her a patronizing look. "You like to perform and be the center of attention, don't you? I understand. But we are finished now."

"I see misfortune coming to you," Samia replied.

"Indeed? And when is this dire thing to befall me?" Charlotte drawled.

"Soon, perhaps. I can't say."

"Of course you can't. Because it does not exist. But if I

tripped and fell, say, you could point and declare, there it is, the misfortune. Just as I predicted."

"Charlotte," said Harriet and Sarah at the same time.

Samia stood up. Harriet expected her to be hurt or offended, but she showed no signs of that. "I will say good-bye to you, Miss Finch. And your friends. We may be gone the next time you come here."

"I'll try to see you again," replied Harriet.

"Thank you for the reading," said Sarah.

"You are welcome." With a regal bow of her head, Samia walked away.

Sarah turned on Charlotte. "How could you be so mean to a child?"

"I have no patience with that sort of gibberish."

"She's probably six years old!"

Charlotte looked guilty. "When she talked, she seemed older."

Harriet started toward the path through the woods. The rest followed. As they passed under the first trees, Charlotte added, "She didn't like me, so she gave me an ominous prediction."

"Just be careful not to trip and fall," replied Sarah caustically.

Charlotte sighed. "All right, I was too sharp with her. Shall I go back and apologize?"

"I don't think Samia cared too much," said Harriet.

"She is a very self-possessed child," agreed her mother.

They took the shortest way back, there being no need to evade the watchers in this direction. The man on duty was startled to see them emerge from the woods and watched them pass by as if they might be apparitions.

"I suppose Papa has been looking for us to complain about the plants," said her mother as they reached the Winstead Hall garden. "He put in the order himself."

"And I'm sure he solved the problem on his own," answered Harriet. "He always does. He never wishes to hear anyone else's opinion."

Her mother gave her a nervous glance and said her farewells. Harriet watched her slip off to look for a way to sneak into her supposed home.

She had passed out of sight when Cecelia, Duchess of Tereford, appeared from behind a bush that obscured a bend in the garden path. "There you are," she said. "I called to see you, and you couldn't be found. I was just heading back."

She'd been lonely when they first came here, Harriet thought. Now Winstead Hall was as busy as an inn yard when the mail coach was due. She wished new arrivals would announce themselves with a blast from a yard of tin.

"We were visiting the Travelers' camp," replied Sarah. "So interesting. A little girl, Samia, read our palms."

Cecelia looked amused. "I hope she saw good fortune."

Charlotte snorted.

"Have you heard anything from Ferrington?" Harriet asked. Her attempt at disinterest fooled nobody, she noted.

"Not a word. I am a bit puzzled. James said he mentioned Tunbridge Wells…"

"What?" Harriet blinked. "We used to live in Tunbridge Wells. Mama and I."

"That's right," said Sarah.

"James had forgotten because he despises the place," said Cecelia. "Begging your pardon, Harriet."

"I have no affection for it," she answered.

"Can he have gone there?" wondered Sarah.

"Why?" asked Charlotte. "To visit the scenes of Harriet's childhood?"

"I was eleven when we went there," said Harriet. "And, of course, that is ridiculous, Charlotte."

"As my tone was meant to indicate," her friend replied.

"He can't have gone to get a marriage license," Cecelia said. "Tunbridge Wells would not be the correct location. I checked."

Three sets of eyes focused on Harriet. "I can't break it off until he returns," she snapped.

"Are you certain that is what you want?" asked Sarah.

"There is the matter of kisses," said Cecelia.

Harriet tried not to wince as Sarah and Charlotte gaped at Cecelia and then turned to stare at her. She failed.

"I have come upon you embracing more than once," Cecelia added.

"Harriet," exclaimed Sarah. "You never mentioned that."

"Did he accost you?" asked Charlotte, clearly ready to be outraged.

"No." Harriet decided she sounded younger than Samia at this moment.

"The embraces looked...mutually enthusiastic to me," said the duchess. "And to James as well."

Charlotte put her hands on her hips. "That seems a rather important bit to leave out, Harriet."

Her face must have told them everything.

"You are in love with him!" declared Sarah.

She couldn't deny it. Yet she couldn't quite admit it either. "I've made a complete hash of things." She waited for Charlotte's mockery.

It did not come. "We will just have to set them right then," Charlotte said instead.

Sarah agreed. "But we must know *everything*."

Harriet sighed. These were her friends, old and new. She trusted them, and she believed they had her best interests at heart. She also knew them to be wise and kind. They would understand even if she did not come out well. Taking a deep breath, Harriet related her entire history with the rogue earl.

"That is a very romantic tale," said Sarah when she was done.

"Indeed," said Charlotte dryly. "A saga of bucolic chivalry."

Harriet wrinkled her nose at her.

"I like that neither of you were vying for social advantage when you met," said Cecelia. "There's nothing of the marriage mart there."

"He did lie to me," said Harriet. But even she could hear that the anger had drained out of that accusation.

"I might have done the same if Lady Wilton was after me," said Sarah. "She makes me quake in my boots."

"And you hid your true motives from him when you… encouraged his offer," said Cecelia.

"Are you suggesting that the two deceptions…cancel out?" Harriet asked her.

"Two wrongs don't make a right," intoned Sarah.

"But any number of rights can make a wrong," put in Charlotte.

"What does that mean?"

Charlotte shook her head and shrugged. "It seemed witty, and then it…wasn't."

"No," Harriet agreed.

"Well, you and Ferrington have both told the truth now," said Sarah. "You have a clean slate."

"So this is what a slate feels like when you have wiped every marking from it," replied Harriet.

Their looks were sympathetic.

The comparison actually felt apt. Harriet's mind was a blank. She also felt surrounded. Was it possible to be offered too much help? "I begin to see why some people have found us annoying."

"What do you mean?" asked Sarah.

"We rather…leapt upon people to solve their mysteries. Whether they wished us to or not."

"They required our help," said Charlotte.

"You can be a bit like a bull seeing a red flag," Harriet replied.

"What? No, I am not. I am simply determined."

"So is the bull."

"Oh, pish."

"We won't do anything you don't like," said Sarah, as always the bridge. "We will work together as we always have. Cecelia can take Ada's place."

"Which is?" The duchess looked amused.

"Organization."

"But what does that mean in this situation?" Harriet wondered. "There is no work to be done."

"We'll find something," said Charlotte.

That was what worried her.

"Nothing you don't like," repeated Sarah.

"Sometimes one doesn't know what one doesn't like until it happens," Harriet said.

"That is quite true," said Cecelia, looking struck by the statement.

"What's wrong with you, Harriet?" Charlotte shook her head. "You used to be the most sensible of us all. If this is being in love, I am glad I never shall be."

"Oh, Charlotte," said Sarah.

"Yes," said Harriet. "Oh, Charlotte indeed. I look forward to the day when I can remind you of those words."

"There will be no such day."

As they glowered at each other, Cecelia said, "I still don't understand just what you intend to do."

That reduced the group to silence.

Sixteen

JACK RETURNED TO FERRINGTON HALL LATE THE FOL-
lowing night. Having tended to his horse, he let himself in
and moved quietly through the sleeping house. It felt a bit
more like home, but he realized this was because he was
more at home in himself after this foray into the world. He
had used his skills and resources to take action, as he was
used to doing across the sea. Perhaps this was the real meaning of home, he thought as he undressed in his bedchamber.
A person confident in himself could be at home anywhere,
even in the country of a critical great-grandmother.

His business had gone smoothly, and he had a marriage
license in his pocket. This might be overreaching. But if the
document was not required, it could be torn up. He needed
now to see Harriet at a time and place where they could talk
and were not surrounded by prying eyes.

The next morning, Jack woke early and wrote a note to
her, suggesting such a meeting. As he sent it off with a sta-
bleboy, he felt like a gambler risking all in a final throw. He
didn't wait for a reply, wishing to avoid the Terefords until
his fate was decided. Instead he went out and walked to the
Travelers' camp.

He found them gone. Only trampled grass and charred

fire circles remained from their visit. Jack was sorry not to have bid them farewell. Mistress Elena had suggested they would come again next year, and he hoped to greet them then as a settled man.

Movement caught in the corner of his eye, and Jack turned to see Harriet, ethereal in pale-sprigged muslin, approaching from the wood, her face half-hidden by one of her parasols. He moved toward her, and they met in an open space where a caravan had been.

"Here you are," she said.

"I am." It lifted his heart to see her. As much of her as he could see at any rate. He purely hated her parasols. They were like portable draperies, ready to hide her face at a moment's notice. "Let us go and sit in the shade," he said. Where she could shut the dashed thing. He didn't wait for agreement, just strode off to the shelter of the trees.

He led her to the little clearing near the edge of the camp, where they had sat before on the large, dry log among the murmur of leaves. That had been an easier time. "You won't need that here," he said, pointing at the parasol. He did not intend to talk through it or to it.

Harriet closed the lacy barrier and set it aside. "I was glad to receive your note," she said, speaking quickly. "I am sorry for what happened. I wanted you to understand."

"As I did about the things I told you when we first met," he couldn't resist saying.

She bowed her head, then gave one nod.

Sitting near her was unsettling. She'd roused him and hurt him, touched his heart and bruised his spirit. Her familiar face and figure brought back moments they'd shared. He'd thought she was his. Then he'd been ejected from that happy state. Yet she'd come to see him when he asked. "I wanted to—" he began.

She held up a hand to stop him. "Before anything else, I would like to tell you why I acted as I did."

Seeing that she was trembling to do so, he nodded.

Harriet folded her hands, released them, gazed into the wood. "I don't think you know. My mother was rejected by her family, just as your father was by his. My grandfather didn't approve of her marriage to my father, even though Papa was a valued employee of his business. He wanted her to make a grand match."

She spoke like someone repeating an old tale, one she'd chewed over many times before.

"He thinks that is what females are *for*," she added with obvious bitterness.

Including Harriet herself, Jack knew.

"So he cut her off. From his money and his society. And more than that, he did everything he could to make sure Papa failed at any venture he undertook. There was a great deal Grandfather could do to ruin him. He is very influential."

"How can you live with the man?" burst from Jack. The tale was worse than he'd realized.

Harriet's face was stony. She didn't look at him. "It is the most difficult thing I have ever done. But he approached Mama, you see, and offered to leave me all his money."

"Which should have been partly hers from the beginning."

"Yes. And she…"

"Couldn't resist," Jack put in. "Like a man thinking he was to be welcomed back into the family that had thrown his father out."

Finally, she turned to him. He saw surprise and what might have been tenderness in her green eyes. They filmed with unshed tears as she nodded. She blinked them away.

"And perhaps, like that man, she found things weren't so simple."

"They were in fact the same as ever," she replied. "Only now my grandfather's ambitions focus on me, while he treats Mama like a pathetic failure."

"You should turn your back on him and walk out the door." It was what he had done in the face of Lady Wilton's insults. Surely it was the only response to such tyranny?

"I would like to!" Her voice was fierce. "I would gladly go back to our small, frugal life. But Mama spent all our capital on my London season. Without consulting me." Her fists clenched in her lap.

Jack's urges to defiance died on his tongue. He had resources, an earldom. Her case was not the same. How right he'd been to take action.

"So Mama is terrified when Grandfather threatens to throw her out again," Harriet added. "As he does if I try to oppose him in any way."

The man deserved a thrashing.

"He is...was driving Mama to distraction with his threats. She'd taken to laudanum to ease her fears."

A thorough thrashing, to be terrorizing that nice little lady in such a way. His own daughter, too!

"I had to do something," Harriet said. Her tone and her eyes held pleading. "You must see that. I would do anything for my mother, as you would for yours, I'm sure."

His bright, antic mother had died a slow, hard death, with disease eating at her insides. He'd done what he could, which hadn't been enough, of course. That cruel process had certainly left him familiar with laudanum.

Harriet sat straighter. "And so, I…pushed for the engagement, the sort Grandfather insists upon, to a title."

She spoke as if it could have been any match, any man, as long as he was noble. The idea brought a sharp pain.

"He's so eager to climb the social ladder," she added. "He thinks the high sticklers will welcome him in if I am a countess." Her laugh was harsh. "I would almost do it, just to watch when he realizes he's wrong."

"But it wouldn't be worth it," said Jack. He kept emotion out of his voice, but he couldn't help hoping for some contradiction. Marriage to him could not be such a grim prospect? Could it?

Harriet turned and blinked at him as if startled. "I didn't mean… I wasn't speaking…"

"Of me." Had he been reduced to a mere counter in her game to best her grandfather?

"I was desperate about Mama. I followed an impulse. It was wrong of me. I'm sorry."

He appreciated the apology. But it was not enough, any more than his regrets had been for her.

"I didn't see how it would involve…"

"Me," he said again.

"A number of complications," she corrected. She bit her lower lip in the way she did when torn. "And you. I am very sorry, Lord Ferrington. I will make things right at once..."

"If you had simply told me all this in the beginning, I would have agreed to help," he interrupted. He didn't want to discuss how the engagement was to end.

She stared at him, lips slightly parted. "You would?"

"Of course. Why not?"

"But it... Why would you?"

"Because I despise domestic tyrants? Like Lady Wilton. And would be glad to see them all thwarted."

She looked a bit dazed.

"I would have been happy to join in the, er, rebellion," Jack added.

"It didn't occur to me that I might..."

"Ask for help?"

Those three words appeared to startle her, as if they were in a foreign language that she ought to know but didn't. Then she shook her head. "With Grandfather? No."

"Because he seems to hold all the power."

"He doesn't *seem* to. It is a fact."

"Perhaps not..."

"If you had seen what he did to my father! You know nothing about it." She made a slashing gesture. "It is so much easier for you."

He acknowledged it with a nod. "Still, we could have plotted together." He rather liked the sound of that.

"We are not speaking of some children's game," she answered wearily.

Jack caught a glimpse of how she would look in future decades, when life had piled on even more trials—still lovely, perhaps even more so in her courage and determination.

"I have to find some other…"

"I see how a false engagement fit your circumstances perfectly," he interrupted.

"False," she echoed.

"Your grandfather is satisfied, and your mother seems happy."

"She's delighted," said Harriet in a toneless voice.

"That's good then."

"How? Neither of these things will be true in the end."

It would feel like an end indeed if he was rejected by Harriet Finch. But she didn't look happy about her statement. And what about the kisses? The kisses didn't fit into this story. His senses flared at the memory. They had been real kisses, not feigned embraces to lure him in. He could not have been deceived about that. He knew passion when he experienced it. His spirits stirred. There was more to all this than she was saying. How to discover it? He racked his brain. The silence had stretched on too long, and Harriet started to reach for her parasol. "I came to England because I longed for a family," he said.

Her hand went still.

"Not to swan about being an earl. I don't care about that. But to become part of a clan. I've always wanted that, since I was a boy. My own family was so fractious, you see. Often more a thing to be endured than enjoyed."

Her green eyes were fixed on him.

"I did not find what I was looking for, of course. Lady Wilton had no welcome for me. Quite the opposite."

"We cannot choose our families," said Harriet tonelessly.

"Lady Wilton will always be my relation," Jack acknowledged. "And I doubt we will ever feel much affection for each other. But here's the thing I've been thinking recently: I should like to build another sort of family."

"Build?"

Jack nodded. He had been pondering this subject. "I think it would be…will be work. Not an easy task. But well worth it."

Harriet sighed. "It sounds grand. And, of course, one's friends can be a kind of family. But in the end, the 'relations' determine what can be done." Her lips turned down. "For females, at least."

"I understand that."

This earned him a flashing glance.

"You did not ask where I have been," Jack went on.

"I have no right to do so." But there was curiosity in her tone.

"Tunbridge Wells," he told her.

"The duke thought… Why would you go there? It is a dreary place."

"Did you find it so?"

"Yes, I was so glad to leave for school. I only regretted abandoning Mama there."

"She's quite fond of the place, actually. She told me so."

"What? You must have misunderstood her. Mama often says things to be polite."

"She had no need to do so with me. I'd never heard of the town until she told me the happiest time of her life was at a house in Tunbridge Wells."

Harriet tried to take in this incredible assertion.

"It was after you had gone off to school," he added apologetically. "She had a room at the front of the house to show off her fancywork, which was very much admired."

Harriet remembered that chamber. She hadn't thought much about it, being wrapped up in her own youthful concerns.

"And, indeed, I found many ladies there remembered her fondly," said the rogue earl. "They all wanted to know how she was getting on. You, too, of course."

Harriet doubted that last statement.

"So I purchased the house for her."

"You...you what?" She couldn't have heard him properly.

"I shall settle an income on her. I asked my new man of business about it. That sounds grand, doesn't it? I recently acquired an advisor on Tereford's recommendation. Someone up to every rig and row of English practice, as he put it. He'll set things up."

"You can't," she declared.

"It's quite possible. And will be legal and permanent. So there can be no threatening to take it away later as your devilish grandfather does. That will put a spoke in his wheel," he finished with evident satisfaction.

"Wheel?" echoed Harriet, still astonished.

"If your mother has an income and a household of her own, your grandfather can't threaten to throw her out." He shrugged. "Well, he could, but she can ignore him."

"I can't allow you to do that," Harriet said.

"Why not?"

"It's not right."

"I don't see that."

"You are not… We are not… People make such arrange-ments for family members or old retainers."

"You mustn't call your mother that. She'd be livid."

"Will you be serious?"

"I'm perfectly serious." He certainly looked it.

"What would people think?"

"The matter won't be published in the newspapers," he said. "It will be a private transaction. No one will know unless we tell them."

"No. I forbid it."

"Well, you know, you can't really stop me."

Harriet groped for words.

"What's the point of having a fortune if you don't do what you like with it? That's what I say."

"Lord Ferrington," she began and stopped. "This just isn't done."

"In fact, it is done. I saw to that before I returned."

"This isn't a matter of wordplay!" Harriet cried. "It is out-side the bounds of…"

"Polite society?" he interrupted.

"Exactly."

"People who are interested in being accepted by polite society would be moved by that consideration," he replied. "I'm not. Are you?"

"Not moved?" asked Harriet, bewildered.

"Not interested in being accepted." He held her gaze. "You spoke once of running away to a different sort of life."

It had felt like flying, Harriet remembered. "Then I found I could not abandon Mama."

"Of course not. But if her future is settled, perhaps we could talk of…"

"Running away?" He could not mean that, yet Harriet's heart beat faster at the idea.

"If you like," he answered. "But before that—love."

For the first time, her rogue earl looked anxious. Harriet went still.

"We talked and danced and even became engaged without mentioning it," he continued. "I am sorry for that. I ought to have said long before now that I love you with all my heart."

Harriet's breath caught. She'd longed to hear those words. And to tell him she felt the same. Except. "You decided my mother's future and went off to settle it without telling me or asking my opinion."

"I didn't think you would…"

"Would what?" she asked when he stopped. "Agree with you?"

"I thought if I eased your mother's worries, we could… consider the future without impediments."

"And so, you acted for Mama and me. In our best interests."

Ferrington clearly caught her tone.

"Much as I did when I forced our engagement without including you," Harriet continued. She nodded at his evident surprise when she acknowledged the similarity. "If I could build a different sort of family—as I, too, have dreamed of doing—it would require mutual decisions," she continued.

The rogue earl nodded. He raised his right hand. "I solemnly promise that from this moment, we will always conspire together rather than separately."

Harriet liked the sound of that. Even though he was presuming a bit.

"If that is, you consent to conspire with me."

"I...believe that I do."

Looking as if he didn't quite dare to hope, he said, "To be perfectly clear, when we say *conspire*, we mean as husband and wife." He shifted. "Should I kneel?"

"You needn't. And yes. That is what we mean."

Ferrington's smile was brilliant. "So, we have a deal?" He offered his hand, as he would have to seal a commercial bargain.

Harriet did not take it. "I hate that word," she said. "It is my grandfather's word."

He gestured as if warding off all such associations. "What do you prefer?"

She leaned closer. "This," she said and kissed him.

His arms came around her and pulled her closer. This kiss was sweeter than any before it as they gave themselves up to the promise of the future. They were both breathless when it ended.

"A pact well sealed indeed," said the rogue earl. "We shall make every agreement precisely so."

Harriet laughed.

"But there is something you have not said," he added.

She did not pretend to misunderstand. "I love you," she answered. "I have loved you for a long time, since soon after I met Jack the Rogue."

"And I fell head over heels for Miss Snoot. Perhaps we will name our children thus. Rogue and Snoot."

"No, we won't," replied Harriet, flushing a little.

"As you wish, my love. Now and always."

This required another kiss, which inspired several increasingly torrid embraces. It was quite some time before they reluctantly left the clearing.

"This place seems so empty now," Harriet said of the Travelers' field. So much of their history together had involved the camp and its environs. An ending and a beginning, the crushed grass seemed to say.

"They'll be back. They found a safe haven on my land."

He said *my land* quite naturally now. He was settling into his position as an unconventional earl. Could there also be a rogue countess? Harriet wondered. She didn't see why not.

Seventeen

"You are keeping something from us," Charlotte said to Harriet as the three friends went down to dinner at Winstead Hall that evening.

"I do not share every little detail of my day," Harriet replied. She hadn't told them about the note from Ferrington, not knowing how the meeting would go. How wonderfully it would turn out. She hugged that knowledge to her for now.

"You do seem especially cheerful," said Sarah.

"Suspiciously cheerful," said Charlotte.

"What can you mean by that?" Harriet couldn't resist teasing Charlotte a little after the way her friend had twitted her during this visit.

"Something's happened," said Sarah.

"How was today's solitary walk?" Charlotte asked.

They were on the scent. But they'd reached the dining room now, and Harriet was not required to answer.

As usual, Harriet's grandfather dominated the dinner table conversation. He was full of the final plans for the ball, having crushed the vendor who'd sent the wilted greenery. "He will not palm off shoddy goods on anyone again," he gloated. "Ha! Palm off potted palms."

Harriet was in such a good mood that she laughed at his feeble jest.

Her grandfather swung around to look at her, looking more surprised than gratified. It was true that Harriet didn't usually appreciate his witticisms. "Have the ball gowns arrived?" he asked.

"Yes, Grandfather." He'd insisted all the young ladies have new dresses for his ball, ordered from the fashionable modiste who'd made Harriet's clothes for the season, and that he pay for them.

"Yours must be the finest at the ball," he'd told Harriet. He'd tried to dictate the design, urging Harriet to demand lavish decoration. It had taken all her efforts to persuade him the seamstress knew best about these things.

"They're lovely," said Harriet's mother.

"Huh." He consumed most of a slice of roast beef in one bite, and silence reigned while he chewed. "Ferrington's procured the license," he said then. "So that's all right and tight."

"Oh," said Charlotte. "Is the earl... You have heard from him?"

"That's what I said."

Charlotte and Sarah turned to look at Harriet. She concentrated on her dinner.

Naturally, they pounced on her as soon as the meal was over, congregating around the pianoforte in the drawing room again to put their heads together. Fortunately her grandfather had not joined them this evening.

"Tell," demanded Charlotte in a sibilant whisper.

"You saw Ferrington on your walk, didn't you?" asked Sarah.

"And you didn't break it off," said Charlotte.

"No. We decided we…may as well marry."

"May as well?" Sarah's voice rang out.

"What is it?" asked Harriet's mother from the sofa across the room.

"Nothing, Mama," said Harriet. "We are looking for music to play."

"May as well?" muttered Sarah.

"As we are so much in love," Harriet answered with a radiant smile.

"Oh, Harriet." Sarah hugged her.

"And that is what you want," said Charlotte.

"With all my heart."

"Then I'm happy for you."

"Harriet?" said her mother, clearly sensing more was going on than she was being told.

"Yes, Mama." Harriet handed Charlotte a sheet of music and went to sit beside her mother. "I wanted to speak to you," she told her.

"Is something wrong?"

This was always her mother's first assumption, Harriet thought sadly. "No. It is just a new idea. Or a possibility really. For you to consider."

"Me?"

Was she asked so seldom to choose? That should not be. "I was talking to Ferrington today, and he told me of your conversation about Tunbridge Wells."

Her mother blinked. Had she been anxious all Harriet's life? Perhaps so, but not to this extent.

"He said… He got the idea you were quite happy living there. After I'd gone off to school."

"I missed you very much, of course," replied her mother, as if this had been an accusation.

She'd had little reason to miss such an oblivious daughter, Harriet thought. Well, she would not be that way anymore. "And he thought…wondered if you might like to return. Our old house is…available. And he would be glad to procure it for you." She did not say he had already done so. They'd agreed that arrangements were to be all up to her mother. If she didn't want the house, it could be let. She was to be where she wished to be.

"Tunbridge Wells?" she said.

To Harriet's horror, Mama's eyes filled with tears. "You are most welcome at Ferrington Hall, of course. Indeed, we want you there. Absolutely. Both of us. Ferrington only thought…"

"But how could I return?" her mother interrupted. "I've been so foolish about our money." Her hands clasped convulsively.

"He would like to settle an income on you. A permanent one that could never be withdrawn."

"Oh, Harriet!" The tears spilled over. "So generous."

"So that is what you would like?" Harriet still wasn't certain.

"More than anything. Oh, Harriet, can it really be true?"

"Quite true."

Her mother's breath caught on a sob. "I never dared dream… I would visit you, of course. It is not too far away. But to have my own… You say our old house can be taken?"

"Ferrington has bought it," Harriet replied.

"Bought!" Her mouth fell open. "Bought?"

"Yes, Mama. For you."

She stared, astounded, wordless.

"What has happened?" asked Charlotte, coming over to join them. Sarah trailed along behind.

"Harriet is marrying the most wonderful man in the world," said her mother.

"Really?" Charlotte rested her satirical dark eyes on Harriet.

"I think perhaps I am," she agreed.

❧

The Winstead ball took place on a balmy summer evening when a full moon made nighttime travel easy for the neighbors. And notables from miles around made it their business to attend, drawn by the promise of meeting a duke and duchess and the affianced wife of their local earl. Not to mention Ferrington himself, who had not yet made the acquaintance of many of them. The guests flowed into the just-constructed ballroom, greeted by Harriet, her mother, and her grandfather at the door. From there, they fanned out to examine every nook and cranny of this ambitious addition to Winstead Hall. Jack circulated among them, supported by the Terefords. The duchess had made a list of all those invited and their positions, and Jack had done his best to memorize it. All was going smoothly, and Jack was confident his own plans were firmly in place, when he heard the butler announce an unexpected name.

"Lady Wilton Cantrell," the man intoned.

Jack spun around. It was true. His wizened great-grandmother stood in the doorway, frowning, of course, resplendent in lavender satin. Jack met Harriet's stunned gaze. Clearly, she hadn't known about this either.

"Did they invite Grandmama?" asked the duke at his shoulder.

"Not that I ever heard." He would have vetoed the idea.

"Do you suppose she is crashing the party?" Tereford wondered. "*I* did not tell her of it."

"I would guess Mr. Winstead asked her," said the duchess, who had joined them. "He wanted as many nobles here as possible."

"He said nothing of it," Jack objected.

"He's a sly old bird," she pointed out.

"We'll have to go and greet her," said the duke.

Jack set his jaw. "I don't have to do anything for *her*."

"It's more for Harriet, really," the duchess responded. "To show she's welcomed into the family."

If one called it that. Which Jack did not. But he would do anything for Harriet, even this.

"We'll stay with you," said the duchess.

He'd like to see Lady Wilton be rude to her.

They walked across the ballroom. Lady Wilton waited for them, leaning on her cane. "Hello, Grandmama," said the duke when they reached her. "What an unexpected pleasure."

"I didn't see your name on the guest list," said Jack.

The old lady raked them all with her gaze. "Winstead invited me. Told me about the engagement as well, which none of you bothered to do." Her bilious look settled on Jack. "If you think this match excuses your treatment of me, you are quite wrong."

"His treatment of *you*?" murmured the duchess.

Jack waited for the fury Lady Wilton had roused in him before. It did not come. He remembered Harriet's distinction. Lady Wilton was a relation but not his family. And he needn't care what she thought.

"You might have done better if you'd waited for me to take a hand," the old lady continued. "But the girl's not bad, and a great deal of money washes off the stink of trade."

Here was the anger. "*Never* speak of Harriet in that way again," Jack replied, in the cut-glass accent of his father's haughtiest moments.

"She is my friend, Lady Wilton," said the duchess. "A splendid person."

"Petty spite becomes no one, Grandmama," added the duke.

A startled Lady Wilton faced their united front. "I only meant…"

"I don't care," Jack interrupted. "If you talk of Harriet with anything but respect and admiration, we shall never have anything to do with you. And I'll do my best to make you regret it."

The old lady snorted. "I don't know what you think you could do."

"No, you don't. I have the manners of a barbarian, remember?" He gave her glare for glare, and after a long moment, Lady Wilton's eyes dropped.

The duchess leaned closer to the small, wizened figure. "It seems foolish to deride one's own family," she murmured. "Malice is likely to reflect back on the speaker."

"Will you allow them to speak to me this way, Tereford?" Lady Wilton asked the duke.

"I think you rather deserve it, Grandmama."

"Well!"

Some of his relations qualified as family after all, Jack thought with warm gratitude. The Terefords, certainly.

He turned to find many in the crowd watching them, waiting for an opportunity to meet the most illustrious guests. Everyone seemed to have arrived. Or if they hadn't, too bad. He didn't care. This felt like the moment. "If I may have your attention," he called. He had to repeat this before all the chatter died and everyone was looking at him. "Since you are all here, in your finery, we decided to make this ball even more momentous."

As they'd planned, Harriet had come to stand at his side. Charlotte and Sarah had taken their cues and were approaching from the left with a particular guest.

"And be married here and now before you," Jack added.

"What?" exclaimed Lady Wilton and Mr. Winstead in chorus.

Charlotte and Sarah pulled the vicar into place. He looked nervous, but he'd examined and approved the license two days ago and was primed for his role.

"Just one minute," Mr. Winstead began. The duke went to take his arm and quell his objections. Only a duke could have, Jack thought.

"This is outrageous," said Lady Wilton. "Out of the question."

The duchess herded the old lady away from the central couple and metaphorically sat on her.

And so Jack and his love were married in a most unconventional way, which heralded the sort of life they intended to lead. People in the crowd were appalled, charmed, outraged, or amused according to their natures. Most agreed, however, that this ball would be unforgettable and that the celebrations following the ceremony were the liveliest the neighborhood had ever seen. The food was certainly splendid.

As the guests were tucking into the grand spread, Mr. Winstead and Lady Wilton came face-to-face over the lobster patties. "I hope you know I had nothing to do with this wedding," he said.

"Most improper," she declared.

"Yes, indeed. I suppose we will find many things to agree on now that our families are joined."

She annihilated him with a glare that made those he gave his employees pale in comparison. "Joined," she snorted and stomped away, punctuating each step with her cane.

Jack and Harriet twirled on the dance floor in a waltz. "We've scandalized the neighborhood," she said.

"We have that."

"When can we do it again?"

He threw back his head and laughed. "After the honeymoon," he promised.

"Have the newlyweds gone?" the Duke of Tereford asked his wife over breakfast the following morning. Jack and Harriet were to sail for Boston, where Ferrington would wrap up his affairs and his countess would meet his American friends.

"Yes. They were up at dawn and off soon after."

He nodded. "Shall we follow their example? Not at dawn, however."

The duchess nodded. "I've told the servants to pack up our things and ready the carriage for tomorrow."

"And so we're off to Cornwall?"

"To Tresigan, yes. I've had word the house is buried in ivy."

"When you say *buried*?"

"Completely smothered by a jungle of vines," said the duchess.

"Of course it is."

Don't miss book one in
The Duke's Estates

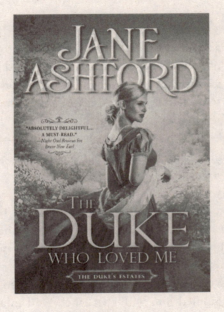

Available now from
Sourcebooks Casablanca

One

THREE DAYS AFTER HE INHERITED THE TITLE DUKE OF
Tereford, James Cantrell set off to visit the ducal town house
just off London's Berkeley Square. He walked from his
rooms, as the distance was short and the April day pleasant.
He hoped to make this first encounter cordially brief and be
off riding before the sunlight faded.

He had just entered the square when a shouted greeting turned his head. Henry Deeping was approaching, an
unknown young man beside him.

"Have you met my friend Cantrell?" Henry asked his
companion when they reached James. "Sorry. Tereford, I
should say. He's just become a duke. Stephan Kandler, meet
the newest peer of the realm as well as the handsomest man
in London."

As they exchanged bows James silently cursed whatever
idiot had saddled him with that label. He'd inherited his
powerful frame, black hair, and blue eyes from his father. It
was nothing to do with him. "That's nonsense," he said.

"Yes, Your Grace." Henry's teasing tone had changed
recently. It held the slightest trace of envy.

James had heard it from others since he'd come into his
inheritance. His cronies were young men who shared his

interest in sport, met while boxing or fencing, on the hunting field, or perhaps clipping a wafer at Manton's shooting gallery, where Henry Deeping had an uncanny ability. They were generally not plump in the pocket. Some lived on allowances from their fathers and would inherit as James had; others would have a moderate income all their lives. All of them preferred vigorous activity to smoky gaming hells or drunken revels.

They'd been more or less equals. But now circumstances had pulled James away, into the peerage and wealth, and he was feeling the distance. One old man's death, and his life was changed. Which was particularly hard with Henry. They'd known each since they were uneasy twelve-year-olds arriving at school.

"We're headed over to Manton's if you'd care to come," Henry said. He sounded repentant.

"I can't just now," James replied. He didn't want to mention that he was headed to Tereford House. It was just another measure of the distance from Henry. He saw that Henry noticed the vagueness of his reply.

"Another time perhaps," said Henry's companion in a Germanic accent.

James gave a noncommittal reply, wondering where Henry had met the fellow. His friend was considering the diplomatic corps as a means to make his way in the world. Perhaps this Kandler had something to do with that.

They separated. James walked across the square and into the narrow street containing Tereford House.

The massive stone building, of no particular architectural distinction, loomed over the cobbles. Its walls showed signs of neglect, and the windows on the upper floors were all shuttered. There was no funerary hatchment above the door. Owing to the eccentricities of his great-uncle, the recently deceased sixth duke, James had never been inside. His every approach had been rebuffed.

He walked up to the door and plied the tarnished knocker. When that brought no response, he rapped on the door with the knob of his cane. He had sent word ahead, of course, and expected a better reception than this. At last the door opened, and he strolled inside—to be immediately assailed by a wave of stale mustiness. The odor was heavy rather than sharp, but it insinuated itself into the nostrils like an unwanted guest. James suspected that it would swiftly permeate his clothes and hair. His dark brows drew together. The atmosphere in the dim entryway, with closed doors on each side and at the back next to a curving stair, was oppressive. It seemed almost threatening.

One older female servant stood before him. She dropped a curtsy. "Your Grace," she said, as if the phrase was unfamiliar.

"Where is the rest of the staff?" They really ought to have lined up to receive him. He had given them a time for his visit.

"There's only me. Your Grace."

"What?"

"Keys is there." She pointed to a small side table. A ring of old-fashioned keys lay on it.

James noticed a small portmanteau sitting at her feet.

She followed his eyes. "I'll be going then. Your Grace." Before James could reply, she picked up the case and marched through the still-open front door.

Her footsteps faded, leaving behind a dismal silence. The smell seemed to crowd closer, pressing on him. The light dimmed briefly as a carriage passed outside. James suppressed a desire to flee. He had a pleasant set of rooms in Hill Street where he had, for some years, been living a life that suited him quite well. He might own this house now, but that didn't mean he had to live here. Or perhaps he did. A duke had duties. It occurred to him that the servant might have walked off with some valuable items. He shrugged. Her bag had been too small to contain much.

He walked over to the closed door on the right and turned the knob. The door opened a few inches and then hit some sort of obstacle. He pushed harder. It remained stuck. James had to put his shoulder to the panels and shove with the strength developed in Gentleman Jackson's boxing saloon before it gave way, with a crash of some largish object falling inside. He forced his way through but managed only one step before he was brought up short, his jaw dropping. The chamber—a well-proportioned parlor with high ceilings and elaborate moldings—was stuffed to bursting with a mad jumble of objects. Furniture of varying eras teetered in haphazard stacks—sofas, chairs, tables, cabinets. Paintings and other ornaments were pushed into every available crevice. Folds and swathes of fabric that might have been draperies or bedclothes drooped over the mass, which towered far above his head. There was no room to move. "Good God!" The stale odor was much worse here, and a scurrying sound did not bode well.

James backed hastily out. He thought of the shuttered

rooms on the upper floors. Were they all...? But perhaps only this one was a mare's nest. He walked across the entryway and tried the door on the left. It concealed a larger room in the same wretched condition. His heart, which had not been precisely singing, sank. He'd assumed that his new position would require a good deal of tedious effort, but he hadn't expected chaos.

The click of footsteps approached from outside. The front door was still open, and now a fashionably dressed young lady walked through it. She was accompanied by a maid and a footman. The latter started to shut the door behind them. "Don't," commanded James. The young servant shied like a nervous horse.

"What is that smell?" the lady inquired, putting a gloved hand to her nose.

"What are you doing here?" James asked the bane of his existence.

"You mentioned that you were going to look over the house today."

"And in what way is this your concern?"

"I was so curious. There are all sorts of rumors about this place. No one has been inside for years." She went over to one of the parlor doors and peered around it. "Oh!" She crossed to look into the other side. "Good heavens!"

"Indeed."

"Well, this is going to be a great deal of work." She smiled. "You won't like that."

"You have no idea what I..." James had to stop, because he knew that she had a very good idea.

"I know more about your affairs than you do," she added.

It was nearly true. Once, it certainly had been. That admission took him back thirteen years to his first meeting with Cecelia Vainsmede. He'd been just fifteen, recently orphaned, and in the midst of a blazing row with his new trustee. Blazing on his side, at any rate. Nigel Vainsmede had been pained and evasive and clearly just wishing James would go away. They'd fallen into one of their infuriating bouts of pushing in and fending off, insisting and eluding. James had understood by that time that his trustee might agree to a point simply to be rid of him, but he would never carry through with any action. Vainsmede would forget—willfully, it seemed to James. Insultingly.

And then a small blond girl had marched into her father's library and ordered them to stop at once. Even at nine years old, Cecelia had been a determined character with a glare far beyond her years. James had been surprised into silence. Vainsmede had actually looked grateful. And on that day they had established the routine that allowed them to function for the next ten years—speaking to each other only through Cecelia. James would approach her with "Please tell your father." And she would manage the matter, whatever it was. James didn't have to plead, which he hated, and Nigel Vainsmede didn't have to do anything at all, which was his main hope in life as far as James could tell.

James and Cecelia had worked together all through their youth. Cecelia was not a friend, and not family, but some indefinable other sort of close connection. And she did know a great deal about him. More than he knew about her.

Although he had observed, along with the rest of the *haut ton*, that she had grown up to be a very pretty young lady. Today in a walking dress of sprig muslin and a straw bonnet decorated with matching blue ribbons, she was lithely lovely. Her hair was less golden than it had been at nine but far better cut. She had the face of a renaissance Madonna except for the rather too lush lips. And her luminous blue eyes missed very little, as he had cause to know. Not that any of this was relevant at the moment. "Your father has not been my trustee for three years," James pointed out.

"And you have done nothing much since then."

He would have denied it, but what did it matter? Instead he said, "I never could understand why my father appointed *your* father as my trustee."

"It was odd," she said.

"They were just barely friends, I would say."

"Hardly that," she replied. "Papa was astonished when he heard."

"As was I." James remembered the bewildered outrage of his fifteen-year-old self when told that he would be under the thumb of a stranger until he reached the age of twenty-five. "And, begging your pardon, but your father is hardly a pattern card of wisdom."

"No. He is indolent and self-centered. Almost as much as you are."

"Why, Miss Vainsmede!" He rarely called her that. They had dropped formalities and begun using first names when she was twelve. "I am not the least indolent."

She hid a smile. "Only if you count various forms of sport.

Which I do not. I have thought about the trusteeship, how-ever. From what I've learned of your father—I did not know him of course—I think he preferred to be in charge."

A crack of laughter escaped James. "Preferred! An extreme understatement. He had the soul of an autocrat and the temper of a frustrated tyrant."

She frowned at him. "Yes. Well. Having heard something of that, I came to the conclusion that your father chose mine because he was confident Papa would do nothing in particular."

"What?"

"I think that your father disliked the idea of not being… present to oversee your upbringing, and he couldn't bear the idea of anyone *doing* anything about that."

James frowned as he worked through this convoluted sentence.

"And so he chose my father because he was confident Papa wouldn't…bestir himself and try to make changes in the arrangements."

Surprise kept James silent for a long moment. "You know that is the best theory I have heard. It might even be right."

"You needn't sound so astonished," Cecelia replied. "I often have quite good ideas."

"What a crackbrained notion!"

"I beg your pardon?"

"My father's, not yours." James shook his head. "You think he drove me nearly to distraction just to fend off change?"

"If he had lived…" she began.

"Oh, that would have been far worse. A never-ending battle of wills."

"You don't know that. I was often annoyed with my father when I was younger, but we get along well now."

"Because he lets you be as scandalous as you please, Cecelia."

"Oh nonsense."

James raised one dark brow.

"I *wish* I could learn to do that," exclaimed his pretty visitor. "You are said to have the most killing sneer in the *ton*, you know."

He was not going to tell her that he had spent much of a summer before the mirror when he was sixteen perfecting the gesture.

"And it was *not* scandalous for me to attend one ball without a chaperone. I was surrounded by friends and acquaintances. What could happen to me in such a crowd?" She shook her head. "At any rate, I am quite on the shelf at twenty-two. So it doesn't matter."

"Don't be stupid." James knew, from the laments of young gentleman acquaintances, that Cecelia had refused several offers. She was anything but "on the shelf."

"I am never stupid," she replied coldly.

He was about to make an acid retort when he recalled that Cecelia was a positive glutton for work. She'd also learned a great deal about estate management and business as her father pushed tasks off on her, his only offspring. She'd come to manage much of Vainsmede's affairs as well as the trust. Indeed, she'd taken to it as James never had. He thought of the challenge confronting him. Could he cajole her into taking some of it on?

She'd gone to open the door at the rear of the entryway. "There is just barely room to edge along the hall here," she said. "Why would anyone keep all these newspapers? There must be years of them. Do you suppose the whole house is like this?"

"I have a sinking feeling that it may be worse. The sole servant ran off as if she was conscious of her failure."

"One servant couldn't care for such a large house even if it hadn't been…"

"A rubbish collection? I think Uncle Percival must have actually been mad. People called him eccentric, but this is…" James peered down the cluttered hallway. "No wonder he refused all my visits."

"Did you try to visit him?" Cecelia asked.

"Of course."

"Huh."

"Is that so surprising?" asked James.

"Well, yes, because you don't care for anyone but yourself."

"Don't start up this old refrain."

"It's the truth."

"More a matter of opinion and definition," James replied.

She waved this aside. "You will have to do better now that you are the head of your family."

"A meaningless label. I shall have to bring some order." He grimaced at the stacks of newspapers. "But no more than that."

"A great deal more," said Cecelia. "You have a duty…"

"As Uncle Percival did?" James gestured at their surroundings.

"His failure is all the more reason for you to shoulder your responsibilities."

"I don't think so."

Cecelia put her hands on her hips, just as she had done at nine years old. "Under our system the bulk of the money and all of the property in the great families passes to one man, in this case you. You are obliged to manage it for the good of the whole." She looked doubtful suddenly. "If there is any money."

"There is," he replied. This had been a continual sore point during the years of the trust. And after, in fact. His father had not left a fortune. "Quite a bit of it seemingly. I had a visit from a rather sour banker. Uncle Percival was a miser as well as a..." James gestured at the mess. "A connoisseur of detritus. But if you think I will tolerate the whining of indigent relatives, you are deluded." He had made do when he was far from wealthy. Others could follow suit.

"You must take care of your people."

She was interrupted by a rustle of newsprint. "I daresay there are rats," James said.

"Do you think to frighten me? You never could."

This was true. And he had really tried a few times in his youth.

"I am consumed by morbid curiosity," Cecelia added as she slipped down the hall. James followed. Her attendants came straggling after, the maid looking uneasy at the thought of rodents.

They found other rooms as jumbled as the first two. Indeed, the muddle seemed to worsen toward the rear of the house. "Is that a spinning wheel?" Cecelia exclaimed at one point. "Why would a duke want such a thing?"

"It appears he was unable to resist acquiring any object that he came across," replied James.

"But where would he come across a spinning wheel?"

"In a tenant's cottage?"

"Do you suppose he bought it from them?"

"I have no idea." James pushed aside a hanging swag of cloth. Dust billowed out and set them all coughing. He stifled a curse.

At last they came into what might have been a library. James thought he could see bookshelves behind the piles of refuse. There was a desk, he realized, with a chair pulled up to it. He hadn't noticed at first because it was buried under mountains of documents. At one side sat a large wicker basket brimming with correspondence.

Cecelia picked up a sheaf of pages from the desk, glanced over it, and set it down again. She rummaged in the basket. "These are all letters," she said.

"Wonderful."

"May I?"

James gestured his permission, and she opened one from the top. "Oh, this is bad. Your cousin Elvira needs help."

"I have no knowledge of a cousin Elvira."

"Oh, I suppose she must have been your uncle Percival's cousin. She sounds rather desperate."

"Well, that is the point of a begging letter, is it not? The effect is diminished if one doesn't sound desperate."

"Yes, but James…"

"My God, do you suppose they're all like that?" The basket was as long as his arm and nearly as deep. It was mounded with correspondence.

Cecelia dug deeper. "They all seem to be personal letters. Just thrown in here. I suppose they go back for months."

"Years," James guessed. Dust lay over them, as it did everything here.

"You must read them."

"I don't think so. For once I approve of Uncle Percival's methods. I would say throw them in the fire, if lighting a fire in this place wasn't an act of madness."

"Have you no family feeling?"

"None. You read them if you're so interested."

She shuffled through the upper layer. "Here's one from your grandmother."

"Which one?"

"Lady Wilton."

"Oh no."

Cecelia opened the sheet and read. "She seems to have misplaced an earl."

"What?"

"A long-lost heir has gone missing."

"Who? No, never mind. I don't care." The enormity of the task facing him descended on James, looming like the piles of objects leaning over his head. He looked up. One wrong move, and all that would fall about his ears. He wanted none of it.

A flicker of movement diverted him. A rat had emerged from a crevice between a gilded chair leg and a hideous outsized vase. The creature stared down at him, insolent, seeming to know that it was well out of reach. "Wonderful," murmured James.

Cecelia looked up. "What?"

He started to point out the animal, to make her jump, then bit back the words as an idea recurred. He, and her father, had taken advantage of her energetic capabilities over the years. He knew it. He was fairly certain she knew it. Her father had probably never noticed. But Cecelia hadn't minded. She'd said once that the things she'd learned and done had given her a more interesting life than most young ladies were allowed. Might his current plight not intrigue her? So instead of mentioning the rodent, he offered his most charming smile. "Perhaps you would like to have that basket," he suggested. "It must be full of compelling stories."

Her blue eyes glinted as if she understood exactly what he was up to. "No, James. This mare's nest is all yours. I think, actually, that you deserve it."

"How can you say so?"

"It is like those old Greek stories, where the thing one tries hardest to avoid fatefully descends."

"Thing?" said James, gazing at the looming piles of *things*.

"You loathe organizational tasks. And this one is monumental."

"You have always been the most annoying girl," said James.

"Oh, I shall enjoy watching you dig out." Cecelia turned away. "My curiosity is satisfied. I'll be on my way."

"It isn't like you to avoid work."

She looked over her shoulder at him. "*Your* work. And as you've pointed out, our…collaboration ended three years ago. We will call this visit a final farewell to those days."

She edged her way out, leaving James in his wreck of an inheritance. He was conscious of a sharp pang of regret. He put it down to resentment over her refusal to help him.

∽

Thinking of James's plight as she sat in her drawing room later that day, Cecelia couldn't help smiling. James liked order, and he didn't care for hard work. That house really did seem like fate descending on him like a striking hawk. Was it what he deserved? It was certainly amusing.

She became conscious of an impulse, like a nagging itch, to set things in order. The letters, in particular, tugged at her. She couldn't help wondering about the people who had written and their troubles. But she resisted. Her long association with James was over. There were reasons to keep her distance. She'd given in to curiosity today, but that must be the end.

"Tereford will manage," she said, ostensibly to the other occupant of the drawing room, but mostly to herself.

"Mmm," replied her aunt, Miss Valeria Vainsmede.

Cecelia had told her the story of the jumbled town house, but as usual her supposed chaperone had scarcely listened. Like Cecelia's father, her Aunt Valeria cared for nothing outside her own chosen sphere. "I sometimes wonder about my grandparents," Cecelia murmured. These Vainsmede progenitors, who had died before she was born, had produced a pair of plump, blond offspring with almost no interest in other people.

"You wouldn't have liked them," replied Aunt Valeria. One never knew when she would pick up on a remark and respond, sometimes after hours of silence. It was disconcerting. She was bent over a small pasteboard box. It undoubtedly contained a bee, because nothing else would hold her attention so completely. A notebook, quill, and inkpot sat beside it.

"You think not?" asked Cecelia.

"No one did."

"Why?"

"They were not likable," said her aunt.

"In what way?"

"In the way of a parasitic wasp pushing into the hive."

Cecelia stared at her aunt, who had not looked up from whatever she was doing, and wondered how anyone could describe their parents in such a disparaging tone. Aunt Valeria might have been speaking of total strangers. Whom she despised.

She felt a sudden flash of pain. How she missed her mother! Mama had been the polar opposite of the Vainsmedes. Warm and affectionate and prone to joking, she'd even brought Papa out of his self-absorption now and then and made their family feel—familial. She'd made him laugh. And she'd filled Cecelia's days with love. Her absence was a great icy void that would never be filled.

Cecelia took a deep breath. And another. These grievous moments were rare now. They'd gradually lessened in the years since Mama died when she was twelve, leaving her in the care of her distracted father. She'd found ways to move on, of course. But she would never forget that day, and feeling so desperately alone.

Until James had come to see her. He'd stepped into this very drawing room so quietly that she knew nothing until he spoke her name. Her aunt had not yet arrived; her father was with his books. She was wildly startled when he said, "Cecelia."

She'd lashed out, expecting some heartless complaint about his financial affairs. But James had sat down beside her on the sofa and taken her hand and told her how sorry he was. That nineteen-year-old sprig of fashion and aspiring sportsman, who'd often taunted her, had praised her mother in the kindest way and acknowledged how much she would be missed. Most particularly by Cecelia, of course. After a moment of incredulity, she'd burst into tears, thrown herself upon him, and sobbed on his shoulder. He'd tolerated the outburst as her father would not. He'd tried, clumsily, to comfort her, and Cecelia had seen that there was more to him than she'd understood.

A footman came in and announced visitors. Cecelia put the past aside. Aunt Valeria responded with a martyred sigh.

Four young ladies filed into the room, and Cecelia stood to greet them. She'd been expecting only one, Miss Harriet Finch, whose mother had been a school friend of her mama. Mrs. Finch had written asking for advice and aid with her daughter's debut, and Cecelia had volunteered to help Miss Harriet acquire a bit of town polish. Now she seemed to be welcoming the whole upper level of a girls' school, judging from the outmoded wardrobes and dowdy haircuts. "Hello," she said.

The most conventionally pretty of the group, with red-blond hair, green eyes, a pointed chin beneath a broad forehead, and a beautiful figure, stepped forward. "How do you do?" she said. "I am Harriet Finch."

According to the gossips, she was a considerable heiress. Quite a spate of inheritances lately, Cecelia thought, though she supposed people were always dying.

"And these are Miss Ada Grandison, Miss Sarah Moran, and Miss Charlotte Deeping," the girl went on. She pointed as she gave their names.

"I see," said Cecelia.

"They are my friends." Miss Finch spoke as if they were a set of china that mustn't on any account be broken up.

"May I present my aunt, Miss Vainsmede," said Cecelia.

Aunt Valeria pointed to one ear and spoke in a loud toneless voice. "Very deaf. Sorry." She returned to her box and notepad, putting her back to their visitors.

Cecelia hid a sigh. Her aunt could hear as well as anyone, but she insisted on telling society that she could not. It must have been an open secret, because the servants were well aware of her true state. But the ruse allowed Aunt Valeria to play her part as chaperone without making any effort to participate in society. Cecelia had once taxed her with feigning what others found a sad affliction. Her aunt had informed her that she actually did not hear people who nattered on about nothing. "My mind rejects their silly yapping," she'd declared. "It turns to a sort of humming in my brain, and then I begin to think of something interesting instead." Cecelia gestured toward a sofa. "Do sit down," she said to her guests.

The girls sat in a row facing her. They didn't fold their hands, but it felt as if they had. They looked hopeful and slightly apprehensive. Cecelia examined them, trying to remember which was which.

Miss Ada Grandison had heavy, authoritative eyebrows. They dominated smooth brown hair, brown eyes, a straight nose, and full lips.

Miss Sarah Moran, the shortest of the four, was a smiling round little person with sandy hair, a turned-up nose, and sparkling light blue eyes. It was too bad her pale brows and eyelashes washed her out.

The last, Miss Charlotte Deeping, was the tallest, with black hair, pale skin, and a sharp dark gaze. She looked spiky. "I thought you didn't have a chaperone," she said to Cecelia, confirming this impression.

"What made you think that?"

"We heard you went to a ball on your own."

"I met my party there," Cecelia replied, which was nearly true. She had attached herself to friends as soon as she arrived. That solitary venture had perhaps been a misjudgment. But it was a very minor scandal, more of an eccentricity, she told herself. She was impatient with the rules now that she was in her fourth season. "My aunt has lived with us since my mother died," she told her visitors.

"I thought it must be a hum," replied Miss Deeping. "It seems we are to be stifled to death here in London."

Cecelia could sympathize. Because her father paid no attention and her aunt did not care, her situation was unusual. She'd been the mistress of the house for nine years, and manager of the Vainsmede properties for even longer. Her father left everything to her, too lazy to be bothered. Indeed Cecelia sometimes wondered how she ever came to be in the first place, as Papa cared for nothing but rich meals and reading. She supposed her maternal grandmother had simply informed him that he was being married and then sent someone to drag him from his library to the church on the day. But no, he had cared for Mama. She must believe that.

"Every circumstance is different," said Miss Moran.

She was one who liked to smooth things over, Cecelia noted.

"And Miss Vainsmede is older than…" Miss Moran blushed and bit her lip as if afraid she'd given offense.

"Three years older than you," Cecelia acknowledged. "Do you all want my advice?"

"We must have new clothes and haircuts," said Miss Grandison.

The others nodded.

"We're new to London and fashionable society, where you are well established," said Miss Finch. "My mother says we would be wise to heed an expert."

"Which doesn't precisely answer my question," said Cecelia. "Do you wish to hear my opinions?"

They looked at each other, engaged in a brief silent communication, and then all nodded. The exchange demonstrated a solid friendship, which Cecelia envied. Many of her friends had married and did not come to town for the season. She missed them. "Very well," she began. "I think you, Miss Moran, would do well to darken your brows and lashes. It would draw attention to your lovely eyes."

The girl looked shocked. "Wouldn't that be dreadfully *fast*?"

"A little daring perhaps," said Cecelia. "But no one will know if you do it before your entry into society."

"Don't be missish, Sarah," said Miss Deeping.

Cecelia wondered if she was a bully. "You should wear ruffles," she said to her. She suspected that this suggestion would not be taken well, and it was not.

"Ruffles," repeated the dark girl in a tone of deep revulsion.

"To soften the lines of your frame."

"Disguise my lamentable lack of figure you mean."

Cecelia did not contradict her. Nor did she evade the glare that came with these words. They either wanted her advice or they didn't. She didn't know them well enough to care which it was to be.

"You haven't mentioned my eyebrows," said Miss Grandison, frowning.

"You appear to use them to good effect."

Miss Grandison was surprised into a laugh.

"And I?" asked Miss Finch. There seemed to be an undertone of resentment or bitterness in her voice. Odd since she had the least to fear from society, considering her inheritance.

"New clothes and a haircut," Cecelia replied. "We could call on my modiste tomorrow if you like."

The appointment was agreed on.

"Oh, I hope this season goes well," said Miss Moran.

"There will be another next year," Cecelia said. She heard

the trace of boredom in her voice and rejected it. She was not one of those languishing women who claimed to be overcome by ennui.

"I shan't be here. It was always to be only one season for me." Miss Moran clasped her hands together. "So I intend to enjoy it *immensely*."

About the Author

Jane Ashford discovered Georgette Heyer in junior high school and was captivated by the glittering world and witty language of Regency England. That delight was part of what led her to study English literature and travel widely. Her books have been published all over Europe as well as in the United States. Jane was nominated for a Career Achievement Award by *RT Book Reviews*. Born in Ohio, she is now somewhat nomadic. Find her on the web at janeashford.com and on Facebook at facebook .com/JaneAshfordWriter, where you can sign up for her monthly newsletter.

FORTUNE FAVORS THE DUKE

First in the sparkling new Cambridge Brotherhood series of Regency romance from author Kristin Vayden

Quinton Errington is happy teaching economics at Cambridge. But when his eldest brother dies in a tragic accident, Quinton becomes Duke. Between being head of his family, mourning his brother, and trying not to fall in love with his late brother's fiancée, Quinton will need some help…

"Flawless storytelling! Vayden is a new Regency powerhouse."
—Rachel Van Dyken, #1 *New York Times* bestselling author

For more info about Sourcebooks's books and authors, visit:
sourcebooks.com

AN EARL TO ENCHANT

Dazzling opposites-attract Regency romance
from bestselling author Amelia Grey

Arianna Sweet knows her father's death was anything but acciden-
tal. Someone is after his groundbreaking medical discovery and
now they're after her. Alone and with no one to turn to, Arianna
has almost given up searching for an ally—until a chance encounter
leaves her and her father's research in Lord Morgandale's strong and
trustworthy hands…

"What romance dreams are made of."
—*Love Romance Passion* for *A Dash of Scandal*

For more info about Sourcebooks's books and authors, visit:
sourcebooks.com

THE PRINCESS STAKES

Smart, sexy, and beautiful Regency romance
from bestselling author Amalie Howard

Born to an Indian maharaja and a British noblewoman, Princess
Sarani Rao has it all: beauty, riches, and a crown. But when Sarani's
father is murdered, her only hope is the next ship out—captained
by the man she once loved…and spurned.

Captain Rhystan Huntley, the reluctant Duke of Embry, is loath
to give up his life at sea. But duty is calling him home, and this is his
final voyage. Leave it to fate that the one woman he's ever loved has
stowed away and must escape to England on his ship…

**"Vivid, sensual, and beautifully written—
impossible to put down."**
—Lisa Kleypas, *New York Times* bestselling author

For more info about Sourcebooks's books and authors, visit:
sourcebooks.com

THE DUKE WHO LOVED ME

The Duke's Estates series brings you sparkling Regency romance from bestselling author Jane Ashford

When James Cantrell, the new Duke of Tereford, proposes a marriage of convenience, Cecelia Vainsmede doesn't understand how he can be so obtuse. He clearly doesn't realize that he's the duke she's always wished for, so his offer is an insult. But when a German prince arrives in London and immediately sets out to woo Cecelia, James will have to come to terms with his true feelings. Is running away worth the cost of losing her, or will the duke dare to win her once and for all?

"Impossible to put down... The story crackles with clever dialogue and humorous scenes."
—*Historical Novel Review*

LADY EVE'S INDISCRETION

Captivating, steamy Regency romance from *New York Times* and *USA Today* bestselling author Grace Burrowes

Lady Evie Windham has a secret to keep, and a wedding night would ruin everything. She's determined to avoid marriage, but with her parents pushing potential partners her way from every direction, she needs a miracle. Perhaps old family friend Lucas Denning, the newly titled Marquis of Deene, could be the answer to everything.

"Grace Burrowes is terrific."
—Julia Quinn, *New York Times* bestselling author of the Bridgerton series

For more info about Sourcebooks's books and authors, visit:
sourcebooks.com

Also by Jane Ashford